FLYING BLIND

Colin Bowles was born in London in 1953, and educated at Southend High School, where he was trained to become a pillar of the community. On leaving school he travelled round Europe, fell in and out of love in Sweden, and had his hopes of becoming an international soccer star dashed after trials with Southampton and Gillingham.

He emigrated to Australia when he was twenty, where, after several false starts and after meeting his wife Helen, he took up his writing career. Since then he has written extensively for radio and television, including contributions to *The Two Ronnies*. He has had several flirtations with the world of advertising, where he is currently employed as a freelance copywriter. However, he insists the relationship is purely platonic.

He has one daughter. He does not have a villa in the south of France, and has never been interviewed by Clive James. At present he is working on a seven-part comedy series for ABC Television in Sydney.

FLYING BLIND

Colin Bowles

ARROW BOOKS

Arrow Books Limited
62–65 Chandos Place, London WC2N 4NW

An imprint of Century Hutchinson Limited

London Melbourne Sydney Auckland
Johannesburg and agencies throughout
the world

First published in Great Britain by Century 1986

Arrow edition 1988

© Colin Bowles 1986

Typeset by WBC Print, Bristol

Printed and bound in Great Britain by
Anchor Brendon Limited, Tiptree, Essex

ISBN 0 09 956730 X

For Helen, my wife
Without you, no book.

AUTHOR'S NOTE

There is no such place as Preston in Western Australia, although towns very much like it exist right through the Kimberley region.

The characters in this book are also purely fictional; it has not been my intention to portray anyone living or dead.

However, some of the incidents are based on fact; drawn from the excellent histories of the service of Harry Hudson, Ion Idriess and Michael Page and the records of the courageous and dedicated people who have worked for the RFDS, men and women such as Allan Vickers, Clyde Fenton, Robin Miller, Harold Dicks and many others.

There are many in Australia's outback who owe them a debt that can never be repaid.

CHAPTER 1

I was up to my knees in mud.

I stopped a moment to catch my breath. It was raining harder now and I was exhausted. How much further could it be?

I had been called out on Christmas Day before. Which doctor hasn't? But it had never been like this. Oh, I'd slipped grumbling behind the wheel of my air-conditioned Holden in my shorts and open-necked shirt and driven a few miles in bright and glorious sunshine to attend a heart failure or sunstroke or a sick infant; once I had raced next door halfway through my turkey and cold ham to help deliver twins.

But it had never been like this.

This was the first Christmas that my housecall had taken me a hundred and twenty miles through a tropical storm in a tiny, shuddering frame of airborne metal and bolts; and then required me to slosh another three miles through wet, clinging mud to my patient's bedside.

It hadn't said anything about this in the advertisement, oh no. It had fleetingly referred to the beautiful, dry, mild winter climate which had seemed so tempting with the rain spattering against my surgery window; there was not a word about the damp, suffocating summer heat or the fierce seasonal cyclones. In their picture, the Flying

Doctor was a smiling, tanned young man surrounded by small children who gazed up at him adoringly like they do to Jesus in illustrated Bibles; he wasn't sleep-starved and dirty with sweat and rain dripping down into his eyes in the middle of a plain somewhere on the high Kimberley.

It was getting dark. Clouds hung low over the sky in a dismal, grey shroud. The air was as moist and thick as warm treacle, and grimy perspiration ran in tiny rivulets down my chest and back. My legs ached from the sucking, clawing effect of the mud.

I closed my eyes and forced myself to keep walking. 'How much further, Jackie?'

The Aboriginal youth turned and grinned at me. He seemed to be enjoying himself; he hadn't stopped smiling since he had run up to meet us on the ridge.

'Him long way yet boss,' he said, and continued bounding through the cloying mud, almost with abandon. I took a deep breath and struggled after him.

The call had come through over the radio earlier that afternoon. A pregnant woman on a cattle station at Hawkestone had fallen badly and gone into premature labour. The Australian Inland Mission nurses at Fitzroy Crossing were unable to get through because of the 'wet'. After a hurried consultation with the woman's husband over the radio, I had made the decision to go.

My pilot, a gloomy Irishman named Joe Kennedy, had been apprehensive – with good reason. A cyclonic depression was sweeping across the north-west and visibility was down to half a mile. As we took off from the Preston aerodrome the ominous rumbling of thunder had echoed around the mountains and for an hour we had bounced and pitched through heavy, turbulent air. We had found our way to the station by following the bush tracks, our wings barely skimming the tree-tops, watching the wheel ruts in the roads below rapidly filling with water.

Joe had been concerned from the start that the airstrip at the station would not now be safe for a landing; sure enough, when we got there, it was under six inches of water. The only dry ground was on a ridge some three miles from the station and Joe had landed the Cessna there in buffeting crosswinds. After we had finished pegging down the plane, we were met by a couple of the native hands from Hawkestone, and we set off for the long march to the homestead.

As we trudged through the swamp I thought again of that comfortable little practice I had had in Collaroy and wondered why I had ever left.

I turned round, peering back across the flat, grey plain. Joe was well over fifty yards behind, his head down and his shoulders hunched, as if he had just fought a long battle, and lost. He and the other native boys were carrying the stretcher between them. Retreat from Passchendaele? I would have liked to have shouted something encouraging to him, but I couldn't think of anything.

Soon we reached a patch of dryer ground. It was a relief to be clear of the mud and we began to make better time. The light was fading rapidly now. I searched the horizon ahead for a light, something to indicate the journey was nearly over.

Nothing.

'How far now, Jackie?' I said. I was finding it very difficult now to keep up with his strong, youthful legs.

He turned round, the ever-present grin powder-white in the gloom. His eyes speculated. 'Him little bit long way,' he said at last. I digested this new piece of information and meditated on its possibilities.

I waited for Joe to catch up.

The long, sorrowful face was etched with tragic self-pity, and even in the grey light of dusk I could make out the expression of sorrowful resignation in his eyes. Joe had a theory, and he called it Kennedy's Law: 'If anything can go wrong, it will happen when I'm there, and if it possibly can, it will happen to me.'

Most of the time he was right.

I forced myself to smile. 'What a way to spend Christmas, eh?'

He gave me a sparse bitter look and kept walking. 'Just my luck,' he muttered. 'Just my luck.'

Jackie led us across the plain in the gathering darkness with nothing more sophisticated than a single flashlight to help him. Joe and I followed him with a blind faith and absolute confidence in his knowledge of the terrain, and the arcane bush instinct that these people seem to possess.

How he did it, I haven't a clue; but half an hour later we stood on the banks of the Hawkestone River, looking across at the kerosene lamps shining welcomingly on the porch of the homestead.

For most of the year the Hawkestone River is a dry creek bed, a dark orange gash in the blistered ground. But now, eighty feet wide and four feet deep, a dark roaring mass, it presented a formidable obstacle.

'What do we do now, Jackie?' I said. The young boy grinned and started peeling off his trousers and his white T-shirt.

I looked at Joe. 'Oh Christ,' he muttered. 'We really got the rough end of the pineapple this time.'

I started to strip off my shirt too, and then thought better of it. I couldn't get any wetter than I was already. Then a more sinister consideration cast its shadow across my thoughts.

'Any crocodiles in there, Jackie?'

'Oh no, boss,' he grinned back at me. 'Not many.'

'You go first.'

'Orright, boss. Crocydile he only eat white feller anyway.'

Thus reassured, I waded in after him, holding the precious medical kit high over my head. Joe and the other boy followed behind me. The water was blood-warm, but I had to struggle to keep my balance against the swirling, eddying current. I was frightened. I felt alone and very vulnerable in that black, fast-flowing river. I knew that crocodiles weren't the only danger – I had not long ago treated a man left in agony after a bite from a water snake. I searched the water around me for any sudden movement; the lamps outside the house threw a little light over us, although the far banks of the creek threw most of the river into shadow.

I hurried after the flickering torch ahead of me, my ears straining for any tell-tale splash that would mean a crocodile had picked up our scent and was in the river with us.

I was halfway across when I saw it coming.

It was moving towards me from upstream, a dark, gnarled shape, its snout just above the water as it swam swiftly along with the current. I tried to yell out but the sound caught in my throat and all that came out was a stifled sob. I made an attempt to run but the drag of the water was too strong. I couldn't see Jackie but I saw the torchlight suddenly spin in my direction as I threshed through the river towards him.

I looked round. It was nearly on top of me. There was nothing I could do. I was still holding the medical kit above my head, leaving my ribs exposed, but something inside me refused to let it drop. I imagined the rows of small yellow teeth moving towards me and braced myself for the terrible crushing blow as the jaws closed around my chest.

Now.

The mulga bark stung a little as it caught me a glancing blow just under the fifth rib, before being carried out of sight by the strong current. I stood there panting, my heart hammering inside my chest, staring down dazed at where the piece of driftwood had struck me. It took a few seconds before I realised that there had been no crocodile, no sharp rows of teeth, outside of my own imagination.

And then Jackie was beside me, shaking me by the arm, his voice hoarse with alarm. 'You okay boss?'

I felt suddenly very stupid. 'It's okay Jackie,' I said. 'Crocodile him belong tree.'

I saw two more 'crocodiles' before we made the far bank. The Ancient Mariner couldn't have been happier to feel solid earth beneath his feet than I was just then.

The homestead perched on the brow of a hill overlooking the creek. Jackie led us up the path towards the verandah of the old stone building, two or three dogs growling and snapping at our heels. Finally, at the top of the pathway. I made out the silhouette of a man on the porchway, watching our arrival.

Tom Doyle and I knew each other well; it wasn't the first time I had been on an emergency call to Hawkestone.

Tom looked me up and down as I stood on his verandah, spattered with mud, pools of water forming around my feet. If I had been expecting a hero's welcome, I was to be sadly disillusioned.

Tom put his hands on his hips, his face creased into an expression of sour impatience. 'You took your time, didn't ya?'

I put a stiff rein on my temper and tried at a smile. I made allowance for the fact that the poor man's wife was just inside the house going through an early labour.

'Wrong time of the year to have babies,' I said, as cheerfully as I could. Tom nodded silently. He was a big man, with forearms like legs of mutton and a dark stubble on his chin. He was built like a heavyweight boxer, and under his cotton shirt his body looked as hard and as bulky as a sack of potatoes.

'You'd better come in and get cleaned up,' he said, turning and walking into the house. 'Me missus is gonna drop the kid any minute.'

As we entered the house, I took in the familiar sight of the sparse furnishings – the single chest of drawers in one corner, the old black and white photograph on the stone fireplace, the jarrah table with the straight-backed chairs, the smell of dough and tobacco. It was dour and spartan, like Tom himself.

From one of the bedrooms leading off from the rear passageway, two pairs of eyes peered out at me. I smiled in their direction and the two little faces disappeared, giggling.

'Cut it out, you pair o' buggers,' Tom yelled. 'Let's have a bit of quiet. Your mother's not well.' He turned to me and pointed to one of the other bedrooms. 'I've put out a couple of me dry shirts and some daks. And there's plenty of hot water ready on the range.'

Though physically exhausted, my mind was instantly alert. Everything else was forgotten as I brought my concentration to the immediate medical problem to hand. As I followed Tom down the passage I asked him what had happened.

'I dunno,' he said. 'I wasn't here. I was out musterin' some strays. They found her at the foot of the steps by the verandah. Jackie had to come and get me.'

'Is she bleeding?'

He shrugged. 'Seems all right.'

'How long between the pains?'

'Hard to tell,' Joe said, as if to say – you're the doctor, you should know. 'You'd better give her somethin' doc. She says it's hurtin' her something fierce.'

It was a strange thing about Tom. Seemingly impervious to pain himself, he couldn't bear the thought of anyone else suffering any sort of discomfort. (Except me, of course.) And although he was quite adept at delivering baby calves to his own herd on occasion, my predecessor informed me that he had fainted when his eldest daughter was born and had refused to attend the births of the other two.

I started to strip off my wet clothes. One of Tom's shirts and a pair of his trousers were laid out on the bed. I could hear Kate Doyle's groans in the next room. 'I'll want some blankets and clean towels,' I said to Tom.

'They're all ready,' Tom said.

The shirt fitted me like a bell-tent. I knew it would be pointless trying to get into the trousers so I slipped my surgical gown over the top of the shirt and put on a pair of the dry woollen socks. I was privileged with a glimpse of my reflection in the mirror. My hair was wet, and plastered across my forehead; the green surgical gown was set off nicely by the red check shirt and a pair of bristly knees.

Still, now was no time for vanity. 'Okay,' I said. 'Let's see how your wife is.'

'Don't forget, doc', Tom said. 'I want a boy this time.'

Suddenly Tom's eleven year old daughter Linda ran into the room. Her face was shockingly pale.

'I thought I told you to stay with your mother,' Tom said.

'Daddy, Mummy's bleeding awful bad.'

Tom looked at me. His face paled too under the dark growth of beard.

15

We rushed off down the passageway to the next bedroom.

Kate Doyle lay on the bed, panting. Her white nightgown was pulled up nearly to her shoulder, her thick mass of black hair matted around her forehead and in her eyes, a blank appeal for help. Her small pale hands were screwed into fists of terror and pain.

The sheets around her lower body were covered in bright red blood.

I picked up one of the towels lying in readiness on the bedside table and used it to staunch the flow of blood. 'It's all right,' I whispered to the terrified woman. 'It's all right,'

And I thought *What the hell am I going to do?*

'What's the matter, doc?' Tom said from the doorway. I turned round. The little girl was standing behind him, wide-eyed.

'Mummy's okay now, Linda,' I said, trying to sound as reassuring as I could. 'Why don't you go and play with your sisters?'

It was unbelievable. Of all the things that could possibly have happened here, now, this was the one thing I was not prepared for. Poor Kate was haemorrhaging badly, and the birth of the baby was just hours away. I tried to control a wave of panic.

What the hell was I going to do?

If I had been in a hospital I could have performed a Caesarian, delivered the child and repaired the site of the haemorrhage. There would have been a ready supply of blood for Kate. But this was not a hospital, and there was no blood – and both Kate and the baby were in mortal danger.

I had to make a quick decision. Ideally I wanted to

16

get Kate to Preston as soon as possible. But between us and the plane was a flooded creek and three miles of swampy ground. And if the baby came while we were in the middle of the plain . . .

Yet what could I do?

The rain was still falling outside, and there was a danger that the plane would get bogged on the ridge. But if we waited until I had the chance to operate, we might find ourselves stranded on the station and Kate would almost certainly die from loss of blood.

I made up my mind.

I turned to Tom, who was staring at the blood-stained sheets with undisguised horror. 'Where's Joe?' I said.

'Jackie took him to the bunkhouse to get some dry clothes.'

'Well tell him not to get too comfortable. We're leaving again right now.'

CHAPTER 2

Tom's three small daughters huddled around him as he bent down to say goodbye. 'Now you girls be good till Daddy gets back. I'll bring Mummy home as soon as I can, all right?'

Emma said in a hushed whisper 'Where's Mummy going?'

'She's going in the aeroplane so she can get well again, like you did.'

'She can take Miss Suzy if she wants,' Emma said, offering the tattered, one-eyed doll.

'No, you keep it love,' Tom said, softly.

'Will the baby in her tummy get better too?'

'Yes, the baby will get better too,' Tom said. He looked up at me, the big ruddy face grim and fearful. I stood by the door watching. Poor Tom, I thought. He's trying to reassure them, and he's as frightened as they are.

And I'm frightened too.

I had slipped back into my wet clothes, ready for another swim in the creek. 'We'd better be going,' I said.

'Right.' Tom looked at the man standing next to me in the doorway, his foreman. 'Put them straight to bed, Harry. Make sure they're good, okay?'

'I will, Tom.'

'Let's go,' Tom said, and he kissed them all quickly and six large brown eyes watched as we

18

went out into the darkness and then the door closed behind us.

As we ran down through the mud towards the creek I began to question my decision. It was one thing to test your judgment in the clinical atmosphere of a hospital with all the drugs and equipment that modern-day science could provide at your fingertips; quite different to pit that decision against the alien world of the outback. The whole situation was nightmarish. Here we were, attempting to ferry a pregnant woman with a uterine haemorrhage across a swollen creek in the middle of the night – hoping to God that the baby didn't choose to be born before we could get them both to safety. The responsibility of that decision was mine and mine alone. I only prayed that it would turn out to be the right one.

I reminded myself again that if I had attempted surgery on the spot, there was a good chance we would get stranded at the homestead by the rising floodwaters. The best chance for the mother and the baby was to get them to the Hospital straight away.

As long as Kate didn't go through labour in the middle of a flooded paddock.

There were flashlights and the sound of voices ahead of us as we reached the foot of the hill. Jackie and the other native boy were down by the creek with Joe Kennedy. They had carried Kate down with them.

I knelt down beside the stretcher. 'How are you feeling?' I whispered.

'I'm okay,' Kate said.

'I'll be right here the whole way.'

I checked to make sure she was strapped tightly

19

on to the stretcher and we set off.

This time as I clambered into the swirling muddy water there was barely a thought about crocodiles or water snakes. It is strange how concern for another human being can override fear. With one of us at each of the grips, and Tom supporting his wife's weight underneath, we carried the stretcher above our heads across the river. Tom growled at each of us in turn; he cursed angrily at Jackie when the poor boy stumbled and nearly pitched his end into the water.

Nobody growled back.

It took five long minutes to struggle through the current to the far side of the creek. Tom and Jackie and the other boy carefully lifted Kate up the muddy bank on the stretcher. Joe was the last to emerge and I stopped to help him clamber up. As he reached up, his hand slipped out of mine and he slid back through the mud, face down, and fell back into the creek again.

It was insult to injury for a man who had once helped to fly luxury passenger aircraft on the domestic route.

'There were sixty-nine applicants for this job,' Joe said bitterly when he finally crawled up on to the bank. 'Why the bloody hell did they pick me?'

It took another weary hour to reach the plane. The mud squelched underfoot, thick and tacky as porridge; occasionally I would hear Tom whisper a word of encouragement to his wife. Mostly we walked in silence. I stayed beside the stretcher the whole way, dreading the worst. It seemed an endless journey . . . at any moment Kate might begin the final stages of labour.

She was a woman of incredible courage. She bore what must have been terrible distress with stoical silence, only crying out a few times, when the jolting and the pain became too much.

Once again the young native boys somehow led us back through the darkness to the Cessna moored on the ridge overlooking the plain. The ground there was still quite firm. Thank God, I thought. I turned to Joe.

'Looks like we've made it,' I said.

'I'll believe it when I see it.'

We strapped the stretcher onto the deck behind the pilot's seat and the three of us clambered in. Jackie and his partner wished us good luck and set out to return to the homestead, their fourth trip across the plain that night. I noticed that Jackie had stopped smiling by this stage.

I got the Verey gun out of the rear of the cockpit and fired one of the flares into the night sky. It burst high above the ridge and for a moment our makeshift airfield and the surrounding plains and the dark brooding clouds above were illuminated in a brilliant flash of white light. I jumped back into the cockpit, slamming the door behind me.

As the engines roared to life and we started to move off, I said a small prayer. Well, this is it, I thought. If we can get off this ridge, our troubles are nearly over.

I strapped myself into the seat next to Joe, as the Cessna lumbered across the grass. The light of the flare was already starting to fade.

'Come on girl,' I said, as we began to gain speed. 'Come on, come on!'

I looked at Joe. 'I bet we get stuck in some mud,'

he said, 'that'd be just my luck.'

But we didn't bog in the mud. Joe opened up to full throttle and a few seconds later the ground slipped away beneath the wheels. As we flew up into the night clouds I leaned back in my seat and let out a long, grateful sigh of relief.

I should have known better. After all, it was I who had propounded the theory, known as 'Hazzard's Law': 'If a woman is going to have a difficult birth, she will have it at night'. And I should have been aware of its corollary: 'If a baby is going to be born it will do so at the worst possible time and in the worst possible circumstances, and if it does, it will be a girl.'

Right again, Doctor Hazzard.

We were halfway between Hawkestone River and Preston when Kate began panting harder and she let me know that the baby was not going to wait any longer.

Tom was kneeling at her side, patting her hand with one of his enormous paws. 'It's okay, old girl,' he whispered. 'You'll be okay.'

'*Ooooohhhh!*'

Joe turned on the cabin light and I put on a pair of sterile gloves from the kit and slipped a surgical gown over my soiled shirt and trousers. These were hardly sterile conditions, but I would have to make the best of it.

Tom was still patting Kate's hand. 'You'll be okay, love.'

'It's coming!' Kate suddenly yelled, and Tom's hand whipped back to his side as if he had been stung. He looked up at me in fear and shock and for a moment I thought he was going to start sucking his thumb. He looked at me. 'Do something,' he said.

I pushed him out of the way and removed the linen plug. Fresh bright blood started to pour forth. I had to staunch the flow at the site of the haemorrhage with the back of my hand as the baby pushed its way down the birth canal. Kate screamed and started to convulse and I had to get Tom to hold her shoulders down. The poor man, seeing the blood and his wife screaming, thought she was dying and he started to cry. The plane dipped and reeled through the rainclouds, and somewhere in the front of the cockpit, Joe started crying too.

The moment was as surreal as a fresco by Dali. A sudden flash of lightning illuminated the cabin – the two men crying, the woman screaming, and the little black head appearing very easily, wet with mucus and blood, and slipping out onto the stretcher.

'Quick Tom, hold the baby!' I yelled. The poor man just looked at me. I didn't have enough hands! I needed to cut the umbilicus, but one hand still plugged the bleeding while the other was around the slippery, writhing little bundle that had caused all the trouble.

Tom, paralysed with fear, just stared at the blood and the baby, and his jaw fell open.

'Here, Tom! You fly the plane,' Joe shouted from the front of the cockpit. 'I'll hold the baby!'

Tom stared at him as if he'd gone mad. Perhaps he had. Joe started to get out from behind the controls but then the plane hit an air pocket and dropped like a big dipper and we all screamed, including the baby.

I realised I would have to go solo.

I held the baby still between my elbows while I

plugged the bleeding as best I could with a towel. The flow stopped. Quickly I cut and tied the umbilicus and wiped the mucus from the baby's eyes and mouth, wrapped it in a clean blanket and laid the child on Kate's chest.

With a sigh of relief I whispered the Flying Doctor's prayer; 'Please God, don't do this to me again.'

Poor Kate, agonised and weary from her shocking ordeal and the loss of blood, and very close to unconsciousness, seemed to come alive with the feel of the child on her breast and a few minutes later she was cradling the child on the crook of her arm, and patting Tom's head with her other hand. 'It's all right now, darling,' she whispered to him. 'you can go and rest now.'

Tom nodded, crawled into a corner of the cabin, and fainted.

Kate arrived at Preston Hospital forty-five minutes later. She went straight into surgery and the baby was put into intensive care. Four hours later they were out of danger.

When I gave Tom the good news, he jumped up and gave me a hug that almost collapsed my ribcage.

But the really unnerving part came as we were getting into my car outside. He opened the door, turned to me and said, 'Doc, you know I love my daughters, but what do you reckon about us trying again for a boy?'

I don't know, I just couldn't seem to think of an answer for him.

CHAPTER 3

It was just two years before the birth of Tom Doyle's fourth daughter that I had first arrived in the Kimberley.

It was a time of change in Australia. Two weeks before Robert Menzies had resigned as Prime Minister and leader of the Australian Liberal Party after a reign of sixteen years, to be replaced by Harold Holt. It was the end of an era. Decimal currency was about to be introduced to replace the old pounds, shillings and pence. And in a tiny Asian country called Vietnam, Australian servicemen had begun to fight their first war since Korea.

When I got off the plane and stepped out onto the tarmac, I had the sensation of walking into a sauna bath. I sucked in lungfuls of the thin, moist air; it was as though all the oxygen had been scorched out of it.

It was the middle of summer in north-west Australia, and so humid that the shirt on my back turned to wet cotton in a few minutes. The sun was high overhead, blistering the tarmac and the dry, red earth, beating down on the few white single-storey buildings and the assortment of huts and Quonset hangars that comprised Preston aerodrome.

The town lay on the rim of a huge gulf in the north-west of the Kimberley region of Australia, a rugged, arid and desolate area of vast cattle stations, Aboriginal reserves and gold and mineral claims. It was a place of huge distances, subject to flood and tropical storms during the 'wet' from November to March – when the temperatures soared high into the hundreds, but dry and parched the rest of the year.

Preston itself was a small town of about five thousand people, one of the two main cattle ports for the region. Down by the quay there was a long wooden jetty where cattle were herded on to the steamers for export to Perth and overseas; at low-tide it was left exposed on the mud flats, like the skeleton of some dark, ancient fossil.

It was all very different from what this doctor from Sydney was used to.

As I walked across the concrete apron towards the main building, I contemplated the things I had given up to come to this quiet little backwater. After three years on a microsurgical team at St George's Hospital in Sydney I had entered into private practice in Collaroy with two partners; we had a busy surgery and a handsome income. At the age of thirty-six I found myself with wealth, a family and a respected position in the community. I should have been happy – instead I was bored and restless. There is something in a man's spirit that seems to leave him dissatisfied with things that other men would welcome; I did not even know what more there was to want. But I would probably have continued my life of comfortable disenchantment in Collaroy until the day I retired if Life itself had not come along to tear down my little house of cards and force me to move on.

It was just a few months before, in September,

26

that my world collapsed around me.

My wife Angela and my young son were both killed in a smash on the Pittwater Road. All at once there was nothing left to live for.

In the weeks that followed there was little to do but go through the daily process of eating, drinking, breathing, sleeping. When I finally came to accept what had happened, I sold all that would remind me of my former life, and resolved to leave the old world behind – the house, the partnership, Collaroy, even the friends and family who had shown me so much kindness. I started to look round for something that would take me away from Sydney, something in which to immerse my energies and my thoughts, helping me to forget my own personal unhappiness.

And then one day, thumbing idly through a medical magazine I saw the advertisement for a medical officer with the Royal Flying Doctor Service in the the north-west of Australia. I applied for the position, and with surprising speed I was interviewed and accepted. In a few short weeks I had been whisked away from the traffic jams and the bustling shopping malls to the vast and lonely tracts of the Kimberleys.

Clifford Trenton, the man I was to replace reminded me of a retired English major. He was a tall, slim man with sandy-coloured hair and a luxuriant moustache. He wore a khaki shirt and shorts and long white socks, a uniform that was to become almost a necessity in the damp, tropical conditions. He ambled across the airfield to meet me, his pipe clenched between strong white teeth, grinning broadly and revealing a huge gap between his front two teeth that was at once comic and appealing.

'You must be Hazzard,' he said, pumping my hand energetically. 'Cliff Trenton.' I thought I detected a trace of an Oxford accent.

'Mike Hazzard,' I gasped. 'Nice to meet you.' Perspiring heavily in my jacket and long slacks I was happy to hand over my bags and climb gratefully into his white Holden, parked in the shade of a white gum behind the terminal building.

'Good flight?' Trenton asked.

'Not bad. Had to wait three hours for my connection in Perth. I'm glad to be here at last.'

'You won't feel like that for long,' Trenton said, and laughed.

As we drove I got my first glimpse of the town that was to be my home for the next two years.

After the busy streets of Collaroy and the central metropolis of Sydney, Preston was something of a shock. Although it was the middle of the day, the main street was deserted, except for two Aboriginal women who were shouting obscenities at each other on the verandah outside a chemist's shop. A few old cars, smeared with the orange dusty stain peculiar to Northern Australia, were parked haphazardly along the street. As with many country towns in outback Australia, Preston reminded me of a set from a Wild West picture, with its shaded sidewalks, balconies and two-storey red brick buildings.

'That's the main watering hole,' Trenton was saying as we passed a huge edifice on the corner, with the sign 'Union Hotel'. 'The publican's a pretty decent sort of bloke. Gets bad arthritis occasionally so I slip him some phenylbutazone. He'll see you right for a free bottle of spirits occasionally.'

'I'll bear it in mind,' I said.

We drove down past the quay, and Trenton pointed out the long wooden jetty disappearing far out into the Sound on the mud flats. Further out of town, the houses were mostly tin and asbestos and the sealed roads gave way to hard, rutted dirt tracks.

'This is the Hospital just coming up on our right,' Trenton nodded towards an assortment of white-painted buildings huddled between some cypress trees. 'The main building's a bit further on. They have some pretty good equipment there. An EEG and a kidney machine – that sort of thing.'

'Who's in charge?'

'A Doctor Fenwick. Charles Fenwick.' Trenton's voice had a sardonic edge to it as he said the name and I looked round at him quizzically.

'What's he like?' I asked.

'Charming fellow. Absolutely charming.' And he smiled, a broad grin, the pipe clenched firmly between the Terry Thomas teeth.

We had turned into a long, quiet street of white-painted asbestos homes. 'Well, here it is,' Trenton suddenly announced. 'Preston Palace'.

The doctor's Residence was like all the others in the street, perhaps a little larger. It had a wide, shady verandah and shutters on all the windows. It looked tidy and well-kept, but a little spartan compared to the air-conditioned comfort of my home in Collaroy. Still, I thought, when in Rome . . .

I opened the creaking wooden gate, which obligingly came off in my hand.

'I've been meaning to fix that,' Trenton laughed.

I looked around. There was a small patch of garden out at the front – couch grass battling dourly with the hot sun and sandy soil, bordered by a few native bushes and a handful of dried-up begonias.

I felt suddenly depressed.

Inside the house it was thankfully a little cooler, and the fly mesh on the doors and windows kept the busy, buzzing insects outside at bay. Most of them, anyway.

'I'll put your cases in your room,' Trenton said cheerfully. 'It isn't the Taj Mahal, but it's pretty comfortable. Have a look round.'

Trenton was right, it wasn't the Taj Mahal.

There was a large living room, decorated with an odd assortment of teak and mahogany furniture, and at the window were some faded blue curtains. In the middle of the room stood a large, lumpy yellow sofa that looked as though it had fallen in through a hole in the roof and nobody could be bothered to shift it. There were some badly-painted landscapes in inadequate frames and a few Aboriginal artefacts hanging from nails in the plasterboard. It was a room that had been furnished with a view to covering up the spaces.

I wandered out into the kitchen. From the back door I could see the small patch of grass leading off from the verandah, the outside toilet, the banana palms, the fringe of mulga trees that backed directly onto virgin bush, and a full-blood Aboriginal trotting up the steps in a cowboy hat and army surplus shorts, followed by an emu with a deformed foot.

'Yo-i, boss,' the man said, and walked in, went

30

straight to the fridge and took out a can of beer. 'You the new doc?'

'That's right,' I stammered, studying the apparition warily. Perhaps I had sunstroke already.

On the verandah the emu was pecking not very gently at the fly wire. 'Doan worry,' the man said, showing me a mouthful of gold fillings. 'You be okay. Any'ow, I'm George.' He grinned and slapped me heftily on the back.

'Mike Hazzard.'

'Good on yer. I better go see Ethel,' the man called George said. 'She doan like me leavin' her alone too long.'

And the apparition went back outside and as he descended the steps I saw him stop and offer the can to the limping emu, who sipped gratefully at the contents with her long beak.

Trenton came into the kitchen. 'I see you've met George,' he said.

'Who is he?'

'George? I don't know really. He just sort of hangs around. He can be very useful.'

'How did he get here?' I asked watching the gangly native saunter off into the bush with the strange bird following him.

'Damned if I know. He was here when I arrived in sixty-four and he's probably been around much longer than that. He just sort of goes along with the place. He tidies up now and then when he feels like it, and if you're away for a few days he always makes sure you've got plenty of food and beer in the fridge when you get back. Of course you have to leave him the money, and he does take a little as commission.'

'But who pays him?'

Trenton looked at me as if I'd asked him for the square root of three million and five. 'God knows. He sleeps on the verandah and when he wants anything he goes to the fridge. I shouldn't think anyone pays him. He's just George.'

I nodded slowly. 'I see.'

'Want a beer?' Trenton said. He produced a bottle of Swan lager from the fridge and two glasses. I was suddenly aware of the fine dusting of red grit in my mouth that was to become so familiar in the months ahead. I took the beer gratefully, and reflected on my new circumstances.

On the map it's two thousand miles from Sydney to Preston. I was just beginning to realise that it was much further than that.

Clyde Westcott had been with the Royal Flying Doctor Service in Preston for twenty-one years and he had seen a lot of doctors come and go. He was something of an institution in the Service. He had once met John Flynn, the founder, and had worked for a time with Allan Vickers, 'Aspro Allan', one of the colourful and charismatic doctors of the early days. Although nearing sixty he was exceptionally fit, the brown barrel of his body hard and upright. There were no signs of his years in the tanned, mobile face, although the brown putty-like features were a little dented from the boxing tournaments of his early youth.

'Yairs . . .' he was saying, in his slow, agonising drawl as we walked out to the radio station early the next morning. 'I've seen it all 'ere, you know. Been around a bit, you might say. I was with the Royal

Navy before I joined the Service. I was with the pearlers out of Broome before that. That's where I learned me Japanese. I was a radio engineer with the Navy in the war and they looked on me as a sort of secret weapon. Used to talk to the Nips in their own language, to confuse 'em like. Worked wonders in New Guinea. They even loaned me to the Americans once. Nimitz reckoned he would have lost Midway if it wasn't for Senior Signalman Westcott.'

Trenton had brought me out to the base to introduce me to Clyde, and so that I could see at firsthand how the radio system worked. The Flying Doctor base was situated a little out of town to avoid interference from domestic radio sets and other electrical apparatus. It consisted of two buildings – an old rambling brick bungalow with a red corrugated iron roof, where the Westcotts lived and the radio post itself, which was little more than an asbestos hut. There were two rooms. One housed the generator, the other contained the large transmitter/receiver that had brought a voice and a mantle of safety to the isolated backlands of the Kimberley.

'Yairs,' Clyde went on. 'I've got a few stories I could tell you about the war, young man. I got sunk by the Nips three times. They was goin' to give me a medal but I told 'em I didn't want one. Don't agree with medals and ribbons and all that carry on. It's like boastin'. If a man can't be satisfied with havin' served his country without lettin' everyone know about it, he shouldn't do it.'

As we were about to go into the hut, something caught my eye on the wall outside. A pure white pelt hung next to the door. I looked closer. It was a dingo skin.

'Yairs,' Clyde said. 'Shot it meself.'

'Did you? Where?' I said, running my hand across the astonishingly white fur.

'It was trying to get in the window round there. I was sitting on the verandah up at the house one night when I spotted him.'

'He's snow white. Dingo fur is usually yellow, isn't it?'

'Yairs,' Clyde said. 'But we've had so much sun the last couple of years I reckon it's bleached a lot of them.'

'You're kidding,' I said. I looked at Clyde sharply, but his face was as expressionless as a suet pudding.

'Yairs,' said Clyde. 'See where the eyes are missin'? That's where the bullet went through.'

I peered a little more closely at the eye sockets and when I turned round Clyde had gone inside and Trenton was doubled over laughing.

The Royal Flying Doctor Radio was used for far more than simply the relaying of emergency messages. At set hours the doctor had consultations with patients dotted for hundreds of miles around the north-west; it was like a normal surgery except that the physician was not able to actually examine the patient. Minor injuries and ailments could be treated this way, although more chronic or elusive complaints had to wait for the regular clinics that were held around the Kimberley region on a monthly basis.

The Radio Service also acted as a vital communication link in the isolated region, relaying and receiving telegrams from widely-spread stations and minerals exploration teams who would otherwise have been cut off from the outside world. These telegrams were then passed on to the Post Office for normal transmission. For doing this, the Royal Flying Doctor Service received a good commission, enabling them to run their operations without relying totally on government subsidy and donations.

In the radio hut, already warming rapidly to the sun's early rays, Clyde was hunched over the mike, opening the day's transmissions.

'This is Six Victor X-ray, Flying Doctor Preston. The time is seven-thirty. Are there any emergency medical calls? Over.'

Clyde switched the set to 'receive', and there was the crackle of static as he waited for any of the listening stations to call in. After a few seconds, Clyde turned the switch back to 'transmit'.

'We will now relay telegrams. These are the stations for which I have messages . . .'

As Clyde read out the list of radio codes, Trenton showed me the records of the emergency calls over the last twelve months. I was surprised to find that there were long periods of up to a week when he had not been up in the air once; on several other occasions he had been forced to make up to three flights in one day. It was as we were going through these records that I overheard the conversation between Clyde and Six Charlie Foxtrot, Fortune Creek, a name that became increasingly familiar to me over the next two years.

'Telegram for Six Charlie Foxtrot, Fortune Creek – do you read me, over?'

There was a brief burst of static and then, very clear: 'Good morning Clyde. I bet it's from that old bastard, Joe Parker, Over.'

Clyde appeared unruffled by the unorthodox radio procedure. 'Six Charlie Foxtrot, I have a telegram for you from a Mr Joseph Parker, of 23 Glynn Way, Mount Lawley in Perth. Message reads: RECEIVED YOUR MESSAGE STOP GO TO HELL STOP WILL NOT GIVE YOU ANOTHER CENT STOP Message ends. Will you please repeat, over.'

Clyde switched to 'receive'.

'Tell him he's an old . . .'

Clyde deftly flicked the switch back to 'transmit'. There was the shattering whine of the carrier wave and then silence. Finally, in his own leisurely drawl, Clyde said 'Yairs, well, if you wish to reply Six Charlie Foxtrot, I'll be taking telegrams for transmission about eight-thirty. Over and out.'

It seemed appropriate to me at the time that I should get to meet all the people I would be working with in the coming months. One of my chief priorities was the administrator of the local hospital, Charles Fenwick. Trenton seemed amused when I suggested this to him, and showed no interest in introducing me personally. 'But by all means take the car,' he added. 'After all, it is yours now anyway.'

Preston Hospital had fifty-five beds, and five nurses including a matron. There were two junior doctors as well as Fenwick. It was an untidy, rambling place with a central brick building surrounded by a number of smaller huts and annexe wards. The immediate impression was of a sleepy organisation that had suddenly woken up and found itself needed.

As I walked through the main entrance, the receptionist looked up from the pages of *The Fires of Passion* and studied me with a mixture of boredom and irritation, as if I was a fractious employee who had come in to ask for a rise. I smiled and nodded cheerfully.

'I was looking for Doctor Fenwick.'

'Do you have an appointment?'

'I'm the new medical officer with the Flying Doctor Service.' I waited for the information to seep through the girl's consciousness and impress, but instead her expression changed to the look of incredulous disgust one might exhibit having trod on a particularly greasy dog's dropping.

'I'll tell him you're here,' she said and slouched away into the office behind her. After a few moments she reappeared, sat down at her desk and continued to digest *The Fires of Passion*.

'Will he be long?' I said.

'I don't know, do I?'

I smiled and resisted the impulse to shake her by the shoulders. I would content myself with reporting her conduct to Fenwick. I hummed softly to myself, and began to examine the photographs around the wall of the foyer. They were all black and white, neatly framed: 'The Queen visits Preston Hospital, escorted by Dr. C. Fenwick May 20, 1963'; 'The Queen with Dr. C. Fenwick May 20, 1963'; 'The Queen shaking hands with Dr. C. Fenwick, May 20, 1963'. Pride of place on the wall was reserved for an oil-colour portrait of an austere middle-aged man, his brown wavy hair streaked with silver, sombrely dressed in a dark suit. Underneath, in gold leaf, was the inscription: Dr C.C. Fenwick, BM, Ch.D, FRACS.

I heard a voice behind me and I turned round and found myself face to face with the portrait.

'Yes, can I help you?'

I smiled and held out my hand. Fenwick looked at it quizzically as if I was offering him a fish wrapped in newspaper. 'Doctor Michael Hazzard. I'm the new medical officer with the Flying Doctor Service.'

Fenwick continued to stare. His face still had a vaguely enquiring look as if I'd spoken half the sentence in Swahili.

'Yes?' he said finally.

'I came over to introduce myself.'

Fenwick looked irritated. 'You'd better come in,' he said at last, pointedly ignoring my outstretched palm. Obviously the treasured digits were reserved for royalty only.

I followed him into his office. I was impressed.

It was more like the office of a dean or a professor than the administrator of an obscure country hospital. I found myself surrounded by textbooks, framed diplomas and more pictures of the Queen at Preston Hospital on May 20, 1963 with Fenwick grinning epileptically over her right shoulder. It was a wonder there wasn't a snap of him elbowing Philip out of the way.

Fenwick slid into a brown leatherette chair and I found myself standing on my own halfway across the room, looking at Fenwick's silhouette against the sunlight streaming in from the window directly behind him. It made him look as if he had a halo, which is probably exactly the impression he wanted to give.

'Well,' he said. 'State your business.'

I sat down in the chair across the desk from him, squinting slightly into the glare.

'As I said, Doctor Fenwick, it was just a courtesy call. I thought, as we would be working fairly closely together from now on . . .'

'I think that's probably a misconception on your part,' Fenwick cut in. He had a silver pen between the forefingers of each hand and surveyed me grandly, like a psychiatrist studying a particularly neurotic patient.

I was stumbling for words. 'Well, we will be treating the same patients some of the time.'

'Correction, Doctor . . .?'

'Hazzard.'

'Yes. I will be treating my patients. Your job is simply to bring them here when they require treatment beyond the scope of your little black bag. I hope that is understood.'

There was a heavy silence in the room. I momentarily considered wrapping the Queen at Preston Hospital, May 20, 1963 across his skull and going back to Collaroy. Then there was a knock on the door and someone burst into the room behind me.

'Oh, I'm sorry, Doctor Fenwick . . .' It was a woman's voice.

'That's quite all right,' Fenwick said. 'Doctor Hubbord is just going.' He got up and went towards the door.

'Hazzard,' I said heavily.

'Yes. This is Matron Margaret Renford. Margaret, this young man is taking over the running of the Black Man's Ambulance. He came to introduce himself.'

Matron Renford was a stern, robust woman of early middle age. She smelled of antiseptic. I smiled quickly in her direction. I knew better than to hold out my hand in this place.

She gave me a quick, searching glance and turned back to Fenwick. 'Mr Reynolds is having respiratory problems, doctor. I'd like you to have a look at him.'

'Of course.' Fenwick turned back to me. 'You must excuse us doctor. Unlike yourself, we haven't the time to visit anyone but our patients.'

And they left me standing there.

As I got in the car outside the Hospital I thought again of Trenton's comment and found myself echoing his sentiments as I drove away. 'Charming fellow. Absolutely charming . . .'

CHAPTER 4

I think you'll understand that it was a little unnerving
to discover that my pilot was accident-prone.

He limped towards us from under the wing of the
single-engine Cessna, his left hand heavily bandaged
and his face a mass of cuts and bruises. Joe Kennedy
was in fact older than he looked – preoccupation
with his impending doom hadn't aged him a bit. He
had a mop of unruly sandy hair and a bulbous,
plum-coloured nose that sat square in the middle of
his face as if it had nowhere better to go. His eyes
had the forlorn expression of a basset hound.

'Joe,' Trenton was saying, 'I'd like you to meet
my replacement, Michael Hazzard. Mike, this is Joe
Kennedy. He'll be your pilot,'

'You poor sod,' Joe said. He held out his left
hand, and with some difficulty, I shook it.

'What happened to you?' I said. The man called
Kennedy looked back at me with a querulous
expression as if unaware of his own appearance.

'Nothing.'

'He fell down some steps at his bungalow,'
Trenton explained. 'He never looks where he's
going. Clumsiest bugger I've ever come across.'

Thus reassured about the competence of the man
who was supposedly entrusted with my life, I followed the two of them across the tarmac to the plane.

The Cessna had been in service at Preston for four

41

years, and it had proved to be an ideal machine for the conditions, although the cabin space was small and a little cramped. The cockpit had been adapted for use by the Service with the doctor seated next to the pilot at the controls, and room for a stretcher case and another seated passenger behind.

It was stiflingly hot in the cabin, and we were all anxious to be away. I helped Trenton load our equipment aboard and in a few minutes we were taxiing along the runway for the short flight to Brookton Downs.

We received clearance from the tower and soon we were speeding away down the tarmac strip and then we were clear of the ground, soaring high into the pale blue sky. The Kimberleys spread into a panorama around us, as the shadow of the Cessna gradually dwindled to a small black cross on the ochre earth below us, no larger than a postage stamp.

Suddenly, we were looking out over the Stirling Sound, with the gleaming tin roofs of Preston away to our right. Joe banked the plane to port and we turned towards the mainland and the Van Gelten plateau. We flew in over the tangled mangrove swamps and teeming wildfowl of the Sound, and the clear blue waters of Frenchman's Bay; directly ahead of us lay the dramatic contours of the Kimberley plateau.

Joe seemed unmoved by it all. He continued to stare out of the cockpit with morose concentration while Trenton chattered aimlessly at him from the next seat. He made no appearance of listening, although he did sneeze occasionally to let us know he was still alive.

'I think I'm allergic to the sky,' he muttered once,

then lapsed again into silence.

For better or worse, I was on my first Flying Doctor operation. Not, as I had imagined, an errand of mercy to some beleaguered station in the middle of the outback to save a dying stockman named Clancy, but, as it turned out, a routine flight to one of the larger and more hospitable of the cattle stations in the Kimberley to treat two cases of arthritis, an Aborigine with haemorrhoids and to lance a boil.

'Joe,' I said, after we had been in the air for about fifteen minutes, 'How long will it take to reach Brookton?'

'About another forty-five minutes,' Joe said. 'If we don't crash.'

'Well, would you mind if I have a spell at the controls later on? I used to fly a Cessna in Sydney.' I had flown one once.

Joe's sad grey eyes looked at me as if I was a voodoo death curse that had just been pushed under his door.

'You serious?' he said.

'I do have a private pilot's licence. I had a Piper in Sydney.'

'All right,' Joe said wearily. 'Why not? Who wants to get old?'

'You mean you can handle one of these things?' Trenton asked. He looked impressed.

'I've been flying for years. Just for pleasure.'

Joe frowned. *'For pleasure!'* I heard him mutter. 'I'll let you have a spell later on, okay?' he said, but of course he conveniently forgot my request and I didn't press the point as it was my first time up with him. But I was determined that later on I would put in some hours at the controls of the aircraft.

Besides, I was absorbed with the scenery below

us. After the green parks and forests I had flown over in the Blue Mountains bordering Sydney, it seemed a very wild and desolate landscape indeed. The high savannah grasslands uninhabited but for the herds of roaming cattle and sheep, were dotted with white gum, boabs and paper bark; the wide plains were etched with deep, rock-walled gorges and rivers flowing over shallow pebbled beds. Occasionally, we would see flocks of pink and grey galahs rise screeching high into the air as the noise of the engine disturbed their primordial quiet.

Suddenly, Trenton turned round in his seat. 'You're not married, are you Mike?'

'No.'

Trenton nodded. 'Well, you'll like Brookton then,' he said with a sly grin.

'What do you mean?'

Trenton just grinned. 'You'll see.'

Brookton Downs was one of the largest cattle stations in the west Kimberley. It covered a distance of over thirteen hundred square miles, employing twenty stockmen and boasting over ten thousand head of cattle. The homestead was a hundred miles from Preston across the Van Gelten plateau and twenty-five miles from the Gibb River Beef Road. It was run by a man named Hoagan, a descendant of one of the original settlers in the region over a hundred years before.

As we passed over the station I could make out the name BROOKTON painted proudly in white on top of one of the sheds.

We landed on a wide, dusty strip some two miles away. Joe turned the plane round and we taxied to a halt a few yards from a battered blue utility, driven by two half-caste stockmen.

We waited in the ute while Joe secured the plane with guideropes and pegs. 'A cockeye bob come along, it would turn the plane over as easy as flipping a coin,' Joe had said. 'That'd be just my luck.'

Then we were bouncing away across the plain, between the boabs and gum trees, to Brookton Downs.

The station consisted of a couple of sheds, a few barns for the horses, a storehouse and a large rectangular wooden hut that I guessed was the men's quarters. The homestead itself was a large grey-stone building, with a sturdy chimney of red brick. Pack and riding saddles hung over the rails under the wide bark verandah that extended right around the house. Half a dozen battered and dusty vehicles and a couple of old Ford trucks were parked outside the house; on the porchway about a dozen men sat around in the shade awaiting our arrival – the day's customers.

As soon as the ute pulled to a halt in front of the house, we were instantly surrounded by a mass of small, brown-eyed Aboriginal children and scrawny, yapping dogs.

Suddenly, the front door of the house burst open and Jesse Hoagan clumped out onto the balcony. Immediately the children and the dogs disappeared.

'You're late,' he said, squinting into the bright midday sun.

'Hello Jess,' Trenton said cheerily, ignoring the reproach. 'How's it going?'

'Orright. Who's the white skinny bloke?' he said, nodding in my direction.

'That's Doctor Hazzard. He'll be taking over from me at the end of the week. He's just out from Sydney.'

Hoagan gave me a long, appraising look.

He was a short, red-faced man of beefy Irish stock, his skin the colour of old leather from a life lived in the saddle. He had quick, shrewd eyes and I had the uncomfortable feeling that his preliminary inspection of me wasn't to his liking.

'You just get used to one bloke, and they change 'em round.' he stared at me for a moment as if it was my fault. Finally he said 'Well – don't just stand there. You'd better come in.'

The house was a fair reflection of the man. Stockwhips and branding irons hung on nails around the walls. The furniture was good quality but mostly drab, solid and spartan; there were no cushions on any of the chairs and no curtains on the windows. The only real decoration hung over the fireplace: a pair of huge bullock horns, finely polished – the symbol of a proud cattleman.

'I've set you up in the corner over there, as usual,' Jesse Hoagan said, indicating a pitcher of water and a few towels neatly laid out on a polished mahogany table.

'I'll go and tell the first one to come in, shall I?'

'Not so fast, Jess,' Trenton said. 'I want to find out how you are first.'

'Me? Never been better.'

'I heard you've been having chest pains again.'

'Who told you that?' Hoagan said. Suddenly his expression changed and he looked for a moment like a schoolboy who'd been caught smoking in the lavatory.

'Never mind who told me. How about we have a look at you?'

Hoagan thrust his thick thumbs into the belt at his waist and stuck out his jaw. 'Look here, Doctor Trenton, there's nothing wrong with me and I don't care what she says. There's enough blokes what are crook round here without worryin' about blokes what ain't.' And he stormed out, slamming the door behind him.

After he'd gone, Trenton turned to me. 'I want you to keep an eye on him. I think he's got a bad ticker but he won't come into the hospital to have it checked out. Obstinate old bastard. He could be dying of pain and he wouldn't tell you. And he fusses around everyone else like a mother hen.'

Our patients that afternoon were all from the surrounding area, mostly from other, smaller cattle stations; there were a couple of station hands, half-castes, from Brookton itself. All of them had been on Trenton's consultation list, and he had been in touch with them regularly over the Flying Doctor radio. One of the Brookton hands had file cards an inch or more thick; he was a hopeless hypochondriac and everyone knew him as Aspirin. 'He comes with the job,' Trenton grinned at me after the man had left with a phial of sugar pills for his 'smallpox'.

It was late into the afternoon when he finished. Jesse Hoagan, Trenton and myself were sitting in the kitchen of the old house, each of us with a glass of cool beer. It was more than welcome after the languid heat of the afternoon.

Suddenly we heard shouts outside. The door burst open and I got my first glimpse of Megan Hoagan.

Outback women can be handsome, but they are rarely pretty. They are mostly thick-set and broad-shouldered, even as girls, built for a life of hard work and childbearing. They are often raucous and good humoured but seldom do you find the poise of a city girl.

Which is why I was so totally unprepared for Megan Hoagan.

As she was led into the room, I could see straight away that she had not inherited her looks from Hoagan's side of the family. She was slim, tall and fair-haired; it was difficult indeed to imagine what part Jesse had played in her conception. She wore no make-up and her face was streaked with grime and perspiration, yet despite her plain jeans and cotton check shirt she still looked good enough to make a film starlet spit. I could see Trenton grinning at me across the table and I knew then why Brookton was such a great attraction for unmarried men.

One of the station boys helped her into the room. There were cuts on her face and she was grimacing with pain and holding her arm. Jesse Hoagan was out of his chair in an instant.

'What happened?'

'Her horse fell, boss,' the boy was saying as he helped Megan into one of the chairs. 'I think she broke her arm. It wasn't my fault,' he added, glancing warily at Jesse.

Hoagan looked angrily at Trenton. 'Well, come on! This is an emergency.'

Trenton looked lazily in my direction. 'Your first case,' he said.

At his words, a swift memory passed through my mind of the first consultation I ever performed as a

48

green young intern. It involved a man with a cracked bone in his leg. The hospital's chief surgeon leaned over my left shoulder and asked me what I thought was wrong. I could feel his hot breath on the back of my neck. I stammered out that I thought it was popliteus tendonitis and tried to manipulate the leg. The man screamed and so did the chief surgeon, only for different reasons. It is one of those emotional scars that I suppose every young intern carries away with him from medical school . . .

While I was examining Megan's arm I had what was almost a déjà vu experience. Only as I held the frail and swollen arm it wasn't the chief surgeon's breath on the back of my neck, it was Jesse Hoagan's. I remember thinking 'One scream and you're gone.'

I heard an ominous growl in my ear. 'Are you sure you know what you're doing?'

Trenton's voice came from somewhere behind me: 'Mike's a bone specialist,' he lied. 'Your daughter couldn't be in better hands.'

'How did it happen?' I asked.

'Sherri – my mare – slipped. I don't know . . . it must have been a rabbit hole. She fell forwards. I just remember putting my hand out and then I was on the ground.'

'Well, there don't appear to be any broken bones.'

'Are you sure?' Hoagan said, close to my left ear.

I restrained from the urge to say, 'No, it's a wild guess,' and took some mercurochrome out of the medical kit to treat the cuts on her forehead, 'Now, this might sting a bit.'

'Be careful with her,' Hoagan breathed.

As I smeared the vermilion-coloured antiseptic on

the cuts I was able to get a closer look at the girl. She was older than I had thought at first glance, perhaps twenty-two or twenty-three. She had blue eyes and high, perfectly-chiselled cheekbones. Perhaps her mother was French, I mused, certainly there had to be European blood in the family. I looked round at Hoagan and wondered at the miracle of genetics.

'Did you black out at all?'

'No. No, I don't think so.'

'All right, we'll give you a couple of Dispirin for your arm and put it in a sling for a few days to make sure you rest it. It should be fine in about a week.' I looked up at Jesse. 'Keep an eye on her. If she has any nausea or clouding of vision, get on to me straight away. I'll contact you tomorrow during the consultation times.'

Hoagan looked at me dubiously and gave a long sigh. 'Are you sure you know what you're doing?' he said.

A quarter of an hour later as the utility drove us back to the bare sandy strip of the airfield, I asked Trenton about the girl.

'Bit of a mystery to me too,' Trenton said. 'God knows, I think enough men have tried to get her off the station but she doesn't seem interested. A few have come close – so I'm told. I don't know – maybe she just doesn't like men. Dreadful waste.'

'Who was her mother?'

'Young English girl. Died when Megan was just a kid, I believe,' Trenton looked at me seriously. 'You'd better keep a close check on that arm. Make sure complications don't set in.'

And of course, complications did set in, but not the physical kind.

CHAPTER 5

It was on the way back from Brookton Downs that I was called out to my first emergency. I very nearly made it my last.

Trenton and I were chatting casually about the day's events. I had a feeling of complacency and well-being, a sensation I was to recognise later as a sure sign of impending disaster.

'So what do you think so far?' Trenton was saying.

'Not much different from the practice in Sydney really,' I said smiling smugly. 'Except the consulting rooms aren't as comfortable.'

'Yes, well today was a pretty easy day. don't forget you haven't been on an emergency call yet.'

The Cessna was fitted with a two-way radio tuned to the Royal Flying Doctor frequency and in the background we could hear Clyde's monotonous drawl reading out a long list of telegrams to outposts all around the west Kimberley. The volume was turned right down to little more than a drone. Suddenly an urgent, strident voice broke in.

'This is Disaster Creek here, we need help. Can you hear me out there?'

Clyde's leisurely, unflustered tones came back next. 'Yairs, all stations off the air, please. We have an emergency medical message here. Will that station please come in again. Everybody silent please.'

'This is Disaster Creek. Our cook's had a bad accident. We need the doctor out here quick, over.'

'This is Six Victor X-ray, Flying Doctor Preston, we have received your message. Did you get that, Six Charlie Tango? Over.'

Trenton picked up the intercom and pressed the relay switch. 'Six Charlie Tango. I've got it Clyde.' Trenton called up the man at Disaster Creek and asked him to explain what had happened.

'Cook's had an accident,' the voice said, over the crackle and whine of the static. 'Very nasty.'

'What sort of accident? Over.'

'It's our lady cook. She's had a fall.'

'What injuries does she have? Over.'

'Can't tell.'

Trenton looked at me. Frustration was apparent on his face. 'Why not? Where is she? Over.'

'We can't get to her,' the voice said. 'It's very nasty.'

'Why can't you get to her? Over.'

'She's down 'ole.'

Trenton looked at Joe. 'What do they do at Disaster Creek, Joe?'

'They got a mine there,' Joe said. 'Copper and tin, I think. Maybe she's fallen down a shaft.'

Joe considered a moment. 'About twenty minutes. It's just to the north of here. But it means we might have to make our way back in the dark. That's always dangerous,' he added gloomily.

'We don't have any choice,' Trenton said. Then he turned to me. 'Well, looks like we're in business.' He pressed the transmit button on the intercom.

'This is Six Charlie Tango, Flying Doctor Mobile calling Disaster Creek. Do you read me?'

'I've got ya, sport.'

'We'll be there in about twenty minutes. What sort of condition is your landing ground in?'

The voice came back with the time-honoured catchphrase of outback Australia: 'Oh, she'll be right,' it said. 'Over and out.'

Disaster Creek was tucked away at the foot of a wide gorge in the Taylor Range sixty miles to the north-east of Preston. Twenty minutes later we were flying over the tiny array of tin huts and sheds where the miners lived, bordered on three sides by steep rocky walls. The landing strip, a small brownish scar near the foot of the gorge, looked painfully small. Joe flew low over the site a couple of times to check the strip itself.

'It's going to be tricky getting up again,' he said, 'especially if it's dark. We'll probably fly straight into one of those mountains.'

'Take her down, Joe,' Trenton said wearily.

'All right. It's your funeral,' Joe said. 'And mine, of course,' he added heavily. He turned the plane through a hundred and eighty degrees at the far end of the gorge and took the Cessna down in a steep descent.

I soon learned that despite Joe's melancholy demeanour, he was nevertheless a very good pilot. Just as it seemed we were going to nose-dive into the scrub below he pulled the nose up and settled the wheels down onto the makeshift runway. Although it had looked fairly smooth from above, the surface was far from ideal, being strewn with small stones and potholes, and our tiny plane shuddered and bumped like a bicycle on a corrugated iron roof, until it seemed that the frail little craft must tear apart. Finally we braked to a halt about thirty feet from a massive boulder that marked the end of the runway – one way or another.

'My God,' I whispered. 'Are all the strips like this one?'

'Oh no,' Joe said. 'Some are a lot worse.'

The airstrip was just a hundred yards or so away from the settlement. Even before we had rolled to a halt I could see a small barrel of a man running towards us across the scrub, his bush hat dancing crazily on his head, his round belly jumping up and down inside his shirt like some monstrous beanbag.

Trenton jumped out of the cockpit first.

'S'truth, I'm glad to see you guys,' the man said. 'She's screamin' her bloody lungs out over there.'

Sure enough we could hear someone yelling, off in the distance. I pulled our emergency equipment out of the back seat and jumped down to the ground beside Trenton.

'Harry Barham's the name,' the man said.

'Hello, Harry. I'm Doctor Trenton and this is Doctor Hazzard.'

'Right, well, you'd better follow me,' Harry said.

'Now, what happened here?' Trenton asked, as we hurried across the scrub towards the tiny settlement, little Harry Barham scurrying ahead of us.

'It's our cook,' Harry babbled. 'She's been screamin' something terrible ever since it happened. I'm glad you blokes got here as quick as you did. Jeez, it's nasty.'

'Well, what exactly happened?' Trenton repeated.

Harry Barham continued to be vague. 'She fell down 'ole,' he said. 'I think she must have busted somethin'.'

When we reached the camp a group of men were standing around in the middle of the clearing like a gang of unemployed round a dole office, waiting for the cheques to arrive. There was a low murmur as we reached the group and for a few crazy moments Trenton, Harry and I stood on the fringe of the crowd, looking at each other, waiting for someone to do something.

The yelling now was very close. 'OH CHRIST ORMIGHTY! WHERE ARE YOU, YOU BAS-TARDS?'

Other expletives followed. Trenton and I stared at each other. Harry stared back at us. Nobody moved. Then Trenton said 'Well? *Where is she?*'

Harry Barham nodded towards a wooden build-ing at the edge of the clearing. Trenton blanched. 'Oh my God, no.'

Suddenly I too realised what it was we were staring at.

'She hasn't fallen *in*?' Trenton gulped, staring at Harry.

'I'll get you blokes a torch, shall I?' Harry said.

'Why didn't you tell us?' I said angrily.

'I was afraid you wouldn't come.'

'OH JEEEEESUS! SOMEBODY GET ME OUT OF THIS . . .' The obscenities echoed around the gorge as the late afternoon sun started to fleck the steep walls of the gorge with a rosy pink glow.

'How did it happen?' Trenton asked.

'Well she's a big girl,' Harry said. 'The white ants must have got at the wood. I suppose she sat down and the thing collapsed. First we knew was when we heard her scream.'

'How badly is she hurt?' I said.

'Dunno.'

'What do you mean, you don't know?' Trenton growled.

Harry shrugged.

'Hasn't anyone been down there?' I said.

'We didn't see any point,' Harry said sheepishly. 'We thought we'd wait for you.'

'Thank you very much,' Trenton said.

Trenton and I approached the wooden building like two sappers about to defuse a mine. Trenton pushed the door open with his foot and we peered in. The WC was a large affair with two wooden holes for communal comfort – or it had been once. Now there was one small hole, and one large jagged one, opening onto the cesspit several feet below. The screams from the murky depths were deafening. The lady in question obviously possessed a very fair set of lungs.

I turned round to Harry. 'What's her name?'

'Bessie,' Harry said. 'She's a good cook. We'd hate to lose her.'

I braced myself and took a few steps inside.

'OH CHRIST ORMIGHTY! GET ME OUT!' Another long string of expletives followed.

Gingerly I cleared my throat. 'Hello? Bessie?'

'GET ME OUT OF HERE YOU BASTARDS! Ow, me bleedin' leg!'

'Bessie, this is Doctor Hazzard here. Hold on, we'll have you out soon.'

'OW GAWD, 'URRY UP!'

Trenton turned to Barham who was hovering anxiously at his shoulder. 'We'll need a torch and some lengths of good strong rope. Can you fix that?'

'Sure,' Harry said and he was gone.

I looked at Trenton. 'What are we going to do?'

Trenton looked round at the group of men who were gathered outside the WC doing their best to avoid his eyes. He licked his lips thoughtfully. 'Well, what would you do if I wasn't here?'

'Well, I suppose I'd have to go down and get her out myself.'

Trenton looked pleased. 'Exactly,' he said.

I felt my heart disappear down the hole with Bessie. 'But I can't.' I felt panic beginning to take hold.

'Just like being back in Sydney,' Trenton said with a smug grin. 'Except the consulting rooms aren't as comfortable.'

I searched Trenton's face desperately for some outward sign of compassion. 'You're the new Flying Doctor. I just stayed on to show you the ropes – if you'll pardon the pun.'

At that moment Harry reappeared with some lengths of rope and a torch. With a sour glance at Trenton I took the torch and shone it down the hole. In the thin beam of light I got my first glimpse of Bessie's plight. The poor woman was lying on her back in a pool of nameless muck. Around the lower half of her body were the remains of the wooden seat. She was indeed a big girl. I turned round to Barham, who was already backing out of the door. 'How much does she weigh?'

'I don't know,' Harry said. 'Will you be wanting me for anything else?' But before I could answer, he was gone.

I steeled myself for the ordeal. Trenton lowered me down into the hole on the rope and gingerly I eased myself through the jagged entrance and, torch

57

clenched in one hand, descended into the putrid blackness.

The stench was almost a physical thing. Something wet and warm seeped into my sandals and through my socks. It was appallingly hot and the smell hit me like a wave of gas. For a moment I thought I was going to pass out. I swayed a little against the rope, gagging. By sheer effort of will, I forced myself to get on with the job.

I shone the torch on the beleaguered woman directly beneath me. I tried to sound as reassuring as I could.

'Hello Bessie. I'm Doctor Hazzard.'

'I want to die,' Bessie whimpered. 'I just want to die.'

'Where are you hurt?'

'Me leg. Oh God, get me out of here.'

Bessie was indeed a pitiful sight. Her drawers were still round her ankles, her injury and her enormous bulk denying her even the most limited movement. She had fallen probably little more than eight or ten feet and she might have escaped serious injury altogether if not for the wooden seat which had remained trapped beneath her.

I forced myself down on my haunches. A quick examination revealed that she had broken her thigh down by the knee. I was relieved to find that it was a closed fracture.

I stood up, leaning drunkenly against the rope. We had to get her out, but the problem was – how? The stretcher would never get through that hole. The whole WC would have to go – and quickly.

'You won't leave me here, will you?' Bessie whispered.

'I'll be right back, Bessie.' I shouted to Trenton whose face peered down anxiously a couple of feet above me. 'Haul me up.'

I gasped in the fresh air. The group of onlookers moved further away, muttering. Even Trenton himself took a few paces back.

'Well, how is she?'

'She has a broken thigh. We'll have to get a stretcher down there.'

'It'll never fit.'

I turned to Harry. 'We need to make the hole bigger.'

'We've got small sticks of dynamite in one of the sheds.'

I stared at him. I decided Harry Barham wasn't quite the full quid. 'Look you'll have to get to work on it with axes,' I said. 'I want the front of the WC and the remains of the seat knocked out. Only be careful. And get a couple of blokes to get the stretcher from the plane.'

Harry nodded. He turned and barked out commands to some of his men.

A quarter of an hour later only three walls of the WC remained. Two ropes had been fitted to the stretcher which was now ready to be lowered into the hole. I turned to Trenton.

'I'm going to need a hand.'

He looked panicky. His eyes roamed the horizon as if he'd just spotted something of enormous interest on the skyline. 'What would you do if I wasn't here?' he said at last.

'Exactly what you'd do if I wasn't here. Get someone to help.'

He laughed. 'You don't need me. I'm sure you've

got the experience to handle it all right. One of these other boys will go with you.'

There was an ominous silence.

'You're going down that hole,' I said, softly.

He looked at me, then at the stretcher. He clicked his tongue nervously. 'Okay, if you think you can't handle it.'

Trenton went down the rope first and I followed. Then I shouted to the men above us to start to lower the stretcher.

'We're going to have to lift her onto the stretcher very carefully,' I whispered. I could only see Trenton's silhouette in the darkness. He appeared to be trembling. For a moment I had forgotten about the stench. I was almost used to it.

'*Nnnnnnn*,' Trenton said.

We guided the stretcher down into the putrid sludge and Trenton and I took our positions next to Bessie. I took a deep breath and bent down, vowing not to inhale again until the job was finished. I supported the injured limb while Trenton strained to lift Bessie's enormous bulk a few inches up from the ground and onto the stretcher.

I wanted to gasp for breath, but I wouldn't, even though my chest felt as if it would burst. Finally the stretcher was being lifted up out of the hole.

'We've done it,' I whispered.

'*Nnnnnnn*,' Trenton said.

Back on the surface I drank in the cool, sweet evening air, mentally composing my letter of resignation to the RFDS director in Melbourne.

Bessie lay on the stretcher a few feet from the scene of her tragedy. My heart went out to her. Groaning with pain, she salvaged the vestages of her pride and, raising her head from the stretcher, she looked round at the faces of the group of shifting, shuffling men who had so cruelly deserted her in her hour of need.

'You bloody bastards,' she whispered hoarsely, and lowering her head back onto the stretcher, she closed her eyes.

Harry Barham looked first at me, then at Trenton. He almost held out his hand, then thought better of it.

'Thanks, you blokes,' he said. 'That could have been very nasty.'

Joe Kennedy stood by the side of the Cessna and watched us silently as we climbed into his aircraft. His nose twitched violently as we passed. He looked first at our feet and then at the foul-smelling smears on our clothing. With commendable aplomb he climbed into the cockpit after us, slammed shut the cabin door, got into his seat and pulled down the oxygen mask. He kept it over his face all the way to Preston.

I gave Bessie a shot of morphine to ease the pain but I don't know to this day if she ever outlived the sting of that humiliation. The last I heard of her she had gone to work on an experimental farm in the Libyan desert.

CHAPTER 6

A week later Trenton left, and I was out on my own. Since the incident at Disaster Creek our relationship had become a little strained, but I went out to the airport to see him off, as a sort of parting gesture. As he boarded the Avro Anson that was to take him back to Perth, he stopped at the top of the boarding ramp and made a motion with his foot, as if shaking the dust from his shoes. In retrospect, I can see that the symbolism may have been of a slightly richer nature.

It didn't take long to settle into the routine. Each morning, from nine o'clock to eleven there were my daily consultations. The telephones at the Flying Doctor Residence were linked to the radio base by land lines, and often I took the calls in the small office in the rear of the house. I had to adjust quickly to the unique methods of consultation; I would listen carefully as the patient described his or her symptoms, and with judiciously phrased questions, arrive at a diagnosis. Prescribing treatments was a little easier; all the stations are equipped with a specially numbered medical kit, containing ointments and drugs, as well as essentials such as bandages and a thermometer. If, for example, I wanted to put a patient on a course of pethidene, I would just say, 'One number forty-four after each meal.'

The system did have its drawbacks. There was an obvious lack of privacy, but most of my patients seemed unconcerned that their physical ailments, sometimes of a most intimate nature, were being broadcast over an area of ten thousand square miles to anyone. A case in point was my first conversation with a Mrs Cooper from a place called Bindi station, some three hundred miles to the east.

After she had explained her particular problem to me, I tried to get a few more details from her to help me with my diagnosis.

'And when did you first discover this lump on your breast, Mrs Cooper?'

'I didn't. My husband did, Over.'

'And when did you . . . he . . . first notice it? Over.'

'Last week. About five times.'

'And has it been bothering you? Over.'

There was a moment's silence. 'No. But it's been botherin' him.'

'I see. We'll, I'll be holding a clinic over your way next week, so I'll come and make a proper examination. Is there anything else? Over.'

'My husband wants to know if you've got any of those manuals they sell in the Cross in Sydney.'

Whatever I was expecting when I arrived at Bindi and met the Coopers, it certainly wasn't what I actually saw.

Mrs. Cooper, whose lump incidentally turned out to be quite benign, tipped the scales at seventeen stone, while her husband Bill – a hungry-faced satyr with leering eyes – was a hollow-cheeked little man, half her size and as thin as a rake.

They were known by the station hands as 'The

Needle and the Haystack'.

During the next month there were only two emergency calls; one to deliver a premature baby away on Glenroy station a hundred and sixty miles to the east, the other to bring in an Aborigine who had been speared in the leg after a ritual tribal punishment. My only other flight took me to a station north of Hall's Creek, for a routine clinic.

I learned the meaning of boredom. Although I was on call twenty-four hours a day, I was seldom needed in those first few weeks. I was used to perpetual motion in my practice in Sydney, and then I had treasured my spare time. Now it hung round my neck like a bag of cement. I spent many listless hours staring idly at the bush from the back verandah or hanging round the radio station listening to Clyde's fantastic stories. Ironically, my original purpose in taking the appointment, to find something to absorb me and stop my thoughts wandering back to the past, was the very thing I was denied.

I would have liked to have helped out at the Hospital, which was seriously understaffed, but Fenwick made it painfully clear that my assistance was not required.

There were other privations too, but they were endemic to the whole of outback Australia.

The problem I found hardest to cope with was the dust. It seemed to find its way into everything, a fine orange powder that left a greasy film over everything. Then there were the flies – some as big as ducks and always two or three zooming around the kitchen table. Unlike the domesticated Sydney fly they were quick-witted and brash. In the bush, hordes of the tiny black fiends would descend around your head and attempt to crawl into any available bodily crevice, ear, nose, mouth or eyes, with uncanny persistence. Fly wire netting on the windows and doors was some protection against this terrible air force, but inside the house the infantry divisions were able to infiltrate these feeble defences. Bull ants committed kamikaze in the jam tins and plundered every last crumb from the kitchen table. After a while I stopped worrying about finding them in the food and chewed them whole, dead or alive.

And of course, the ever-present backdrop to this living scenario was the heat. Draining, stupefying, unremitting.

The house was comfortable but a little spartan, apart from the kerosene refrigerator which I would not have traded for its weight in gold for it contained, at all times, an ample supply of cool beers.

Keeping cool on the outside presented a greater problem. We had to use seawater for washing and shaving and as this was stored in the water tank out the back, I could only shower at night. The water got just too hot during the day.

For that first month, the deprivations to a pampered city dweller like me were torture. But it's strange how quickly the human body can adjust when necessity demands it, and slowly I began to torment myself less and less with daydreams about my air-conditioned bungalow in Collaroy and the self-chlorinating pool. I resigned myself to making the most of the next two years.

Unexpectedly, it was my transient self-appointed houseboy George who gave me the most solace during that trying period. I became used to seeing him wander into the house at any hour of the day or night, with the scruffy Ethel, like a wandering dipsomaniac in a fur coat, somewhere close behind. Some evenings, he would join me on the cool of the verandah, help himself to a beer from the fridge, and talk to me in his easygoing, disjointed way. He seemed to have taken onto himself the role of my mentor and confidant, and continually reassured me that I was doing 'orright'.

One night, finding me in poor spirits, he decided he would give me a special treat to cheer me up.

'You like bagpipes, boss?' he asked.

Startled, I stammered that I did.

'You wanna hear George play bagpipes?'

'Well,' I said, a little apprehensively. 'Well, yes, I suppose so.'

His face lit up with an expression of joy that was almost childlike. Suddenly he leaped out of his chair, and with incredible speed bounded across the garden and pounced on a small cat that had strayed near the house and was peering at us from under a bush. Snatching it up, he slung its small, scrawny body under his arm and placed its tail between his teeth.

I watched, awestruck. The cat hissed and struggled and spat but George showed no inclination to relax his hold on the unfortunate creature. He began to march around the garden as though he was on guard at Buckingham Palace.

By varying the degree of pressure of his elbow on the cat's rib, and the effective use of his teeth on its

'Put a blanket under his knees to raise his legs a little, then just keep him as comfortable as you can.'

'Right.'

Clyde had already contacted Joe Kennedy. In thirty minutes the Cessna was out of its hangar and we were airborne, headed for Murray Downs over two hundred miles to the east.

Joe and I were silent as we watched the lights of the aerodrome flash past us. I looked at my watch, the hands glowing green in the darkened cockpit, Just past midnight.

Below us, in the moonlight, lay the wild plateaux and gorges of the Kimberley in ancient, mysterious patterns. This silent land is awesome in the darkness I shuddered to think how men had survived out here before the advent of the motor engine and the aeroplane.

While we were in the air I kept in touch with Simpson over the radio. The patient was getting worse. His temperature had soared to a hundred and five.

'Okay, Mr Simpson, I'm putting our pilot Joe Kennedy, on. Listen carefully, over.'

'Right-ho, doc.'

Joe took the intercom. 'Look Mr Simpson, I want some more information about this landing strip of yours. Has it been cleared recently? Over.'

'Oh yeah, Joe,' Simpson said. And then he uttered the words that struck an icy fear into my heart every time I heard them. 'She'll be right.'

I knew why Joe had asked the question. In the north-west a colony of white ants can build a huge nest during the wet season in just two or three days, and it sets as hard as rock. If a bush airfield is not regularly inspected for those little monoliths, any night landing is fraught with danger.

'Whereabouts is the strip? Over.'

'It's one mile to the south of here.'

'Repeat that please. It's very important. And spell it.'

'One mile south,' Simpson said, very slowly. 'W for wet, U for onion, N for pneumonia.'

Joe was silent for a moment while he digested this latest information. Then he said, 'Do you have any cars?'

'Got a couple of utes.'

'All right, I'll want one at each end of your airstrip facing into the wind with their headlights on. Can you fix that?'

'No worries.'

'Now don't turn the lights on till you hear our engines or you'll run the batteries flat. Got that?'

'Yeah, she'll be right.'

'I repeat. Facing into the wind with their headlights on. Not pointing towards me. Will you repeat that? Over.'

'Sure, you want both cars either side of the strip facing towards you with their headlights on.'

Kennedy groaned. 'No, Mr Simpson. I'll say it again. Now this is very important . . .'

Five minutes later Simpson had it off pat. Nevertheless Joe crossed himself for luck, and kissed the St Christopher around his neck.

There was a strong headwind and the flight took longer than expected. Then, just fifteen minutes from Murray Downs we flew into cloud and light rain. Joe took the plane down under the cloud cover

70

and the dark shadows of trees skimmed past beneath us, seeming almost close enough to touch.

Long minutes went by as we scoured the horizon for the lights. I started to get anxious. What if the headwinds had blown us off course? Perhaps Simpson had still managed to get his instructions wrong. What if he'd left the headlights on the two cars blazing and run down the batteries?

Joe was getting anxious, too. An optimist to the last, he was the first to break the heavy silence. 'Well, that's it then,' he said with a sigh. 'We're lost,'

Suddenly, through the scudding clouds away to our right, we saw them, two tiny specks of light on the lonely grey tract of land. Joe turned the aircraft towards them and took her in. Simpson had done his job after all.

Joe came in low and brought the wheels down just behind and to one side of the first car to give himself the maximum length of illuminated runway. The small craft jumped and jerked through a number of pits and ridges in the hard ground until we finally rolled to a halt just twenty yards from the second car.

As I jumped out of the cockpit I noticed something in the shadows in front of us. It was a termite nest, six feet high and three or four feet wide. If we had hit it, it would have torn the underside of the fuselage completely away.

John Simpson stared at it in the torchlight, scratching his head in wonderment. 'Christ,' he said slowly. 'I wonder how that got there?'

My patient was a young man, no more than twenty

years old. Simpson told me he'd only been working for him about six weeks.

By the time I got there he was in shock. Mrs Simpson had had him moved from the men's quarters to the house so she could nurse him. He was delirious and running a high fever. An examination confirmed my fears: acute appendicitis.

'How is he?' Simpson asked from over my shoulder.

'Not too good. I'm afraid I'm going to have to operate.'

Simpson stared at me wide-eyed. 'What – here?'

'I'm afraid so. If we wait till I get him to the Hospital the appendix may burst and the whole abdomen will become infected. This way he has one chance in ten of making it. If I fly him back to Preston I don't think he'll even have that.'

'Well, I guess you'd better operate here then,' Simpson said and he took off his hat and held it across his chest as if the young man was already dead. He lowered his voice a little. 'What do you need?'

'Hot water and towels. A primus stove, if you've got one. And a decent table. Oh, and I'd better have some straps, too. I don't want him rolling off while I'm trying to operate.'

'Anything else?'

'Yes. One more thing. You'd better get Joe Kennedy in here. He's about to become an anaesthetist.'

Joe kept our patient unconscious by dripping liquid ether onto a face cone, and then holding the mask over the man's mouth. He also played the role of theatre nurse, passing me my instruments which he first sterilised over the primus flame. It was stinking hot in the little room and we had to keep the windows open to make sure the gas from the lamps and the primus wasn't leaking into the room with the vaporised ether. If the bare flame from the stove had ignited any accumulated gases there would have been a nice little explosion, which would have removed the poor boy's appendix quite dramatically – as well as mine, Joe's and everybody else's in the near vicinity.

This however created an additional problem. Attracted by the light, the room soon became full of flying insects, moths, buzzing sand beetles and midges which kept falling into the open wound. So, to lessen the chance of explosion, and to keep the insects away from the incision, we had to move the gas lamps well away from the body, which meant I was operating in near-darkness.

It was a far cry from the operating rooms at St George's Hospital in Sydney. There, I would have been surrounded by hundreds of thousands of dollars'-worth of machinery and trained, expert staff. All I had right now was a few scalpels and a pilot who looked as if he was going to pass out at any moment.

We were in the lap of the gods all right. Flying blind on a wing and a whiff of ether.

The operation took nearly two hours, and by the time I was finished, it was almost dawn. I sewed my patient together again like a piece of sacking and let out a sigh of relief. At least he was still alive. I looked at Joe. He was as white as a ghost, but with manful dedication he continued to watch me with a

73

stare of intense concentration, waiting for the next command.

'It's all right, Joe,' I said, pulling off my rubber gloves. 'We're finished.'

'Can I go outside?'

I nodded. 'And thanks, Joe. You did a good job.'

He turned and staggered towards the door. I was beginning to see a side to Joe Kennedy I'd never seen before. Certainly it had been a fairly messy operation and I doubted if he had enjoyed it much. But he had stuck with it right the way through and I hadn't heard one word of complaint.

As soon as he had gone, Simpson appeared at the doorway and looked in with his large, doleful eyes, first at me, then at the boy. 'Is he dead?'

'He's through the operation. We'll have to get him back to Preston straight away. There's always a risk of infection.'

What I didn't tell him was just how great that risk was. I had operated under the most primitive and insanitary conditions and had pulled at least half a dozen bugs out of the open wound. If the boy made it, he would have his Maker to thank more than me.

I looked at his face. His breathing was shallow, his cheeks tinged with blue, the youthful down on his chin very dark against the pallor of his skin. He looked pitifully young.

I said a prayer for him.

Suddenly, outside on the verandah, there was a loud crash. I ran outside with Simpson and found Joe spread out on the timber. He had fainted clean away.

Miraculously, the boy survived.

'Long ago,' he said, holding the picture to his breast. 'Yes, long ago. In a time when Abdul Ijaz had a string of a hundred camels and gold enough to make a king spit in jealousy.'

From a medical viewpoint, I should have kept him quiet and sedated. But I felt that perhaps it was better for him to get it off his chest. A sort of absolution. For there was no doubt that the old man was dying.

'Tell me about her,' I said.

Back in the Thirties when business was still good, he had decided it was time to marry. He got a station manager that he knew to put an advertisement in a Perth newspaper for him. Even now he could still remember the words off by heart:

'Businessman, transport industry, well-travelled, Oriental complexion, would like to meet well-developed young lady view matrimony. Send photograph.'

'And this girl sent you her photograph?' I asked.

'Oh no. Many hundreds of girls send photographs,' he said, his voice resonant with awe. 'I would have married them all but here a man may only have one wife. What a choice. I lay awake many nights staring at these photographs. A harem of beautiful women before me! But oh – Deirdre Hopkinson – she was the most beautiful of them all.'

'Then what happened?' This time it was Joe's voice.

'I sent her a hundred pounds for her wedding dress and her fare to Broome. I said I would meet her there. And there I waited for a month, damn fool that I was. Craziness! May Allah turn her womb

83

into a palm tree and may she give birth to coconuts!'

'She never showed up, huh?'

'She wrote to me in Broome. She had tripped on the gangplank and fallen in the water as she was boarding the ship. She had spent her hundred pounds on doctor's fees. Doctors! They are the intestines of a rancid sheep! I sent her money and again I waited. Everyday I sat by the docks while my camels grew fat and lazy. May her breath turn into the excrement of a flatulent donkey and choke her!' His face grew bitter as he chewed on the thorny bush of reflection.

I nodded my head knowingly. 'You never heard from her again?'

Abdul Ijaz turned his baleful eyes on me and regarded me with scorn. 'Oh yes,' he said softly. 'Three weeks later I receive another letter. Her boat has struck an iceberg and sunk. She has survived the wreck but needs another hundred pounds to speed her to me. Like a fool, I send her more money. May she trip on her own lying tongue and impale herself on a hundred dead hedgehogs!'

His voice had risen steadily during this speech and a fleck of froth appeared at his lips. Too late, I tried to calm him.

'Take it easy,' I whispered.

But Abdul was determined that we should hear him out. 'For a long month I waited on the docks watching my beard turn white, my turban foul with the droppings of seagulls. Then I receive another letter. Her father has discovered she is to marry a man of the East and has taken away her ticket, vowing she will not disgrace her family by marrying a filthy foreigner who reeks of camel dung.

one hand he nursed a badly swollen jaw.

'Sit down, O'Reilly,' I said cheerfully. 'What's the matter with your jaw? Did you have an accident?' I put my hand out to examine it but he shrank back.

'Ba' toof,' he mumbled.

'It's your tooth, is it? Well look, the dentist is coming out here next week. You'd better wait till then. I really haven't the equipment.'

But O'Reilly continued to sit there, his ham-like fists clenched anxiously on his knee. His face took on an almost pleading expression.

'Pleath,' he mumbled. 'It'th killin' me, the bath-tard.'

I looked at him a moment. He was obviously in some pain. 'All right. Let's have a look. Open your mouth.'

Tentatively he opened his jaw, and let me peer inside. The rotten tooth was right at the back, a deep-rooted brown molar. It was going to take some shifting but poor O'Reilly was going out of his mind with pain. I decided to give it a go.

'I'll have to get some special equipment from the plane,' I said. 'you just wait there.'

I went outside and found Joe. 'Have you got any pliers?'

'In the tool kit.'

'Get them for me, will you? I've got a delicate operation to perform.'

O'Reilly stared at me with unmasked terror as I approached him with the sophisticated medical equipment clutched in my right hand.

'Now this may hurt a bit,' I said.

O'Reilly braced himself. Not trusting his own ability for self-restraint I casually threw my arm around his neck and got a firm grip. After a few moments of cajoling I got him to open his mouth I got the pliers around the offending tooth and started to pull.

O'Reilly yelled and began to struggle almost straight away. I was ready for this so I tightened my grip round his neck and pulled harder on the tooth. He yelled some more and tried to pull himself free from the deathlock I had around his neck. He wanted to close his mouth but he couldn't because the pliers were in them. This made him fight even harder and he threw himself forward off the stool and tried to roll over, like a wild horse attempting to lose its rider. By this time I could feel the molar starting to tear away from its bed and I was ready to announce the success of the operation when suddenly O'Reilly's fist caught me under the nose and I flew backwards across the room hitting my head hard on the kitchen stove.

The next thing I remember, O'Reilly was bending over me, slapping me on the cheek. 'Doc? You orright doc?' he mumbled. 'Jeeth, I'm thorry.'

I put my hand up to my nose. A little blood but the cartilage was still intact. We were both now kneeling by the stove on all fours, confronting each other like two warring mooses.

'Now look here, O'Reilly,' I said, slowly. 'You're going to have to be a big boy about this.'

The pliers had landed on the floor by the sink so I rinsed them with some water from the pitcher on the table. O'Reilly watched me guiltily from his position on the stool. Finally we were ready for round two.

This time O'Reilly wrapped his enormous fists around the seat of the stool and tried to sit tight while I tugged at the tooth. He managed it for a few seconds but then he let out an enormous yell and stood bolt upright. His head caught me under the chin and I flew backwards across the floor spilling a table and two chairs.

The pliers were washed once more. 'This is your last chance, O'Reilly,' I warned. 'One more episode like that and you can suffer till next week.'

'Pleath, doc. It hurth.'

We took up our positions. Round three. O'Reilly struggled and squirmed on the stool, his arms and legs thrashing around as though he were having some sort of epileptic fit. I held onto his neck with grim determination as he bucked underneath me. The tooth was starting to come loose now.

But O'Reilly had had enough. He screamed and threw himself off the stool again, my arm round his neck, and we skidded across the flagstones in an absurd embrace.

We were still writhing on the floor when Jesse Hoagan walked in. 'What the bloody hell's goin' on in here?'

'Just a minor operation,' I said, half my arm still inside O'Reilly's mouth.

'It sounds like you're slaughtering a bullock from outside.'

'No, no bullocks,' I mumbled.

By now O'Reilly had struggled free and was lying sprawled against the cooking range, groaning.

I got to my feet. There was blood still dribbling from my nose and O'Reilly's saliva hanging off my right arm. But I was smiling.

I raised the pliers triumphantly aloft. 'There you are, O'Reily,' I said. 'The doctor always gets his tooth.'

It was soon apparent that O'Reilly was to be my last patient of the day. When I went out onto the verandah the rest of the men had gone, obviously deciding that the symptoms must be better than the cure.

I was putting away my equipment and getting ready to leave when the door opened and Megan Hoagan walked in.

'Hello.'

I looked up, surprised. She was standing over by the door in her jeans and riding boots, her long fair hair falling heavily round her shoulders. This time no sweat, no grime, no cuts and grazes; even a hint of perfume. Breathtaking.

I smiled. 'Hello.' I suddenly realised I was staring, so I said, 'I haven't seen you since you had the fall. How's the arm?'

'It's fine. How are you settling into the job?'

'Getting used to it. It's a bit different from Sydney.' There was an awkward silence. I got the distinct feeling that Megan hadn't come in just to pass the time of day with me. I pulled up a chair. 'Sit down.'

'Thanks.'

'Well, what is it you want to ask me?'

She looked embarrassed. 'Is it that obvious?'

'I'm afraid so.'

She looked at the floor. 'I don't know whether I should be doing this. Dad would have a fit if he

had been neatly sown together with a black thread.

'How did this happen?'

Tom shifted uneasily in his chair. 'Stopped a bullock horn.'

'But who sewed it together?'

'I did,' Tom said gruffly. I looked up at him in astonishment. 'I was out in the bush. Didn't see no sense in getting you running all the way over here. So I sewed it up myself, like you did with Jackie's head when he fell off the horse.'

'But what did you use for anaesthetic?'

Tom shrugged. 'We didn't have any of them fancy drugs with us. Cleaned it out with a bit of brandy first if that's what you mean.' The big bushy eyebrows knitted together. 'What's the matter? Didn't I do it right?'

After I finished the clinic, Kate asked me to look at their youngest daughter, two year old Emma. She had been complaining of pains in her abdomen. Children are always tricky to diagnose correctly. They have a tendency to put anything they find lying around in their mouths, as a sort of random taste test, so they are naturally prone to stomach aches. And their vocabulary is limited, unlike their powers of exaggeration.

I checked her over thoroughly, but I could find nothing wrong. She seemed in good enough spirits. She giggled when the cold metal of the stethoscope touched her chest, and chattered to her doll, a scraggy-haired plastic affair called Miss Suzy, all through the examination. Kate told me that her general health had been good so I put it down to no worse than indigestion and prescribed a small dose of magnesium carbonate. I didn't give the incident another thought.

'Can I take over the controls for a while?' I said to Joe, as we flew over the Harding Ranges on our way back to Preston. Joe looked at me questioningly, and a dark cloud seemed to pass across his face.

'You're sure you know how to handle one of these things?' he asked.

'Come on Joe,' I said persuasively. 'I've been flying for years.'

'May the Good Lord preserve us,' Joe said, but he edged out of the seat, and in the cramped confines of the cockpit, we changed over places.

It felt good to be at the controls of an aircraft once more. It was nine or ten months since I had piloted a plane, and I went through a few simple manoeuvres and was pleased to discover that I had lost none of the skills. Although it was a fine, clear day the air currents rising off the mountains below us were creating a lot of turbulence; not dangerously so, but enough to make it 'interesting'.

Joe sat beside me gripping his seat in terror for the first ten minutes, but finally he began to relax a little as he realised that I was indeed as capable as I made out to be.

Then it happened.

We were just ten minutes out of Preston aerodrome and I was about to let Joe take over the controls once more, when suddenly the engine cut out.

At first there was just an awful, uncanny silence. Then Joe screamed and lunged towards the controls. That was his first mistake.

Now the engine is not the most important thing on a plane. The wings are. If the engine stops, you can still glide to the ground, providing you can find a landing site as you're coming down. The important thing to remember is that you must keep calm, and continue to keep the plane under control.

I'm sure if it had happened while Joe was at the controls, he would have done this; but he was not behind the controls, and that unnerved him.

We were still in a lot of turbulence, and in my opinion it wasn't safe for Joe to take over the controls right then. Besides, I was confident in my ability to bring the plane down, with or without an engine. As Joe leaned across me to grab the controls I tried to fight him off. We banked to port, and the convection currents seized on this opportunity to take hold of the starboard wing and tip us over on our backs.

We very nearly went into a spin. Joe's head rebounded off the roof of the cabin. The altimeter needle started to drop dramatically. Suddenly the browns and yellows and greens of the Kimberley began to swim in and out of focus, getting closer all the time.

'Bring the nose up!' Joe was yelling.

'I can't!'

'Bring her up!' I managed to control the spin, and eventually the nose started to come up again. We may have been dropping like that for just a few seconds, but it might just as well have been hours. As we came out of the dive, Joe lay in a crumpled heap on the floor, staring up at me wild-eyed.

'We're gonna die,' he muttered.

But we didn't. Suddenly the engine spluttered

and came back to life. Two thousand feet from the ground the Cessna roared, like a beast waking from a long sleep and we started to gain height. Immediately Joe reached out and dragged me out of the seat.

Neither of us spoke again till we landed at Preston aerodrome, a few minutes later. My heart was still careening around inside my ribcage like a football getting kicked round a gymnasium. Finally, as we were taxiing up to the hangars Joe turned and gave me an icy look.

'Next time you fly with me,' he said slowly. 'I'm not coming.'

If it had happened to Douglas Bader, he probably wouldn't have even rated the incident worthy of a mention in his memoirs, but it was a severe blow to my self-esteem as a pilot, and Joe didn't help. He made sure that the story spread around town, and I soon found myself with a nickname – 'The Bloody Red Baron'.

After this, I vowed I would never attempt to fly the Cessna again, having come to the rather neurotic conclusion that the machine had something against me personally.

It was a promise I was not to keep.

Joe and I were sitting on the verandah of the house, drinking beer. It was another warm, balmy night but thankfully a little cooler and not as humid as it had been. George was round the side of the house killing off the mosquito larvae in the water tank with kerosene. By now, I had found George to be an invaluable help for a single man like myself, a sort of combined handyman, housekeeper and drinking partner. He was also an excellent cook and a good friend.

He came out onto the balcony just as we were finishing our beers.

'I bin finish the water tank, boss,' George said. 'What I do wid de kero?'

'Is there much left?'

'Not much, boss.'

'Oh, tip it away then,' I said casually. George nodded and went off, Ethel close behind.

Joe went inside and got another couple of beers. When he came out again, he sat down, lit a cigarette, and looked at me thoughtfully. 'That was a close one today,' he said. 'I still don't understand. How did you do it?'

'I didn't do anything. The engine just cut out,' I snapped.

'It's never happened to me,' he murmured.

'Well, I suggest you get the machine thoroughly checked over,' I told him. 'I'm not going in that thing again until we've found out what caused it.'

Joe looked at me with a funny smile, as if to say, 'I know what caused it, and it wasn't anything mechanical.' He said: 'I'm getting the MMA ground crew to go right over it in the morning. Just to be on the safe side.'

'Thanks,' I said bitterly.

George came back with the empty kerosene tin. 'Anything else, boss?'

'No, go get yourself a beer, George. And thanks.'

'Yo-i boss,' George said, and wandered inside. Ethel watched him go with a concerned look on the startled, pointed face and pecked anxiously at the wooden steps.

Joe got up and walked off round the back of the house.

After he had gone I thought again about the Cessna and what had happened. I knew that I was not to blame for the engine stalling. Yet Joe was right. We had had no trouble with the plane before. It was very odd. But I was confident the ground crew would find the source of the trouble.

I was still musing on the possibilities when I heard a bang and a loud yell. Ethel jumped a few feet into the air and bolted. George shot out onto the verandah and stood there, gaping at me.

'What the hell was that?' I yelled.

The noise had come from round the side of the house, from the direction of the lavatory. I jumped down off the verandah and raced down the path. When I reached the back of the house, I could hardly believe my eyes.

The wooden door of the lavatory was hanging off its hinges and smoke rose in a black pall into the night sky. We found Joe inside in a tangled heap with his trousers round his ankles. He opened his eyes briefly and moaned. 'Just my luck.'

George helped me carry him into the house, and into the surgery. I laid him face down on the examination table and inspected the damage. Fortunately, it wasn't quite as bad as it looked. He had minor burns on his buttocks and there was an ugly gash on his scalp that would require stitching. His ankle was swollen and puffy, but there appeared to be no broken bones.

'What happened, Joe?' I said. 'What the hell happened?'

Out of the corner of my eye I noticed George

trying to slink out of the door.

'George!'

George turned in the doorway, his shoulders hunched in shame. The whites of his eyes peered at me from his lowered head.

'George,' I said slowly. 'What do you know about this?'

George just shook his head, suddenly struck dumb.

'How did this happen Joe?' I said.

'I just threw me cigarette stub down the can and the next thing I knew I hit the door,' Joe groaned, 'Oh God, just my luck, just my luck.'

Suddenly, realisation dawned. I turned to George. 'George, you didn't throw the rest of the kero down the dunny did you?'

'Yo-i boss,' George mumbled. 'bin do in the midgie eggs.'

'You nearly bin do in Mister Joe,' I scolded. Then, perhaps out of relief that Joe wasn't badly hurt, perhaps because I'd already had three or four beers or because I don't have true compassion and empathy, I started to laugh. George, relieved, started to laugh too.

Soon we were both collapsed in chairs with tears rolling down our cheeks, slapping our thighs hysterically. For some reason, Joe couldn't quite see the point of the joke.

It was soon evident that I was going to be without a pilot for at least a week, until Joe got out of hospital.

Whatever suspicions Fenwick harboured about the Royal Flying Doctor Service they were almost certainly confirmed when I had Joe admitted to

Preston for observation with his curious assortment of injuries.

I then had a decision to make. I could ask for a replacement to be sent up from Perth but that could take up to a week and by then Joe would be fit for duty anyway. In the meantime I could withdraw from emergency calls and ask for the Flying Doctor at Berwick to cover my area – which was the correct procedure – or I could break the rules and fly myself.

There is a saying, 'What the eye doesn't see the heart doesn't grieve over'. I applied this analogy to the Service Headquarters in Melbourne and decided that I would become a truly Flying doctor – and my own pilot.

The next day I had the perfect opportunity. We received a call from the mission at Goombala sixty miles away that they had an Aboriginal patient there suffering from Hansen's disease. He would have to be flown in to Preston for treatment at the leprosarium. It was a routine flight. The weather was perfect the trip was a relatively short one and I decided it would be an ideal way to start my flying career with the Service.

I took off in perfect conditions. The plane was handling well and there was only one nagging doubt in the back of my mind; the MMA ground crew had checked out the plane and failed to find anything wrong. I told myself that if they had given it a clean bill of health there couldn't be much to worry about but nevertheless I felt a little uneasy as I took the Cessna back into the sky once more.

But the flight out to the mission was uneventful and I arrived at Goombala on schedule. The patient, a full-blood Aboriginal called Tommy was to be accompanied on the trip by one of the nuns from the mission, who was herself returning to Preston. Her name was Sister Theresa; a small grey-haired lady with pince-nez, her lively, ruddy face belying her seventy years.

As we flew back to Preston she chatted to me about Sydney, where she herself had lived for twenty years 'before God called her to the north-west', as she put it.

The sky was clear and blue and the sun glinted on the wild panorama below. I was enjoying myself. I put all thoughts of gremlins in the plane's engines out of my mind.

'Where's Mr Kennedy?' Sister Theresa asked me after we had been in the air about ten minutes. 'Has he left the Service?'

'No, he's still with us. He had a small accident the other day.'

'Nothing too serious, I hope?'

'Not too bad,' I answered. 'But I've advised him to give up smoking,' I added and laughed at my own humour.

'And how long have you been flying?' Sister Theresa inquired.

I grinned. I thought I'd have a little joke. My, I was in good spirits. 'This is my second time,' I said.

I was just about to tell her the full story when the engine cut out.

What happened next is mostly a blur. The same terrible silence, the howling of the wind, then the screaming. The altimeter starting to fall, while I wrestled with the controls, moving fuel selectors, setting ignition switches, mumbling, 'Don't panic, don't panic,' while the sweat oozed down my temples. I do remember that at one point Tommy tried to get out of the door.

It took a little longer for the engines to start up again this time. We had glided down to within a thousand feet of the ground, and I was picking out a site down on the plain below suitable for a crash landing, when the engines burst into life again, the throbbing drone reassuring as a heartbeat.

I turned round. Sister Theresa lay in ungainly fashion on the floor behind me with her habit up round her knees and her right arm circling Tommy's neck, trying to prevent him from making his departure.

I wiped the sweat away from my forehead and licked my lips. I tried to smile. 'Sorry about that,' I muttered. 'Just a little technical trouble.'

'That's all right, young man,' Sister Theresa said graciously.

Tommy showed less restraint. He spent the rest of the trip with his head under the pillow of the stretcher, sobbing.

My conversation with Sister Theresa was at an end. She was mostly silent the rest of the way except occasionally I could hear her whispering her rosary as she fingered the silver crucifix that hung at her neck.

As they got out of the plane – with somewhat indecent haste – I thought I heard Tommy mutter, 'Just my luck', though of course, that might just have been my imagination.

Bill McCormack walked slowly towards me from the other side of the hangar and held out a brittle brown mass for my inspection.

'There you are, doctor,' he said. 'That's what been causing the trouble.'

I took it. Bits of it started to crumble away in my fist. 'What is it?'

'It's a wasp's nest,' Bill said. 'We found it inside the air intake.'

'And this is what made the engine cut out?'

'That's right,' he said, thrusting his hands into his overalls. 'Really had me stumped for a while. Then I was just prodding around with me screwdriver under the cowling and the bloody thing fell out.'

'Do you mind if I hang on to this?'

'I don't care what you do with it,' he said and offered me an anatomical alternative.

Later that afternoon I went to visit Joe at the Hospital. He was lying on his stomach, reading a magazine. He glanced up briefly as I came in and carried on reading.

'How's it going, Joe?'

'Orright,' he mumbled.

'Here, I've brought you something.'

Joe showed an interest in my visit for the first time. 'A beer? A packet of smokes?'

'A wasp's nest.'

He looked at me sharply. 'A what?'

I laid the brown, crumbling mess on the bed beside him. 'That was what made the engine stall the other day. Bill McCormack found it in the air intake.'

He smiled, a strange dreamy sort of smile. 'A likely bloody story,' he said.

I had a funny sort of feeling that Sister Theresa wasn't going to believe me, either.

CHAPTER 9

The cyclone came late in the season, the eye of the
storm situated somewhere over the Timor Sea and
the southernmost edge of the vortex sweeping
down in a wide arc across the Northern Territory
and the north-west Kimberley. The first rains had
hit Preston around midnight, and the palms along
the waterfront were bowing to the first onslaught of
the winds, when the call came in. It was Tom
Doyle. Emma was vomiting and running a high
temperature. As Tom described her symptoms it
became obvious to me that I would have to get her
to the hospital straight away.

'It'll take me about half an hour to get airborne,' I
said. 'How's the strip?'

'She's good. I checked her myself the day before
yesterday.'

'What about the rain? How much water is there?'

'It hasn't started raining here yet,' Tom said. 'The
paddocks are still pretty dry.'

I did a quick mental calculation. Allowing for the
headwinds it was about a ninety minute trip to the
station if I left Preston now. I might just be able to
get there and back before the full blast of the storm
swept over the Kimberley. Fortunately, the airstrip
at Hawkestone was close to the homestead, so I
would be able to land and take off again quickly.

'Okay, Tom. Now listen carefully. I want you to

take your truck to one end of the strip and face her into the wind. As soon as you hear me put your headlights on. And I'll want flares along both sides of the strip. Can you fix that?'

'Sure doc,' Doyle said. 'Only hurry.'

'I'll be about two hours. Don't give her any food or any fluids. Just keep her warm – and don't panic, okay? Over.'

I dressed quickly, threw my medical bag into the car and climbed in behind the wheel. The rain was slanting down from a black sky and in the distance I heard the ominous rumble of thunder. The gentle slap, slap, of the windscreen wipers seemed a very lonely sound as I drove through the deserted streets out to the aerodrome. I was frightened. I had never flown in a storm before, and already I was regretting my decision not to call for a replacement. But it was too late now.

It took just a few minutes to reach the aerodrome. I stopped the car and ran across the black, shiny tarmac to the hangar. Clyde had alerted the MMA ground crew and they were already wheeling the Cessna out of the hangar for me.

I suddenly felt very cold and lonely and tired. I thought: I have this awesome responsibility of a child's life and there is no one I can consult, no nurses to help, no one even to talk to.

I'm alone.

It was then that I saw a dark shape approaching across the tarmac in the grey mist of rain.

'Doctor Hazzard?' It was a woman's voice, and somehow vaguely familiar. 'Surely you remember me?'

I peered into the darkness and suddenly I gasped

as I realised who it was. 'Sister Theresa?'

'I'm a little wet I'm afraid, she said, coming to stand beside me in the hangar and shaking the rain off her umbrella. 'I had to ride over here on my bicycle.'

I was too stunned to speak.

'Clyde Westcott called the mission. He said that you might appreciate a volunteer.'

'A volunteer?'

'You can't fly the plane and care for your young patient at the same time.'

'You're willing to go up there – with me?' I stammered.

'I'm willing to trust the good Lord and His mercy,' she said mildly.

'It's dangerous,' I said. 'I hope you understand that.'

'So is crossing the road, Doctor Hazzard. Even then one must have faith in the Lord.'

I shook my head in admiration. Suddenly my thoughts of despair and abandonment evaporated.

'I really don't know how to thank you,' I murmured.

She shot me a quick embracing glance and a flicker of Irish steel glinted in her eyes. 'Just don't stall the engine again then,' she said and marched past me towards the Cessna, still shaking her umbrella.

The tiny plane bounced and pitched through the air as the storm shook us. The fierce up and down draughts tried to tip the aircraft one way and then the other, and the Cessna floundered at times like a boat going broadside into the waves. The rain spattered against the windscreen in a blinding sheet and often the thunder drowned out even the sound of our own engines. Sister Theresa clung to her rosary and I could see her lips moving in silent prayer. Occasionally she would say 'Well done, doctor!' after we had flown through a particularly bad air pocket, even though at those times I was as helpless as she. I think she just wanted to encourage me.

'Tell me, doctor,' she shouted over the noise of the storm. 'Tell me, how do you know where we are?'

'I get bearings from the radio beacons and the radar.'

'But how will we find Hawkestone in the dark?'

'Well, when I think we're close to the station we just come down out of the clouds and start looking for the lights.'

'What happens if we get lost?'

'Well, in that case I might be very glad I brought you along,' I shouted back to her. 'We might have to get in touch with your Boss.'

'My boss? Oh – I see!' Sister Theresa said, and she pursed her lips thoughtfully.

We were battling against headwinds the whole way and it was almost two hours before we were over Hawkestone. I brought the Cessna down to two hundred feet and we peered anxiously through the blackness for the lights. A couple of minutes later I spotted them dead ahead. I felt a sudden glow of satisfaction. A hundred and fifty miles at night through a raging storm and I had brought the plane to its destination dead on course. I could hardly suppress a grin of triumph.

'How do you like that then?' I said. 'Pretty good, huh?'

'Let us not forget to thank the Good Lord either, Doctor Hazzard,' Sister Theresa chided me gently. Still brimming with my new-found confidence I brought the Cessna gliding down onto the dirt strip at Hawkestone, missing a storage shed by a matter of inches.

Emma Doyle lay in her cot, bathed in her own perspiration and crying softly. Her tattered one-eyed doll still lay clutched under the crook of her left arm. I examined her quickly. Gastro–enteritis. I was sure of it.

I tried to think back. Had I been too careless when I examined her before? It's always easy to blame yourself with the benefit of hindsight. No, my conscience told me that when I had first examined her there had been nothing to indicate the onset of a serious illness. I supposed I could have taken her back to the Hospital 'for observation'. But how could I have justified that to Fenwick when he had a large-scale influenza epidemic on his hands?

'She' goin' to be all right, doc?' Tom said, peering anxiously over my shoulder.

'We're going to have to take her into the hospital straight away, Tom.'

'Is it bad?'

I turned round to face him. His jaw was set in a hard, grim line, but I could see the fear in his eyes. Kate and the two older girls were huddled by the doorway watching. They all looked so lost.

I tried to sound as reassuring as I could. 'It's serious, Tom. But don't worry, she'll be all right as

110

soon as we can get her to the hospital.'

I bundled Emma up in my arms, and covered her with a thick blanket. Tom and I hurried across the paddock to the plane. The wind was much stronger now and the rain was already beginning to churn the ground under our feet into a sticky mud. We would have to hurry.

Sister Theresa was waiting in the plane. I passed her the frail little bundle, jumped into the cockpit and climbed in behind the controls.

I heard Tom's voice behind me. 'Take care of her,' he said softly.

I turned round. He was kneeling beside the stretcher. 'Clyde will keep in touch with you, Tom.'

He nodded and looked down at Emma. He stroked back one of the dark, damp curls and kissed the little girl's forehead gently. 'Goodbye love,' he murmured. And then he clambered out of the cockpit and Sister Theresa slammed shut the cabin door.

'Six Victor X-ray, this is Six Charlie Tango. Do you read me? Over.'

'Yairs, Six Charlie Tango, reading you strength three. Pass your message. Over.' It was Clyde's familiar, comforting drawl very faint against the sharp crackle of static from the storm around us.

'We're just about to take off from Hawkestone River. We have a patient aboard. Alert Preston Hospital. Will signal again when we're airborne. Over.'

'Roger, Six Charlie Tango. And good luck doc.'

The engine roared to life and I turned the plane round at the far end of the strip through the fast-cloying mud. All the dice were loaded against us. By an incredible stroke of fate, the wind had changed direction since we had landed. It meant that we would have to take off in a swirling cross-wind, with only a slight incline in our favour. I calculated that the strip itself was not going to be long enough in these conditions so we would have to try and kick a goal between the barn and an acacia tree soon after we were airborne.

I revved the engine, took a deep breath, and prepared for the take-off.

'Doctor Hazzard.' Sister Theresa tapped me gently on the shoulder. I turned. The nun was pointing out of the window at a dark shape heading towards me across the muddy paddock. I could just make out the silhouette against the flares along the side of the strip. As the running figure got closer I could see that it was Kate Doyle.

Sister Theresa threw open the rear cabin door.

'Doctor Hazzard!' Kate Doyle leaned into the cockpit. She was wringing wet, her dress spattered with red mud. She handed something to Sister Theresa. 'It's her doll – Miss Suzy,' she shouted over the noise of the engine. 'Make sure she has it with her in hospital. She cries without it.'

I nodded. Then the cabin door slammed shut and I watched her run under the wing and back into the darkness.

We were halfway down the field when I suddenly realised we might not make it. The soaking mud dragged on the wheels and the cross-wind began to pit its strength against the power of the engine. We were on full throttle aiming at a spot between the barn and the tree. Fifty yards beyond that was a white fence, and beyond that God knows what.

The barn flashed past.

We started to climb. I held my breath, and waited for the undercarriage to smash into the fence.

But it didn't.

We seemed to keep going so I said 'We're airborne!' and Sister Theresa said. 'Thank God,' and so did I.

I have often wondered since if there are any black tyre marks on that white fence at Hawkestone River – but I've never been game enough to look.

The roller coaster ride began all over again.

Lightning flashed around the plane and I wondered how much longer the Cessna's superstructure could take the terrible hammering. At least now the wind was at our backs.

Once I turned and caught a glimpse of the nun kneeling beside our tiny patient on the stretcher behind me. Her face was deathly white and the fingers of one hand worked furiously at the rosary beads around her neck, while the other hand stroked the child's hair as she murmured words of comfort to the little girl.

It was almost dawn when I spotted the lights of Preston aerodrome looming through the scudding clouds a thousand feet below. Neither the Sister nor myself spoke. Fear works on you like fatigue; after a while your senses become dulled and you start to behave mechanically. As we landed I experienced neither exhilaration nor relief. I just felt numb.

We watched as our young passenger was carried to the ambulance, then I drove the Sister back to the

113

mission on the edge of town. It all seemed very unreal; as she got out of the car she said goodnight as if I was a charitable parishioner who'd just given her a lift home from church.

I drove through the rain in a daze. I had had only two hours sleep that night yet somehow I was no longer tired. I looked at my watch. It was just after five-thirty.

When I got back to the Residence there was a light on round the back of the house. I parked the car and went inside. George was sitting at the kitchen table with two mugs of tea. He grinned as I walked in and passed the steaming mug to me across the table.

I sank thankfully into one of the chairs. 'Thanks, George.'

'Bad wedda,' George observed.

I sipped the hot sweet tea gratefully. 'Wet enough to bog a duck.'

George started to chatter but I paid him hardly any attention. My mind was still on little Emma. I would have liked to have been taking care of her right then myself. The most frustrating part of the job was handing over patients I had cared for – and cared about – to Fenwick. He was too bloody-minded to release much information about them to me, and sometimes they would be transferred down to Perth and I wouldn't see them again for weeks. I would probably have to find out about Emma's condition from Clyde, or perhaps from Tom himself.

I rubbed my hands across my face. All I could see was the ambulanceman carrying the frail little bundle out of the plane . . .

Suddenly I was on my feet, the tea mugs spilling

as I jerked back my chair. George stared at me with his mouth open as I pulled my raincoat back over my shoulders and then he looked sadly at the full mug of tea I had hardly touched.

'Sorry George,' I said, and ran back out to the car.

The MMA boys had already wheeled the Cessna back into the hangar when I reached the aerodrome. Bill McCormack watched me running towards him with a mixture of amusement and surprise.

'You haven't got another call, have ya?'

'I left something behind,' I mumbled. I threw open the cockpit door and peered inside. I found what I was looking for on the cabin floor. Somehow it had slipped under the passenger seat during the flight.

Bill looked at me and at the scruffy one-eyed doll with ironic amusement.

'It belongs to a friend,' I said by way of explanation.

'Sure,' Bill said, and scratched his head in amazement as I ran back to the car with it in my hand.

The first early light was still a grey, grizzled streak away on the horizon when I reached the Hospital. The rain had eased slightly, preparing for the big blow that would come later in the day. I parked the Holden outside the main entrance and went inside. The reception desk was deserted. I walked down the corridor that led off from the foyer and past the startled night nurse.

It was Matron Margaret Renford.

'What are you doing here?' she snapped.

I stopped in the middle of the corridor and spun

round. 'Where's the little girl I brought in this evening?'

Matron Renford raised one delicate eyebrow and gave me a long, cold stare. 'That's no concern of yours.'

'Well, I've just made it my concern. I've got something for her.'

She looked down at the scraggly doll in my hand and then back at me. 'I'll see she gets it,' she said, and held out her hand. Her general manner reminded me of a schoolmistress confiscating a catapult.

'I'll give it to her myself, thanks. Now where is she?'

'If you're not out of this hospital in ten seconds, I'm calling the police.'

'You can do what you bloody well like. Now where's Emma or do I have to pull this dump to pieces?'

For the first time Matron Renford lost some of her aplomb. I saw a flicker of uncertainty pass across the cold, grey eyes. 'Now look here, Doctor Hazzard . . .'

'To hell with you.' I grabbed her by the arm and shook her roughly. A little yelp of surprise escaped her lips. There was a dark shadow of beard on my face, I'd been up all night and my eyes were streaked with pink. I suppose I must have looked fairly menacing, if not demented. I had the satisfaction of watching her wilt.

'Now where is she?' I demanded.

Matron Renford's face had drained of colour. 'Down the corridor. Last room on the left.'

As I let go of her and turned back down the

corridor, I heard her pick up the phone.

Emma lay in a large bed, with tubes in and out of her body. She had been sedated, but I heard her whimper a little as I entered the room. She looked very small, very fragile. I crept over to the edge of the bed.

'Hello Emma,' I whispered. 'I've got something for you.'

I put the doll against her arm under the bedclothes. Her paw closed around the doll's face and she pulled it up to her cheek. I smiled. The whimpering had stopped. I kissed her once on the forehead.

'That's from Daddy,' I said, and tiptoed out of the room.

I was in a fairly loving mood when I came out into the corridor. Charles Fenwick was not.

He looked but a shell of the man I had first met. His eyeballs had a faint yellow tinge and seemed to have retreated into his skull, leaving dark rings around the sockets. His cheeks were sallow and drawn. His distinguished grey-flecked hair was now mussed and untidy and the parting that had traversed one side of his scalp with almost geometrical precision had now all but disappeared. He looked like a starved goat. I guessed that he had been forced to sleep on the premises due to the workload foisted on him by the influenza epidemic. Probably in his own office, on the chaise longue under the picture of 'The Queen inspecting the Maternity Ward with Dr C. C. Fenwick, May 20, 1963.'

He glared at me with undisguised resentment. 'What are you doing in my hospital?' he hissed.

I smiled. 'Having a nice epidemic?'

'I asked you a question.'

'I'm visiting one of my patients.'

'Get out.' I could see Matron Renford peering at me from behind Fenwick's shoulder.

I stared at them both for a moment and the long night of fear and tension suddenly surfaced. 'You're a low bastard, Fenwick,' I growled.

His voice rose to a squeak. 'Get out. Before I call the police.'

I left.

Three weeks later I flew to Hawkestone River once more; this time Joe did the flying and I sat in the passenger seat and admired the view.

I was looking forward to seeing Tom and Kate again.

And so was Emma.

CHAPTER 10

It was a bright warm morning when we landed at Brookton. It was supposed to be a routine clinic but I had something a little special planned. On Megan's urging I was intent on giving Jesse Hoagan a thorough physical examination; it had occurred to me that the only way I might be able to do that was by going through the motions of giving everyone on the station a check-up. It seemed a rather elaborate manoeuvre but I felt it couldn't do any harm, and if Jesse's complaint was as serious as his daughter suggested, it might do a lot of good.

My first customer that morning was Aspirin.

Aspirin was a half-caste Aboriginal, a young boy with smooth, almost feminine skin and perpetually pained expression. He was in the habit of limping, though I never could find anything wrong with his leg. Whenever I was due for a visit he would always come down with some mysterious complaint a few days before. He was my most regular customer, though as far as I could tell he was in excellent physical health. Aspirin however, did not concur with my diagnosis.

He limped in with a baleful expression, and eased himself onto the wooden chair opposite me with the actions of an old man suffering from aggravated gout.

I smiled cheerfully. 'And how are you today?'

119

'Doc,' he said with heavy emphasis. 'Doc, you gotta do something.'

'Why? What's wrong?'

'It's me back, doc. I think I got spina bifida.'

I was not too fazed by this startling piece of information. I knew that Aspirin had had some medical books sent up from the city through the mails. His Bible was *Livingstone's Pocket Medical Dictionary*. He would study the causes and symptoms of a number of diseases and afflictions and sooner or later one of them would inspire him to sickness. He was the only patient I've ever known to get ill alphabetically.

However, this time I realised that he had slipped up. I seized on the opportunity. 'Only children get spina bifida,' I said, with a telling smile.

'That's right. I've had this ever since I was a kid, doc,' he said without missing a beat. 'It hurts bad, real bad.'

'Okay,' I said wearily. Take off your shirt. I'd better have a look.'

As I suspected, his back and spine would have graced an ox. I went automatically to my medical kit to give him the usual phial of placebos, but this time I stopped myself. I decided I would try a new tactic with him. 'Okay,' I said, sitting back in my chair. 'You can put your shirt back on now.'

'What do you think, doc?' he said, eyeing me dolefully.

I looked him in the eye and tried to sound as casual as I could. 'I'm not sure. I'll have to run some tests,' I said, and watched his eyes grow a little wider.

'What is it?' he said, and a hint of panic crept into

120

his voice.

'Oh, it may not be anything,' I said, pursing my lips. I went through the kit and took out an empty syringe casing. 'Look, I want you to go outside and spit into this.'

He looked at me quizzically. 'Spit in it?'

'I want to take a salivary sputum count.' I produced another vial. 'Then I want you to go some place quiet and see if you can cry a little. I need some samples from your eye socket for a hydro-lachrymose litmus test.'

He gaped at me in awe. 'Is it that bad?'

I avoided his eyes, and pretended to make some notes in my consultation pad. 'I won't really know till I've run the tests and got a full cerebral masturbatory analysis from the laboratories in Perth.'

Despite the colour of his skin, I do believe I saw him pale a little. For the first time in his life, someone was telling Aspirin they thought he might really be sick. And not just anyone. A real doctor. I knew it was a bit of a risk; this would either cure him completely or make him worse – but how could he get worse than he already was?

'I'll go and do it now,' Aspirin said softly. 'I think I feel some tears coming on.'

'Be careful not to get any eyelashes in,' I warned him as he went out. 'The hydrocarbons will contaminate the monosodium glutamate.'

Aspirin stared at me, wide-eyed. 'Oh, I'll be careful, doc,' he said and he closed the door softly behind him. I watched him from the window as he walked slowly round the side of the house and retreated to the creek for a good cry.

*

'And what have you done to that lazy good for nothing bastard now?' Jesse Hoagan demanded. 'He's down by the barn blubbering like an old woman.'

'I thought I'd try a new tack with him,' I started to explain.

'The only tack that boy needs is a good sharp metal one, right up the jacksie.'

'Well, that's your job, not mine.'

'That was the wrong thing to say. Jesse's cheeks suddenly glowed a brighter red and the big eyes glared at me across the table like burning coals. 'Don't you tell me my job, you . . .' Epithets sprang to his lips but he contained himself. Whatever his personal opinion of me, the fact that I was the Flying Doctor forestalled name-calling on this occasion.

'I just thought I'd try a few shock tactics on him,' I continued calmly. 'Make him think he really is sick.'

'That's all the bloke needs, someone to tell him he's really sick. Lies in bed half the time as it is. I don't know what I pay him good money for.'

'Then why don't you fire him?'

He looked at me contemptuously, as a man of the land will regard those who know nothing of his arcane art.

'Because, *when* he works, he's the best mechanic for miles.'

'So you'd like to have him fit for work?'

'Of course I bloody would!'

'Well then – let me try my way first, hmmm?'

Jesse Hoagan let out a long, irritable sigh and

started for the door. I stopped him with a polite cough. 'Where are you going?'

Jesse Hoagan was obviously not used to being spoken to that way, least of all in his own kitchen. He glared at me. 'What?'

'I said, where are you going?'

'I'm goin' outside to run me bloody station, where do you think I'm going'?'

'You haven't had your check-up yet,' I said evenly. Jesse stared at me silently for a few moments. I could tell he was considering an appropriate reply from the many and varied possibilities.

'Well,' he said finally. 'Right now I'm busy.'

'I've seen everyone else. You're practically the last on my list.'

Jesse's attitude softened a little. He became defensive. 'Well I feel all right. I don't need a check-up.'

'It's just routine. Prevention is better than cure.'

His voice took on a plaintive whine. 'Look, I'm busy,' he said desperately. 'Can't it wait till next time?'

'All right,' I said, smiling benignly, and making a hurried note in my diary. Jesse smiled triumphantly and turned for the door. 'I didn't realise you were worried about it.'

He shot me a contemptuous glance. 'What do you mean?' He stuck out his chest, suddenly caught between his loathing and mistrust of doctors and his stubborn Gaelic pride.

'A lot of people are frightened of doctors. It's nothing to be ashamed of,' I said mildly. I never took a degree in psychology, but I reckoned you didn't need one with open books like Jesse Hoagan. As I knew he would, he came in spinner.

'I'm not frightened, of you or your bloody examinations, you cheeky little bastard.'

'Good. Then perhaps we can get on with it.'

He straightened, realising he was trapped. 'I told you, I'm busy.'

I played my master card. 'Well, all right then. But Megan will be disappointed when I tell her. She told me you were going to set an example for the rest of the men.'

Jesse Hoagan started to pull off his shirt. He threw it on the chair, and glared at me, the thick, silver-matted chest heaving with rage. 'Come on, then,' he said. 'Let's get this bloody farce over with.'

I gave Jesse a thorough examination, and took some blood and urine samples to take back with me for tests. Jesse worked himself into a silent rage while I examined him, and when I smiled and said, 'Thank you, you can put your shirt back on now,' he scowled and snatched it off the chair in his fist and stormed out of the door, bare-chested. I heard him shouting obscenities at one of the boys and then he jumped in the Landrover and drove away in a spray of dust and small stones.

A few minutes later there was a knock on the door and Megan came in.

'How did it go?' She looked wary. I guessed she had witnessed her father's departure.

'I'm glad to report that he has a very healthy temper.' I was making a few notes on Jesse's card. I indicated the chair opposite mine. 'Sit down, Megan.'

124

'How is he?'

'Well, you're right. He has a very high blood pressure, even allowing for the fact that it probably went up a few points when I asked him to take his shirt off. And I don't like the sound of his heart, either.'

'Did you tell him?'

'Are you kidding?'

Megan nodded thoughtfully. 'What's your professional opinion?'

I stopped writing and looked at her. 'In my professional opinion he should give up the station and take it easy. I believe he's heading for a heart attack.'

She suddenly looked very lost and frightened. I took her hand gently. 'I didn't tell him because I didn't think it would do any good, coming from me. In fact, I think he'd be more likely to stay here, just to prove a point.'

'You're right. That's exactly what he'd do.' She tried to summon a smile. 'What do you suggest?'

'I think you should tell him what I've just told you. He might listen to you. But he has to get away from this station. It's too much for him now.'

Megan looked past me, out of the window. 'It won't be easy to tell him. He lives for Brookton.'

'He's not a young man any more, Megan. He's got to come to terms with that.'

Couldn't you give him some pills or something? Something to make him better?'

'I'll make sure you get some digitalis. They'll help, but they won't cure it. There's nothing that will actually cure it. He just needs to take things easier from now on, and that's it.'

She nodded. There was a long silence. Finally I said, 'he must have considered the possibility of leaving Brookton.'

I've tried to speak to him about it a couple of times and he just gets mad. I don't think he's even willing to consider it. If I'd been a boy it would have been all right. He could have left the heavy work to me and he wouldn't have to leave then.'

'What about you? Do you want to leave?'

She shrugged her shoulders. 'I've grown up here. It's my life. Anyway, Dad needs me.'

I suppose she thought she'd answered my question, but I decided not to let her off that easily. 'You can't stay here for ever.'

'Oh, I suppose not. I'll think about it when the time comes,' she said airily.

'What about boyfriends?'

She smiled, but her eyes were evasive. 'I'm too young,' she laughed, and got to her feet. 'Thanks for looking at Dad.'

'That's okay,' I said, and she left, closing the door quietly behind her.

I sat for a while, thinking. She seemed as reluctant as her father to face the inevitable. But my professional concern for Jesse was complicated by other emotions that had nothing to do with medicine. Ever since I'd first met Megan, I hadn't been able to put her out of my mind. I cursed myself for being a fool. She was thirteen years younger than me, just a girl. Besides, she was also a patient; I could not afford to say or do anything that might compromise my position.

But the fascination remained.

In the next few days I asked myself many

questions about Megan Hoagan and found that I had very few answers. But there was one question that I felt sure would be answered one way or another in the not-too-distant future: how long would Jesse be able to keep running Brookton station?

One of the Aboriginal jackaroos who worked on the station, a man who went by the name of Fish-hook, had volunteered to take the ute and drive Joe Kennedy and I back to the airstrip. We were not far from the plane when we heard shouts and yelling from beyond the crest of a ridge away to our right. It was a shocking racket, something between an Indian war dance and a fight in a Melbourne pub on Grand Final Day.

Fish-hook stopped the truck, jumped out, and went running to the top of the ridge to investigate.

A couple of minutes later, he ran back down the hill, wide-eyed and very excited.

'What's going on?' I said.

'One of dem black bastards!' Fish-hook shouted. 'Bin do in real bad. Better come.'

Joe tugged nervously at my sleeve. 'Let's not get involved,' he muttered.

'What?'

'It's nothing to do with us.'

'Come on, Joe,' I said. 'We'll have to go and have a look.'

'Just my luck,' Joe said.

I followed Fish-hook to the top of the ridge, and the shouts and whooping became deafening.

It was some sort of corroboree. The men were mostly desert Aborigines but several of the station hands had got mixed up with them looking strangely out of place in their T-shirts and long trousers. Most of the natives had ochre patterns painted on to their bodies and white feathers stuck to their skins with blood. Some of them were waving spears and pushing and justling each other. The women, naked and covered in plastered mud, were shrieking and gesticulating and seemed to be urging their men on to feats of violence.

It reminded me of some of the New Year's Eves I had spent down the Manley seafront many years before.

In the middle of this horrifying mêlée was one of the desert tribesmen, lying motionless in a pool of blood.

'What's going on here?' I asked Fish-hook.

'Black bastard bin alonga Sugarbag's woman. Dey wanta kill 'im some of dem.'

'What'd he say?' I asked Joe.

'They're fighting over a woman,' he said.

The speared man was still conscious but seemingly resigned to whatever fate was to befall him. I couldn't understand what the natives were saying but I inferred that they were arguing whether to leave him there or finish him off. The shrieking and jostling had reached a crescendo when I charged down into their midst. When they saw me, there was a sudden hush. They all stood quite still, and stared.

'You bin all go bugger off I think!' I yelled at them. 'Jesse Hoagan belong big fat boss man shoot you all here bang dead if not!'

My attempts to communicate seemed to get through to some of them, and they passed my sentiments on to their brothers. There were a few ominous mutterings, then they fell quiet once more. I bent down beside the injured man and examined the wound. A spear had lodged in his side and although the shaft of the weapon had broken off, the spear was till embedded in his flesh, somewhere near the kidney.

I put my bare fingers into the wound and felt around for the stone head. I located it a couple of inches below the skin. I managed to fish it out and it plopped heavily onto the dirt beside him. Fresh blood oozed out of the wound.

I decided I could do no less for the man than I would for anyone else, despite the rather bizarre circumstances. I would stitch the wound and take him back with me to Preston.

The mumbling band of natives was edging closer around me, and becoming a little restless. Joe knelt down beside me.

'Come on, doc,' he whispered. 'Let's get out of here.'

'Bring my bag over,' I said, turning round sharply.

'What are we going to do?'

'I'm going to sew the wound up to stop the bleeding and then we're going to take him back with us.'

Joe's face drained of blood. 'Oh, Christ. Just my luck.'

The station hands had taken off by this time, but the tribesmen remained. There were about twenty of them, their women keeping off at a distance. They huddled around me, whispering among themselves and watching with astonishment as I injected anaesthetic into the flesh around the wound with a syringe and began to stitch the skin with a suture needle and black thread. The stench from the grease-daubed bodies clustered around me was overpowering; I think I would rather have performed the operation in an Indonesian urinal.

My patient lay silent and uncomplaining through all this, and finally the wound had been closed and he was ready to be moved.

'Okay Joe, give me a hand to lift him here,' I said. Joe took a step forward. But when the natives saw that we were about to make off with their victim, they muttered angrily between themselves and one of them advanced towards us.

Joe looked first at me, then at the man with the spear. 'Awww, shit' he said, and took a step back again.

Encouraged, the rest of the natives fell in behind their bolder blood brother. They obviously weren't going to let us take him; but I was equally opposed to the idea of having them slice my patient up again after I'd gone to all the trouble of sewing him up. I decided I would try and bluff them.

I stood up to my full height and approached the first Aborigine. I tapped him intimidatingly on the chest with my thermometer.

'Now look here you big fat bugger, me whitefeller witchdoctor, I wave this here mighty powerful magic bone you go bang bang all over the shop, you savvy?'

He took one look at the blood-like substance magically suspended inside the transparent tube and his eyes widened in terror, and he shrank back muttering.

Joe, Fish-hook and I took this opportunity to pick

up the wounded man and carry him back to the truck, while I walked in front holding my thermo-meter menacingly in my right hand. The natives cleared a path for us.

Five minutes later, tired and sweat-stained, we scrambled down the rock-strewn ridge and laid our patient face-down on some canvas in the back of the ute. As we drove away the man's blood brothers assembled on the ridge to watch. It reminded me of the final scene in *Zulu*.

I hummed *Men of Harlech* all the way back to Preston.

It was not until my next trip to Brookton that I learned from Fish-hook that on the full moon following that incident, the desert tribe had a corroboree in honour of the witchdoctor birdman and the chief had sacrificed a wild goat in order to appease the wrath of my thermometer.

CHAPTER 11

We were still over the Gulf country when the Cessna's engine first started to give us trouble. I noticed it at about the same time as Joe. A pilot becomes accustomed to the rhythm and pitch of the engine, and even a minor variation in the timing of the blades cannot go unnoticed; by this time I felt as much a part of the machine as Joe did.

He soon confirmed my suspicions. 'We're losing power,' he said, fighting to hold the craft steady in a buffeting updraught. 'Something's wrong. Christ, come on girl.'

Below us the vast swampy inland of the Oxford Gulf appeared, green and dense through the grey, wispy clouds. We were already losing height. I looked at the altimeter: two thousand feet.

Trellis-like patterns of light filtered through the clouds onto the maze of billabongs, creeks and lagoons. Occasionally, the dense matted green would explode into colour as flocks of cockatoos or osprey cranes shot into the air, startled by the heavy drone of our engine.

Rain spattered fitfully against the windscreen, driven by a gusty wind. Suddenly we were into another sodden patch of cloud and the ground below us disappeared into amorphous grey.

Joe and I had never flown that part of the country before. The Flying Doctor team at Berwick had

132

been called away into the Northern Territory on an emergency and a few hours later a woman who was on her own at a small station at Dry Gully began her labour six weeks early. Joe and I had flown out from Preston but by the time we arrived the baby had been born. He was a fine healthy screaming boy, delivered quite competently by the woman's sister, who had driven fifty-five miles from Tweedy. Neither mother nor baby needed our expertise so we took off for the long trip back down the Gulf and over the Kimberley to Preston. It should have been a routine flight – albeit a long and fruitless one – but suddenly we found ourselves in desperate trouble.

I checked the altimeter: fifteen hundred feet. Beads of perspiration stood out on Joe's forehead, his bulbous nose now blushing a deep maroon, like some bizarre warning beacon.

'It's no good,' he muttered. 'We'll have to put her down.'

'According to the map, there should be a landing strip round here someplace. Turner Hill.'

'I'll take her down under the clouds and we'll have a look.'

We came out of the clouds at seven hundred and fifty feet, and began desperately searching the country below us for the tell-tale scar of a landing strip. Nothing. Just the seemingly endless mass of swamp and thick vegetation. Joe snatched up the intercom.

'Six Victor X-ray, this is Six Charlie Tango, do you read me?' Over.'

Clyde came back almost at once. 'Reading you Six Charlie Tango, strength five.'

'Look Clyde – we've got a spot of engine trouble here. We're going to have to put the old girl down somewhere.'

'Yairs, okay Joe. What's your position? Over.'

'Well, we're supposed to be somewhere over Turner Hill but the head-winds may have kept us further to the north. No visible landmarks that I can recognise.'

'Okay, Joe. I'll pass the information on to Berwick air control. Continue radio contact. Over.'

I looked at Joe. 'How much longer can we stay in the air?'

'Only another five or ten minutes,' Joe said.

'We can't be too far from Turner Hill,' I said. The hazy mist that veiled the horizon was keeping visibility down to just a couple of miles in each direction.

Joe, as usual, refused to give up hope. 'You might as well face it. We're lost.'

The minutes passed. We were down to just two hundred feet, the dense mass of mangroves and cypress perilously close.

Joe made his decision. 'There's a clearing just beyond that creek over there. That will have to do.'

It was only a little longer than a football pitch, covered in lush, knee-high grass. There was no way of knowing if the ground below would be firm enough to support the weight of the plane. But, as Joe remarked, it had to be better than a couple of trees and a muddy creek.

Joe fought to bring the Cessna round for a second pass. The engine coughed and for one terrible moment I thought we were about to stall.

'Hold on,' Joe said. 'Here we go.'

We dropped low over the trees, the wheels skimming a row of cypress pines. The strong gusty wind tried to tip the port wing just a few seconds before we landed and we hit the ground with a hard bump. We breathed a sigh of relief as we heard solid ground thundering beneath the wheels, and Joe's face relaxed into a smile.

'It's our lucky day,' he grinned. 'We made it.'

Just then our wheels checked in a swampy patch of mud and bogged. The tiny plane stopped dead at forty miles an hour, somersaulted on its nose and smashed into the ground on its back.

There was a deafening bang and lights of appalling brightness flashed on and off in my head. I felt a sudden terrible pressure on the top of my head.

I remember thinking: 'The plane has turned over and the cockpit is crumbling like cardboard and my skull is splitting apart. I'm dying and there is nothing I can do.' There was no fear; I felt calm and utterly detached, as if I was watching it happen to someone else.

It was all over in a few seconds, and then there was an uncanny silence.

I opened my eyes and found myself hanging from the ceiling like a startled bat. My head was throbbing. There was a soft, tender lump on my crown the size of a baseball; I must have made contact with the roof panel. I unbuckled my lap strap and clambered out into the wet grass, still expecting to float upwards with a heavenly choir to accompany my ascension. But I didn't. Instead, the damp seeped into my knees and my hands sank deeper into the mud and the only sound was the hissing of the hot metal of the engines as they made contact with the swamp grass.

I crawled round to the other side of the plane and found Joe still hanging from his seat, unconscious. He was a sorry sight indeed. His once prominent proboscis had been bent sideways by the harsh embrace of the control column, and thick red blood oozed from it. I clambered inside, unfastened his seat belt, and supporting his weight as best I could, pulled him out onto the grass.

The icy hand of fear tightened around my stomach. Quickly I felt for broken bones and for tell-tale swellings around his abdomen that might indicate a dangerous haemorrhage and internal damage. As far as I could tell, he seemed to have no worse than a broken nose and a badly swollen knee. There was also a good chance that he had a concussion; but in the circumstances it seemed to me that we had both got away pretty lightly.

Joe's eyes fluttered open, like two small butter-flies setting off in spring. 'What happened?' he mumbled.

'Are you all right?'

Joe looked at the plane lying broken on its back a few feet away, and he shook his head, an ironic smile forming on his lips. 'Just my luck,' he said slowly, and passed out again.

We were about a hundred yards from a tangled mangrove swamp that banked onto a muddy creek. My first fear was of crocodiles. I had heard many blood-curdling stories of men and women who had mysteriously disappeared while bathing in creeks in the Northern Kimberley, leaving behind on the bank only their shoes and socks as a poignant memorial. I made a mental note not to venture too near the swamp.

I checked the damage to the aircraft. The propeller had snapped and the fuselage had buckled somewhere near the tail. It looked as though its flying days were over. Worst of all, the radio was out of action. The aerial lay crumpled and twisted beneath the plane.

It was getting late and I estimated that only an hour of light remained. There was little chance of rescue before morning.

Even though it was getting towards evening, it was still humid and stickily warm. I began to consider where we might spend the night. The ground around us was fairly dry and firm but there was the danger that if there *were* any crocodiles in the swamp nearby, they might get our scent and risk coming into the clearing. But it was the advent of another predator that finally decided me against the idea – mosquitoes, hordes of them that descended on us just before dark in a black mist.

I dragged Joe back inside the plane and made him as comfortable as I could on the ceiling of the cockpit. I laid him on the top of a couple of blankets from the stretcher and gave him a small dosage of morphine to dull the pain from his nose.

The air inside the plane was suffocatingly hot. Joe and I lay on our backs, quite still, covered in sweat, listening to the night sounds of the swamp. We talked for a while, about how long it would take the rescue teams to find us, what might have caused the engine trouble, how far we could be from Turner Hill. Then unexpectedly, Joe became quite expansive and started to tell me about his past. Perhaps it was the morphine in his system. But suddenly he said, 'You know, I never wanted to do this for a living. I always wanted to be a solicitor.'

His voice now had a peculiar, honking quality, due to the sudden redistribution of his nasal bones. It was like holding a conversation with an articulate goose.

'Why didn't you?'

'I wasn't smart enough. Anyway I think the teachers had it in for me. So when I left school I went straight into the Air Force. That's where I learned to fly. I'll never forget the first time I went up in a plane.'

'Neither will I,' I said, remembering the thrill of that initiation to the sky. I was nine and my father had taken me for a joy-ride in an old de Havilland Dragon. 'It really gets to you, doesn't it?'

'It certainly does,' Joe said. 'I hated it. I thought I was going to be sick. I still hate it.'

'Are you serious?'

'I don't joke about things like that.'

'Then why the hell did you become a pilot? Why didn't you go into electronics or something?'

I heard Joe give a long sigh. 'They said I had an aptitude. Anyway, the pay was good. My brother was an electrician and I wanted to be better than he was.'

'So how long were you in the Air Force?'

'Three years. Right up until the court-martial.'

'The what?'

'It was the old Kennedy jinx,' he said, 'I sunk somebody's yacht.'

'You sunk a yacht.'

'It wasn't meant to be there,' he went on. 'It had

138

strayed inside our practice range. I mistook it for the target and fired a torpedo at it. Luckily there was no one on board. They'd all rowed to a nearby island for a picnic. But it belonged to somebody important and there was a big furore in the papers and the Air Force decided to make me the scapegoat.'

I hesitated to point out to him that scapegoat or not, he did after all fire the torpedo. But Joe, no doubt inspired by the drug in his veins, was intent now on pouring out his heart to me.

'I tell you there's a jinx on my family. Nothing I do ever seems to go right. When I left the Air Force I went into business with this bloke I met in Queensland. He had this crop-dusting company and he wanted another pilot. We did famous for a while and he made me a partner. Then one day the silly bugger hit an overhead cable and killed himself. That's when I found out he wasn't insured. His widow sued the company and sent me to the wall. Christ, I reckon if it was raining pea soup, I'd get hit on the head with a fork.'

'What did you do then?' I asked.

'For six months, nothing. I was going to shoot me bloody self but I couldn't afford a gun licence. Then a friend of mine got me a job with TAA as a second officer. Not a bad job, if it wasn't for the flying. The pay was steady and there were plenty of holidays. I was there for three months and one of the passengers assualted me.'

'Go on,' I said.

'He was drunk, I reckon. He started abusing me for no reason, and I got mad and stuck his head down a waste chute. He hurt his neck getting it out and claimed damages off the company. I was asked to leave. I was lucky to get this job up here. Now look what's happened. I'll probably get the blame for this.'

He grew silent. I felt compelled to ask the obvious question. 'Why don't you give up flying?'

'You've got to be kidding,' he said. 'It's the only thing I'm good at.'

I slept fitfully. At dawn I moved Joe outside the plane again. The morphine had lulled him into a fairly rested sleep but I had lain awake most of the night, cramped and sticky with my own sweat, and I was eager to be away by the end of the day.

I felt sure that we would soon be found and I had salvaged two distress flares from the aircraft for the first sighting. I would not have felt quite so confident had I known that we were thirty-five miles to the south-east of the estimated position we had given to Clyde on the last radio contact.

At that moment two RAAF Hercules were taking off from Preston and the Flying Doctor Beagle from Berwick was in the air to take part in the search. No doubt they would have found us long before our position became critical . . . but rescue was to come from a quite unexpected quarter.

It was the middle of the morning when we heard the distant rumbling sound; at first I thought I had imagined it. A flock of pigeons whirred overhead and the honking of some geese as they made their way down the creek drowned out the faint noise. Then in the stillness we heard it again.

We assumed it must be one of the search planes but it seemed to be coming from the swamps beyond the creek. It sounded like a jeep or a heavy truck.

I sprang to my feet and raced across the clearing down to the creek. Keeping one eye open for reptiles I picked my way through the twisted roots of the mangroves. I stopped, waited. My breath rattled in my throat. It was very close. I could hear men's voices over the drone of the engine.

Suddenly I saw it, an old mustard-yellow Land-rover flat-top, passing in between the trees just a hundred yards away on the other side of the creek.

I waved my hands and shouted myself hoarse. For a moment I thought they hadn't heard but then I saw the Landrover pull to a stop and two men started picking their way through the undergrowth towards me. Finally one of them, a big man with a red beard, the rest of his face shaded by a khaki bush hat, stood staring at me from the far bank, his hands on his hips.

'Who the bleedin' hell are you?'

'I'm Doctor Hazzard from the Flying Doctor Service in Preston. We crash-landed over in the clearing there late yesterday. My pilot's injured.'

'The Flying Doctor? Well I'll be buggered. They said on the radio you'd come down near Turner 'ill.'

'Where are we?'

'Salmon Creek. Turner 'ill's miles away from here. Look, this must be our lucky day. Our mate's just fallen down a gully an' broken 'is bleedin' leg. We was just goin' back to camp to call for the doctor. You've saved us a trip.'

Joe was leaning up on one elbow, watching me run back across the clearing. 'Did you find them?' he yelled.

'Yeah, it's okay,' I said 'It was a couple of miners in a Landrover. There's a bush track just on the other side of the creek.'

I leaned against the side of the plane, panting.

'Thank God,' Joe said. 'Let's get out of here.'

Supporting him on one arm, and carrying the medical equipment in the other, I helped Joe limp down to the creek. It was a long trip for an injured man and by the time we reached the swampy glades we were both shaking with exhaustion.

The big miner with the red beard and a youth in a shooting jacket were waiting impatiently on the far bank, holding rifles.

''Urry up, doc,' the bearded man said. 'You've got another patient waitin' ya know.'

Joe collapsed onto one of the mangrove roots, gasping for breath, and I trod warily into the muddy waters of the creek, looking up and down the banks.

'Could you guys get hold of a raft or something?' I asked.

'Where we gonna get a bleedin' raft?'

'What about the crocodiles?'

'Look, we got guns, ain't we?'

'But can you use them?'

The big man looked at me as if I was questioning his parentage. The young boy sprang to his defence. 'He won second prize in the Berwick clay shoot.'

I hesitated. The big man spoke again. 'Come on doc, we'll want to be going.'

I hauled Joe to his feet, muttered a quick prayer, and we splashed into the creek. The water was greenish and blood warm. It had a sharp, acrid smell, like urine. My feet sank into the mud below and each step became an effort. Joe groaned and leaned his whole weight against my shoulder.

It was slow progress. The water came up to our

shoulders, and it would have been difficult enough on my own. I was practically dragging Joe along with one arm, and I still had the medical kit with its precious supplies of morphine clutched in my left hand. I was expecting some green-scaled monster with massive jaws to come crashing into the water alongside us at any moment.

The man with the red beard was unsympathetic. 'Christ, 'urry up, doc,' he shouted. 'I don't want to stand 'ere like a shag on a rock all bleedin' day.'

Finally Joe and I scrambled up onto the mud on the far bank, wheezing and coughing. The bearded man and his companion hauled us out of the shallows and onto the dry ground like sacks of potatoes.

'Jeez,' the younger man said suddenly, as I lay gasping at his feet. 'Look at that, Bill.'

We all turned. An enormous crocodile, perhaps nine or ten feet long, was swimming towards the spot where we had so recently emerged, its small, evil eyes and long snout just visible above the level of the water.

The bearded man raised his rifle and fired two shots into the water around its head. The monster turned and with a mighty splash of its tail made off in the other direction.

'You frightened it off,' I managed to mumble.

'I was trying to hit it!'

'Our last two bullets too,' the younger man said.

'You've got a lot of guts you blokes,' the bearded man said, slapping me heftily on the back. 'Don't think I woulda taken a chance like that.'

CHAPTER 12

'I've got a telegram for that old bastard Joe Parker, Clyde. Are you listening?'

'Receiving you strength eight,' Clyde said lazily. 'Repeat your message, Six Charlie Foxtrot. Over.'

'Message reads: LISTEN HERE YOU BASTARD STOP YOU OWE ME A HUNDRED QUID YOU BUGGER AND I'M GOING TO BLOODY WELL GET IT STOP MY LAWYER'S GOING TO CHEW YOUR GUTS IN COURT AND I DON'T CARE WHAT IT COSTS STOP CHEW ON THAT GRISTLE YOU OLD MISER STOP End of message.'

'Right-ho, Six Charlie Foxtrot. Message received. Over.'

'And don't change any of it, ya mug,' the voice at the other end of the line yelled, and the carrier wave ended. Clyde wrote on his telegram form: OUTSTANDING AMOUNT REMAINS AT £100 STOP AM TAKING LEGAL ACTION STOP.

Clyde looked up at me with a sardonic grin. 'It carries the gist of the message without upsetting anyone at the Post Office.'

'How long have they been at it now?'

'More than nine months. Herbie must have spent his hundred quid in telegrams. Don't know why they don't just bury the hatchet.'

It was one of those weeks when I had been

attacked by another fit of indescribable boredom. I had absolutely nothing to do. Joe was almost recovered from his injuries, but the last two weeks had been very quiet and I hadn't moved out of Preston, except to try out the new twin-engine Beagle that had been flown in to replace the ill-fated Cessna, which still lay rusting in the swamp south of Berwick. It was one of three that had been recently flown out from the United States for use in the Service and it seemed ideal; it performed well and it had a little more space than the Cessna. I took it up for a short flight and reported to Joe that he would be well pleased with the new machine. I didn't realise then that I was to be the pilot on its maiden voyage for the Service – and just what a rigorous baptism it was to be.

This particular afternoon I had decided to come out to the radio post for some company and to enjoy some of Mary Westcott's scones. It was another brutally hot day. The temperature had soared into the high thirties and the small radio hut was like a blast furnace. It amazed me how Clyde could work in there day after day.

He finished receiving telegrams and threw the network open for the 'galah session', as it was called. Housewives scattered across the thousands of square miles of the Kimberley got together through the miracle of Marconi for a gossip over the back fence of north-west Australia.

I stood outside, staring idly at the dingo pelt.

'How did you really get this?' I said to Clyde as he came out.

'The truth?'

'Yes, the truth.'

145

'Well, the fact is, it was trying to get in the house one night,' Clyde said, the putty-like face setting as hard as granite as he stared pensively at the white fur. 'It climbed in through the kitchen window and jumped into the sink. Me wife was bleaching some overalls and it drowned. That's how I found it the next morning. All I had to do was nail it to the wall.'

'You don't expect me to believe that.'

'No,' Clyde said, rubbing his chin thoughtfully. 'But if I told you the real story you wouldn't believe it either.'

The next morning I went through my usual consultations, and had the unexpected pleasure of speaking to Jesse Hoagan. Jesse had studiously avoided me since our confrontation three months before, and all my communications with Brookton now went through Megan. I was surprised therefore to hear Jesse's voice coming over the airwaves to ask my professional advice. He had caught his hand on some fence wire and the wound had turned septic. The infection didn't sound too severe and I prescribed some penicillin G.

'And how's your general health, Jess?'

'I'm fine.'

'No dizzy spells?'

'Look, I don't know why you keep pestering me like this. I'm not sick.'

'No more chest pains?'

'I never did have any pains. Look, you examined me yourself! Anyway – what about those damn tests you did? Didn't they tell you what you wanted to know?'

I had sent the specimens down to Perth for testing

but they hadn't been particularly enlightening. The blood-count had been normal, although the sugar level was a little high; and the urine sample was even less use, for as the pathology laboratory reported, the urine had come from some sort of livestock, probably a cow.

I seized on this opportunity. 'There was one very disturbing outcome,' I said to Jesse. 'I don't quite know how to break it to you.'

There was a long silence, the crackle of the static telling its own story.

Finally: 'Have I got something?'

It gave me intense satisfaction to hear the very real panic in his voice. 'Pathology says you're pregnant, Jess. Furthermore, you're going to give birth to a calf.'

The human organism is prone to many malfunctions and diseases and I had come across a wide cross-section of them during my first six months in the Kimberley. However there was one sickness that is endemic in this vast and desolate land that cannot be removed by surgery or treated with drugs.

Loneliness.

Many of the men and women – and the men greatly outnumbered the women – who live in the north-west grow used to their solitary life without realising that they are lonely. After years of bush life most of the men become lost and awkward in the presence of women and never marry: they have their 'mates' and grow accustomed to keeping their own company. Some are prone to episodes of depression that plunge them into fits of drunken violence. Suicides are not uncommon. Worst

147

affected are the Latin races, the 'new Australians', who are by nature garrulous creatures, fond of the society of others.

Occasionally this loneliness can manifest itself in phantom aches and pains, and although these have no physical cause or outward appearance, they do seem very real to the sufferer. My most dramatic encounter with this phenomenon happened at the end of this long, dull week just a couple of days before Joe was passed fit to resume as my pilot.

It nearly cost me my life.

It was a few minutes past ten o'clock when the phone rang. I had settled into bed but a day of inactivity had left me restless and irritable. I snatched up the phone.

'Hazzard,' I fumbled for the light switch and turned on the bedside lamp.

'Doc, I've got a call for assistance from Inglis River.' It was Clyde. 'Some fellow seems to be real bad. I'll put him on.'

'Okay, Clyde,' I said, trying to gather my wits again after my fitful dreams. I heard the crackle of electricity as Clyde fed the reception into the land-lines.

'Hell? Is that the doctor? Can-a anyone hear me?' The voice had a distinct Italian accent and sounded very excited, even hysterical.

'This is Doctor Hazzard. What appears to be the trouble? Over.'

'I'm-a dying. Please come. Oh God, I can't stand it . . .' The rest of the transmission was garbled. I could make out the sound of someone crying.

'Can you give me details of what is wrong, please. I can't make out what you're saying. Over.'

'There's-a pains, just pains all over . . . oh, God, you must-a help me?' More crying. My mind conjured up pictures of a massacre on a par with Hiroshima.

'Who is in pain? Can you please be more precise? Over.'

'It hurts . . . help-a me . . . it hurts . . .'

My mind raced. The carrier wave had stopped, and Clyde cut in on the line. 'It's a strange one, doc.'

'What do you know about the place, Clyde?'

'It's a mine. Copper I think. Three dings run the place. We hardly ever hear from 'em. 'Ello, he's coming on again.'

'Doc, you hear me? Can-a you hear me?'

Clyde put me back on the air. 'Look – I can't come out tonight. I can't land in the dark. Do you understand? Over.'

The man's voice rose to a wail. 'You must-a come. You must. We have-a flares. You can-a land okay. You must-a come.'

I didn't know what to make of it. The man just wasn't making sense. 'Is there someone there with you? Over.'

Silence. Clyde tried to raise the mine again without success.

'I can't raise him,' Clyde said finally. 'Well, that's a funny one. What are you going to do, doc?'

I thought – what if there's been an accident at the mine and the man is badly injured? He had a very strong accent; he might be in real distress and understand very little English anyway, which might explain the strange transmission. I felt I had to risk the night flight: 'When in doubt, go.'

'I'll go out there, Clyde. I must. If I see the flares,

I'll land. If not – well I'll just have to turn round and come back home.'

'Well, be careful,' Clyde said. 'It sounds bloody weird to me.'

It was a clear, starry night and the Kimberleys were bathed in the phosphorescent glow of a full moon, the silent land looking as alien and desolate as the surface of another planet. The shadows of hill and gully contrasted with the luminescence on the brooding mysterious landscape below like craters on the moon. I flew north-east for the ninety minute trip into the Doherty Range. A wild and lonely place even for the Kimberley, it was the province of nomadic Aborigines and a few hardy miners who braved the mountain fastnesses searching for the payloads of precious metal that would make their fortune.

I hadn't expected to find the mine, but to my surprise as I flew over the Christmas River I spotted the glow of seven or eight fires down at the end of a gorge, and headed towards them. As I flew over I saw a car's headlights burning at one end of the strip. Whatever the circumstances, I was expected.

As I took the plane into its approach I lowered the undercarriage and raised the flaps to full trim. Suddenly the flares and the headlights disappeared from view. For a few seconds I didn't realise what had happened. Then I saw it.

I pulled back hard on the controls as a steep ridge suddenly loomed up dead ahead of me in the darkness. There was a high-pitched squeal as I throttled forward and the small plane shuddered as I brought her nose up at almost eighty degrees and sent her shooting up into the night sky towards the stars, the undercarriage clipping stones off the top of the ridge.

My hands were still shaking, as I came in for the second time. I opted for a much steeper approach, flying in high over the ridge and swooping down towards the flares at the last moment. By the time I had corrected the angle for approach I was well past the headlights and the first line of flares, and the Beagle's first bush landing was a bouncing, jarring run through potholes and ruts, hurtling at least fifty yards beyond the last set of flares in almost total darkness. I expected the undercarriage to crumple beneath me at any moment. But finally the Beagle rolled safely to a halt, intact.

I taxied slowly back along the airstrip towards the flares and saw the car headlights speeding towards me.

A man jumped out of the vehicle and helped me from the cockpit. The incident a few minutes before had unnerved me, and I was a little unsteady on my feet. I allowed myself to be led towards a rather beaten-up jeep and I slumped gratefully into the passenger seat.

'Tony,' the man said, pumping my hand enthusiastically.

'Doctor Hazzard,' I stammered.

'You nearly fly into Suicide Ridge, eh?' the man said cheerfully. 'A plane he go bang there like that, two year ago.' To add force to his comment, he punched his fist into the palm of his other hand.

'Why didn't somebody warn me?' I asked, suddenly angry. 'Why didn't you tell me?'

Tony ignored my question. He ran round the

front of the jeep and jumped in behind the wheel.

I was suddenly too tired to be angry. 'Got a cigarette?' I said. I didn't often smoke but I badly wanted something to calm my nerves.

'Sure. You help you self,' Tony said expansively, and handed me a packet of Winfields and a zip lighter, as we sped off across the gully.

Tony was a mean bush driver. We bounced along over the rocks and sandhills at nearly fifty miles an hour. The packet of cigarettes flew out of my grasp and under the seat, but I was more concerned with hanging onto the dashboard now.

The beam of our headlights illuminated a tiny cluster of huts nestled in the shadow of the cliffs. Tony headed towards them and finally we skidded to a halt in front of an old tin shack.

'We arrive!' Tony exclaimed proudly, as if we'd just pulled up in front of the Sydney Hilton.

I nodded, and climbed thankfully out of the jeep. I looked around. It was dark. A gas lamp hung on a hook on the door of the hut; it was the only light in the whole place. Eerie. What the hell was going on?

My companion jumped out of the jeep, went over to the doorway and lifted the lamp off the hook.

'You come in, yes?' he said.

'Okay,' I said warily. 'But where's the patient?'

'You come in,' the man said again.

The lamp cast a peculiar glow across his face, and I was able to make out his features for the first time. He was a young man with a swarthy complexion and black, bushy hair. His teeth glowed white in a happy, almost intoxicated grin. He gave me the impression that he was just on his way to a New Year's Eve party – or just on his way back.

'Where's the patient?' I repeated. 'In here?' I pointed to the door.

'No, no,' he said, with a shy smile. 'Is-a me.'

For a moment there was a silence, then I said, 'But I thought you were dying. There were terrible pains.'

He shrugged. 'Is-a funny. I feel much better since I know you come.'

There was nothing I could say. I considered bawling him out for making me risk my life on a fool's errand but it seemed a pointless and rather hazardous exercise in the middle of nowhere with a man whose mental health remained open to doubt. So I said nothing.

My friend threw open the door of the shack and went inside. 'You hungry, yes? I make us a little something,' he said.

I followed him into the shack; it was like walking into Santa's grotto. As my companion turned on the lamps in the little room, a stunning array of cheeses, salami sausages and black olives came into view. A bottle of wine stood unopened in the middle of the table.

My friend grinned proudly. 'We have-a kerosene refrigerator.' He said the words slowly, carefully. 'Good, eh? Tony prepare special.'

I slumped into a chair. Tony surveyed me happily. Then he said, in almost perfect English, as if it had been well-rehearsed, 'It was good of you to come. I hope I have not been the cause of any trouble.'

'Not at all,' I muttered, thinking of that ridge coming towards me in the darkness. 'Not at all.'

Tony slapped me heartily on the back and started

153

to uncork the wine. 'Now you eat and enjoy. We have-a little party, eh?'

He produced some tumblers and poured two glasses of red wine. He raised the wine to his lips. 'To your 'ealth,' he said.

'I'll drink to that,' I murmured.

Tony and I sat all through the night talking – or rather he talked and I listened. I learned that he was from a small village in northern Italy, not far from Turin. He had six brothers and two sisters. He told me that he had come to Australia in 1963 to seek his fortune, working for a while as a labourer in Perth before buying a share in a mine with two cousins. The other men had abandoned the mine over six months before and since that time he had been there alone.

I offered to take him back with me to Preston but he politely refused. He assured me that he was very close to a vein of gold and that would make him rich beyond his wildest dreams.

So next morning I took off for Preston alone and he waved an enthusiastic *arrivederci* from the bonnet of his jeep. As I waved goodbye from the cockpit of the plane I had a strange feeling that it would not be the last I would be seeing of my Italian friend.

CHAPTER 13

The Coopers' place at Bindi station lay to the east of Hall's Creek. It was a large property with more than five thousand head of cattle. I was on a routine round of the stations, giving inoculations to young children, pre-natal attention to expectant mothers and doling out pills and eyedrops for the seemingly endless lines of small Aboriginal children suffering from various stages of trachoma.

I was again flying solo. Joe had come down with a virus, and rather than postpone the clinics, I set off on my own. I planned to be away for three or four days, and took with me ample supplies of polio, tuberculosis and smallpox serums.

It was perfect weather, and the full panorama of the Kimberleys was spread before me in the warm spring sunshine. The sienna brown earth contrasted with the desiccated yellow herbage in a huge and awesome landscape of monochrome. The surface was dotted with innumerable anthills, some round and squat, others rock-hard towers up to ten feet tall, like the sculpture of some giant primordial artist of Aboriginal dreamtime.

As I touched down on the wide flat strip at Bindi station, I saw a battered blue utility racing towards me in a cloud of red-brown dust, even before the plane had rolled to a stop. It skidded to a halt next to the Beagle and a man jumped out of the vehicle and started running towards the plane. It was Bill Cooper.

He was a small, frail-looking man, shrivelled and brown like an old date. He was no taller than some of his larger fence posts and not a great deal wider – *not* the sort of man you expected to find running a cattle station. And certainly not a man you imagined with a wife weighing seventeen stone.

As I clambered out of the cockpit, he grabbed me by the arm.

'You're just in time,' he yelled. 'We've got an emergency.'

He ushered me over to the utility and pushed me into the seat next to him. 'What's wrong?' I asked, thinking that perhaps a barn had collapsed on a half dozen of his men or the kitchen range had exploded.

He threw the gears of his battered machine into second and almost gave me a whiplash as we took off in a cloud of dust and small stones, making a narrow u-turn and roaring back towards Bindi.

'Can you handle a breech birth?' he demanded.

Well – that's like asking your grandmother if she can suck eggs! 'Of course I can. Who's the mother?' I knew it wasn't Mrs Cooper, as I had seen her just a couple of months before. It had to be one of the Aboriginal women who lived in the station.

'It's Shirley. Me favourite,' Cooper said, shaking his head in panic.

Now I was new to the job, but not new to the world. Was he satisfying his seemingly considerable lusts on the lubras as well? I looked at Cooper and his thin, dried-out body and decided to wait and see for myself before jumping to any outlandish conclusions.

156

We raced across three miles of flat bushland to the sprawling conglomeration of barns, sheds and stone houses that stood on the banks of a winding creek in the middle of the plain. We hurtled through the compound at breakneck speed and skidded to a halt in front of an old wooden barn. While I was picking myself off the dashboard, Cooper ran round the front of the car and threw open the door for me.

'Quick, doc!' he urged, tugging at my shirt. 'We gotta hurry.'

I got out of the ute and stood there, looking at Cooper expectantly.

'Well, where is she then?' I asked.

He gestured in the direction of the barn. 'In there.'

We went into the barn. The heat was stifling and there was a haze of large flies hovering over several piles of animal droppings. The incessant buzzing of their wings filled the air with a monotonous hum. The place stank.

I looked at Cooper, shocked. 'You've got a pregnant woman in here?'

'Not a woman, doc,' he said. He pointed to the far end of the barn. There, in one of the horse boxes, lay a huge chestnut mare. Her eyes were misted with pain, and she seemed scarcely aware of us watching her. Her flanks quivered as she strained against the foal trapped in her womb; she uttered a small whimper of protest, and was still once more.

'She's me favourite,' Cooper whispered. 'She's havin' a lot of trouble with this one. You'll see her right for me, won't ya?'

I suppose none of us are ever too old to stop learning. In my years of medical practice, I have delivered boys, girls, twins and one set of triplets; but this was the first time I had ever participated in the birth of a colt.

There were some difficult moments. I had to insert my arm almost to the shoulder to bring the foal's head round to the proper position, and gave the exhausted mother a shot of pituitrin to help her expel the baby colt. Finally, the tiny thing emerged, alive and healthy. As with any birth, the moment of new life is a beautiful, even awesome moment.

The mother seemed to take it all in her stride but I'm afraid Bill Cooper broke down on my shoulder.

Later that morning I sat in the Coopers' kitchen, celebrating the birth of the colt with a warm beer and a slice of ginger cake baked by Mrs Cooper in the stove oven. I had finished the clinic and was at peace with the world; it was one of those moments when I felt I could stay in the Kimberley as the Flying Doctor for the rest of my life.

The Coopers together were like a pair of lovesick pigeons. He could have climbed into one of the legs of her underwear and still had room to do a barn dance, but their contrasting physiques seemed to be no bar to their love. He doted on her and she in turn absolutely glowed with pride when he was around.

They sat opposite me now, their chairs very close together. While Bill chatted to me about the station and the weather, she stroked his hair and occasionally nibbled his ear. Whenever she did this, he giggled like a schoolboy and told her to stop and I looked out of the window and pretended to be captivated by something of interest over by the creek. I'd never met a couple like them.

They were ridiculous but somehow they made me aware that something was missing in my life, and a sudden pang of loneliness began to dissolve the glow of satisfaction I had felt.

When I finished my third helping of cake I said it was time to go and Cooper got to his feet, kissed his wife goodbye and led me out to his battered 1958 Holden utility. I remembered how on my first visit to Bindi station I had looked at the ute and Bill's tattered brown trousers and assumed that the Coopers were finding it hard to eke out an existence. Joe later informed me that Bill Cooper was a millionaire, on paper at least. I learned that in the outback you can never judge a man's financial position by his clothes and his car, as we do in the city.

As we drove out to the plane, he seemed strangely preoccupied and it was obvious that there was something troubling him.

'Something on your mind, Bill?'

'Don't know how to say it. It's a bit embarrassing, doc.'

'Come on. You know me well enough by now.'

'Well – I'm worried about my lupino.'

'Your what?' Suddenly I had a blinding flash of intuition. 'Oh, your *libido*,' I laughed.

He looked a little offended. 'It's no laughing matter, doc.'

'I'm sorry, Bill. Well, what's the trouble exactly?'

'I dunno. I just can't manage it like I used to,' he mumbled. 'I'm not a young man any more.'

I nodded my head sagely. 'Well, I shouldn't worry too much,' I said. 'These things happen as we get older. We have to learn to adjust.'

'But it's Bessie I'm worried about,' Cooper said. 'She's a normal healthy woman, and she has her needs, if you know what I mean.'

'Well, how often do you have intercourse?' I asked casually.

'How often?' he considered carefully. 'Only about eight to ten times a week these days,' he said ruefully.

I stared out of the window for a long time, trying to clear my thoughts. 'Really, I shouldn't worry about it, Bill,' I repeated at last.

'Well, I was just wondering,' he said. 'if perhaps you couldn't get me some of them vitamin E pills. Or maybe that stuff they advertise in the *Post*. Some sort of ointment.'

'In a professional capacity I'd advise against it,' I told him. 'It could be dangerous.' I looked again at his scrawny arms and sallow cheeks and it occurred to me why the poor man was so thin. 'Just make sure you keep eating enough,' I added.

After I had finished the round of clinics I was asked to make an unscheduled stop at Hall's Creek. I had been notified over the radio that an old miner had died in the town and his last wish had been that he be buried in the family plot in Preston. They requested I stop over at the airport and fly the body back with me. I agreed quite happily to this; I calculated it would add just another thirty minutes to my return trip, and I could still be back in Preston in time for dinner.

The town of Hall's Creek has been built on a flat ten miles away from the original site of the town, which grew up in the mountain ranges away to the west after the discovery of gold in the region in the late nineteenth century. It was here in 1911 that the famous incident with a young stockman called Jimmy d'Arcy took place. Hundreds of miles from proper medical care a postmaster performed a major operation on the injured d'Arcy in the Post Office building, while a doctor twelve hundred miles away in Perth relayed instructions to him by telegraph. D'Arcy died ten days later – ironically enough, of malaria and not his injuries – and it was this incident that was to inspire the Reverend John Flynn to bring about the birth of the Flying Doctor Service many years later.

I taxied across the runway of the Hall's Creek aerodrome towards the hangars, where a solemn little band waited with their grisly cargo. The dead man had no living relatives, and the coffin was accompanied by two of the airport officials, who loaded it aboard the plane. The local doctor handed me the death certificate and in just a quarter of an hour I was airborne once more.

It was a wonderful afternoon. The sun was starting to sink now across the western sky, lending a blaze of pink and orange colour to the high wispy clouds dotted around the horizon. The plains were wrapped in a soft golden cloak, and in the distance the low cliffs of the Haller Range stood out sharp and clear, burnt orange against a background of celestial blue.

I started to hum softly to myself.

Far below, on the rough red-brown country, herds of camel and wild brumby horses scattered as the plane hurtled overhead. The land was littered in places with roaming cattle and occasionally I would

spot emu and kangaroos darting through the under-
brush away from the strange shadow of the aircraft.

Points of light shimmered in the dry sandy gullies
– particles of silica and mica and quartz. Once I
passed over a smouldering fire next to a water hole,
and a group of nomadic natives pointed to the big
white bird as it flew overhead.

Gradually though, my feelings of peace and
well-being started to dissolve. It began with an
uneasy sensation in the hairs on the back of my neck
that worked its way down along my spine. Almost
as if something in me could sense another presence
in the cockpit.

I found myself turning round in my seat and
stealing glances at the polished mahogany box lying
on the cabin floor, as if expecting some ghoul-like
creature to rise up from it and sit there leering at me.
Pull yourself together, I said under my breath. *What's
wrong with you?*

I had practised medicine for many years, and I had
seen a lot of death and dying. The sight of a corpse
didn't keep me awake at night. I was at a loss to
understand this sudden feeling of dread.

I took a few deep breaths. Started to hum a tune.
Tried to concentrate on just flying the plane. But
still something told me: 'You're not alone'.

It was then that the knocking started.

It began with just a gentle tapping and at first I
wanted to believe there was something loose in the
aircraft. You imagined it, I said to myself. You've
got yourself so thoroughly frightened of an inani-
mate corpse that you're starting to have auditory
hallucinations.

I thought back to the psychology I had done at

162

university, and all the documented cases in which men and women had seen and heard things that weren't there, due to the impetus of fear. I thought of the schizophrenic I had treated once for a kidney complaint, and the strange, shadowy world he lived in, a world that had no reality outside of his own mind.

Get a grip on yourself, Mike.

But then I heard it again.

A cold, clammy sweat broke out all over my body and I could hear my heart palpitating in my chest. I swallowed hard and listened carefully. I will do nothing until I hear that noise again, I told myself, and then if I *do* hear it again, which of course I won't, I will take appropriate and rational action.

It came again. This time very loud, very distinct.

I put the plane on automatic pilot and got out of the seat. I tried to get a grip on my emotions. There are only two alternatives, I told myself. Either I am going mad, or the person in that coffin is not dead and someone has made a rather nasty mistake.

More tapping.

I clambered into the rear of the cockpit and fetched the toolkit. I found a crowbar and applied the flat end of the bar under the lid and started to prise it open. I thought briefly of a similar scene that involved Peter Cushing in *Dracula's Revenge*.

Finally, I levered off the lid and peered inside.

I found myself looking at a rather withered, grey-haired old man who blinked and screwed up his eyes at the invasion of the bright sunlight. He put a thin, bone-like claw over his face and peered up at me, squinting. He was obviously very much alive, though I had to admit he didn't seem to be in the best of health.

Neither of us spoke for a long while. I continued to stare and the old man continued to squint. Finally he raised his head a little.

'Young man,' he said slowly. 'I think I would like a second opinion.'

CHAPTER 14

Aspirin looked at me with his large brown doleful eyes and leaned forward in his chair.

'Doc,' he said slowly. 'I've got cholera.'

I took in this information with equanimity and looked dolefully back at him. 'Impossible.'

Aspirin gripped my arm with one clammy paw. 'I've got all the symptoms. Rapid heartbeat, high temperature, abdominal pains . . .'

'Okay, okay. But haven't you been inoculated against cholera?'

He looked at me blankly. 'Huh?'

I made a motion with my finger and thumb in a dumb show of putting a syringe in my arm. 'A needle? Haven't you had one?'

He sat back in his chair, and his face paled a little. 'Oh no,' he said with a grimace. 'I can't stand those things.'

I looked away and out of the window, to the creek where I had sent Aspirin for his 'hydro-lachrymose test' a few months before. The effects seemed to have worn off already. Then suddenly Aspirin's last words hit me: 'I can't stand those things.'

I had an idea.

I looked back at my half-caste hypochondriac and could scarcely conceal a smile of triumph. 'Okay,' I said, picking up the stethoscope from the table.

'Let's have a look at you.'

I gave him a thorough examination. I took his temperature and his pulse and checked his blood pressure – all normal. I tested his eyes, which were twenty-twenty and his reflexes, which would have done justice to a slip fieldsman. Finally I fixed him with a baleful stare and said nothing. The silence went on for a long time and the tension in the room grew. Finally he could stand it no longer.

'What is it, doc?'

'I'm sorry to have to tell you this but I'm afraid it's not cholera. It's "tedious ad nauseum". I've come across it before.'

'Is there a cure?'

'Fortunately yes,' I said, and took a syringe of cholera vaccine from the medical kit and the largest needle I could find. Aspirin shrank back a little in his chair. If this didn't put him off coming to see me, nothing would.

'I don't like needles,' he stammered.

'I'm afraid it's the only way.'

He looked at me for a moment, his face a sick mask of terror. Slowly, very slowly, he started to roll up his sleeve.

'Sorry,' I said. 'We need to get this vaccine straight into the system. The arm's no good . . .'

'You mean . . .'

I nodded.

After some persuasion Aspirin found himself bent over the table with his trousers round his ankles. His buttocks were clenched tight, like a fist. I took my time, making sure he got a good look at the needle before I struck, squirting a little of the serum on the table in front of him.

'We'll have to keep up these injections until the symptoms disappear.'

'I hope it works, doc,' Aspirin said.

'I'm sure it will. Now keep still, this is going to hurt,' I said with relish.

'Quick, get it over with, doc!' he pleaded.

'You're too tense,' I said, and for a split second he relaxed his buttock muscles and I chose that moment to plunge in the needle. There was a deafening scream and five minutes later when Aspirin departed my makeshift surgery I found that the queue of patients which had been waiting to see me had somehow mysteriously disappeared.

Preventative medicine is indeed a wonderful thing.

'You're getting a reputation round here,' Jesse Hoagan was saying, his thumbs tucked into the broad leather belt that contained his ample girth. 'The blokes are gettin' a bit nervy about all this shoutin' and screamin' that goes on every time you have a clinic.'

'I thought your blokes were supposed to be tough,' I said, busily packing away my notes and instruments.

Jesse ignored the remark. 'And what did you do to that bloody no-good darkie? He's really dropped his bundle this time. He's runnin' round the place like a chook with its head cut off, holdin' his arse.'

I smiled, feeling very smug. 'Yes, well I think I found a cure for your Aspirin. I don't think he'll be getting sick too often in the future.'

'Well, that remains to be seen,' Jesse said, hitching one of his heavy brown boots on the back of a chair

167

and peering at me with his large, rheumy eyes. 'But that's not what I've come to see you about.'

I looked up brightly. 'Getting those chest pains again?'

He straightened, and glowered at me furiously. I'm in the best of health. It's Megan I'm worried about.'

'Oh? What's wrong?'

'She's not been herself lately. I want you to take a look at her.'

'Why? Is she sick?'

'Well, not exactly . . . she's been sort of . . . depressed. Moochin' around the place with a long face, and snappin' me head off at breakfast. It's not like her. I think she's pinin' for something.'

'I'm a physician not a psychologist.'

Jesse frowned at me for a moment then, jutting out his jaw defiantly, he said: 'A doctor's a doctor. She's got somethin' wrong with 'er, and I want you to find out what it is and fix it.'

'Oh – is that all?'

It sounded to me as though Megan was upset about something Jesse had done and he was too insensitive an oaf to realise it. Or perhaps she was just having a particularly bad period. But there would be no harm in talking to her – indeed, I thought it would be one of the more pleasant of my duties.

'Where is she?'

'She's out in the store. She's doin' some stock-takin'.'

'All right I'll go and see her.'

A few minutes later I was making my way across the compound to the storehouse, a tall wooden building about a hundred yards from the house. I pulled open the heavy door and went inside.

There were no windows and it was quite dark in there after the glare of the midday sun. A little sunlight filtered in through the wooden slats and the skylight overhead. As my eyes grew accustomed to the grey light, I found myself surrounded by long tiers of shelves containing bags of flour and sugar, and cases of jam, tea and salt. Hurricane lamps were strapped to the rafters overhead and saddles, pack bags, branding irons, horseshoes and stockwhips hung on poles along the walls. Sacks of potatoes and onions littered the slab floor and there was a pervading smell of leather and must.

Megan was standing at the end of one of the shelves, making some pencil notes in a ledger. As the door squeaked open, she looked up and gave me a bright smile.

'Oh, hi.'

'Hello. Jesse told me I'd find you here.'

'He's got me doing the stocktaking. We have to order more supplies this month. He hates book-work.' She looked at me, a dark shadow of concern suddenly passing across her face. 'There's nothing wrong, is there?'

'With Jesse? Not that I can tell. How's he been lately?'

'A lot better actually,' she said. I thought I detected a note of bitterness in her voice but I may have imagined it. 'Those tablets you gave me really seem to have helped. I told him they were for indigestion.'

'Did you talk to him?' I asked. She looked at me blankly. 'About leaving the station?'

She laughed. 'Yes, but it didn't do any good. I told you it wouldn't. Short of putting him in a straitjacket and carrying him off to the Hospital, there's little anyone can do.'

I studied her for a moment. Jesse was right – she *was* looking jaded, and even when she smiled there was a kind of tired resignation in her eyes. More significantly perhaps, her hair, which was normally so beautifully groomed, was tied back in a simple pony tail, and it looked as though it hadn't been brushed.

'Actually you know, I came to talk to you.'

She stopped writing in the ledger and looked up at me. Her face betrayed puzzlement, but something else too. She was flattered.

'That was nice.'

There was suddenly a very real warmth in her face. It surprised me.

'I'm on professional business really,' I said. It sounded arch, and I immediately wished I hadn't said it.

'Oh.' She sounded disappointed.

'Jesse reckons you've been off colour. I think he's worried about you.'

'I'm fine.'

I realised I'd been clumsy. I tried to cover my tracks. 'I told him it wouldn't do any good talking to you. I said you'd tell me you were fine – just like he does.'

'You were right then, weren't you?' She started work with the pencil and ledger again.

'Megan, the two of you have got to work this thing out. You can't keep on like this.'

'Like what?'

'Jesse has no idea how you really feel about the station.'

'Neither have you.'

'Oh?'

'Dad's an old worrier and I don't know why you pay any attention to him. I'm feeling a bit tired, that's all. Now I really have to get this done. I was supposed to order these stores last week.'

I took that as my cue to leave.

I shrugged. Well, at least I'd tried. I turned and left, closing the door gently behind me.

My last clinic that day was at a small township west of Hall's Creek called Leith River. I set up a makeshift surgery at the AIM hostel and while I was there I was approached by one of the Sisters, who asked me to take a patient back to Preston with me. His name was Henry and he had lived most of his life at Leith River. He had recently become blind and was no longer able to take care of himself. Arrangements had been made for him to go to the nursing home just outside Preston.

He made his appearance at the aerodrome that afternoon in a convoy of two battered old Holdens that roared up in a cloud of dust just as I was about to give up and leave without him. The half dozen or so elderly occupants of the two cars piled out and staggered across the dirt strip to the plane carrying Henry along in their midst. They were thirty minutes late – and dead drunk.

It seemed that he had been treated to a farewell party by some geriatric friends down at the hostel that afternoon. By the time he got to me, he absolutely reeked of alcohol and was scarcely able to stand. I was shocked by his appearance. He was easily into his eighties, bald, and with scarcely any of his own teeth. He was wearing a tattered pair of brown corduroy trousers, a grubby cotton shirt and some sandals. All he owned he carried with him in a battered leather case.

The party of decrepit and largely toothless hell-raisers were not eager to part with their compatriot. Farewells were exchanged several times, hands were shaken, we all sang *For He's A Jolly Good Fellow* a couple of times, and then farewells were exchanged all over again. Finally, another bottle of beer was produced and I felt it was time to be firm, so I disentangled Henry from the group, who jeered me loudly, and helped him up into the cockpit. I strapped him into his seat, and at last we were ready to leave.

As I climbed into the cockpit beside him, I had a sudden desperate thought. 'Henry, it's a pretty long flight. Do you want to relieve yourself before we take off?'

'No, she'll be right, young fella.'

'Are you sure?'

'Yeah, she's apples,' Henry said. With some misgivings I started up the engines and waved to the drunken mob of pensioners who were still milling around the two automobiles. To the third incantation of *For He's A Jolly Good Fellow,* we taxied down the runway and Henry said goodbye to Leith River.

Soon after we were airborne Henry confided in me that he had never flown before and the excitement of being in a plane for the first time and the effects of the alcohol made him extremely loquacious.

He needed little encouragement from me to

recount some of his lifetime's experiences, both real and imagined, and he was proving to be a colourful and entertaining companion. He had just finished telling me how he had once found a thirty-pound barramundi wrapped in newspaper in a dried-up creek in the desert when he stopped suddenly in mid-sentence and clutched at his groin.

'Where's the dunny, skipper?'

'I told you, Henry,' I answered, finding it hard to keep the 'I told you so' out of my voice. 'We haven't got a dunny on this plane.'

'No dunny? A plane like this and you haven't got a dunny?' Henry whined.

'There's no room for toilets on small planes like this.'

'You mean this isn't a BOAC Stratocruiser?'

I laughed. 'No, it's a twin-engine Beagle.'

Henry groaned. 'Those blokes told me they'd hired a Stratocruiser, and had it flown up special from Perth. The rotten buggers.'

'This is the Flying Doctor aircraft, Henry.'

'I thought the other passengers were a bit quiet,' he said, and fell silent for a moment. 'Well, look,' he said at last, 'what does a bloke do on this crate when nature calls?'

'He waits till we land,' I snapped.

'I'm afraid I won't be able to do that. My bladder ain't what it used to be.' Henry fidgeted in his seat some more and held onto his groin as if it would burst if he let go. I looked at my watch. It was another forty-five minutes before we reached Preston and it was obvious that Henry would not survive until then. Something would have to be done.

I struck on the idea of putting three air sickness

bags inside each other, as a makeshift container. They are made of fairly sturdy material and I felt confident that in a sort of 3-ply they would do the job. I passed the bags across to him with the necessary instructions.

Henry availed himself the opportunity and after a bit of fiddling around he announced that he was finished and thanked me very much. With considerable aplomb he handed me back the bag with its now weighty contents.

This presented me with a new problem.

Now, by this stage in my career I had clocked up over forty hours of flying while Joe had been grounded, and I now looked upon myself as a fairly experienced bush pilot. I was soon to discover that I was still green behind the ears – in more ways than one.

With my free hand I managed to squeeze open the side window in the cockpit and prepared to jettison the bag and its unsavoury contents. An experienced airman would have reckoned with the formidable air currents at work outside the plane and taken adequate precautions, but this one didn't.

As I threw the bag out of the window, the slipstream picked it up and threw it back at me. I gasped as the contents emptied over me and the bag itself finished up splattered over the rear of the cabin.

I could have accepted this unhappy occurrence philosophically and comforted myself that I had at least rendered some assistance to Henry; but to my horror and indignation the helpless old man soon perceived what had happened and started to laugh. In fact, he enjoyed the joke so much he was still cackling to himself when we landed at Preston.

CHAPTER 15

Relations between Dr Charles Fenwick and myself had been frosty to begin with, and now, after a year's service in the area, they were under several miles of ice. His attitude was not indicative of the majority of doctors towards the Flying Doctor Service. Fenwick was an exception to the rule; my other colleagues worked in an atmosphere of cordiality and cooperation with the hospital staff in their sectors, but I had just been unlucky. Apart from a natural talent for arrogance I suspected that Fenwick had also allowed an unreasonable degree of professional jealousy to colour his opinion of me.

And there were no indications that things were going to improve.

The telephone woke me that morning at seven-thirty. I snatched if off the cradle, expecting it to be an emergency call. Instead it was Fenwick.

'Morning, Hubbord. How's the Black Man's Ambulance?'

I groaned inwardly. It had been a hot and humid night and I had slept only fitfully. He was the last person I wanted to talk to.

'To what do I owe this unexpected pleasure?'

'I understand you've been stealing my patients,' Fenwick said.

'I don't know what you're talking about,' I snapped – though I did have a fairly good idea. Just the previous week I had gone to a motor vehicle accident near the Gilliuga Bridge Roadhouse after reports that a family sedan had ploughed into a tree about a mile down the road. Ordinarily, an ambulance would have been sent out from Preston but the call went out as we were on our approach to the aerodrome, and owing to the nature of the emergency I asked Joe to fly me out there. In just five minutes we were over the scene of the accident and Joe was able to bring the plane down next to the roadway. Fortunately, the victims had only superficial cuts and abrasions which I treated on the spot. It was a minor incident but I knew there would be repercussions. The Gilliuga Roadhouse was inside a fifty-mile radius of Preston and therefore not part of my assigned area. In theory at least, I had acted incorrectly.

I wondered why Fenwick had waited all this time before calling me and then I remembered he had been away on holiday. He must have just got back. I could imagine Matron Renford relaying the details of my transgression with relish.

'I think you know perfectly well what I'm referring to,' Fenwick was saying, his silky tones conveying all the charm of a piece of old pork in the sun. 'I intend to file a complaint with your office in Melbourne.'

'Do what you bloody well like. Unlike yourself, I was genuinely concerned for the people involved, and not your petty bureaucracy.'

'Some call it professionalism. But you wouldn't know about that.'

It was too early in the morning to argue. 'Go to hell,' I snapped and slammed down the phone.

I got up and went to the kitchen, now in a foul mood. The day had got off to a bad start, so I suppose I shouldn't have been too surprised when it got a lot worse.

Just half an hour after Fenwick's call, the telephone rang again. It was Clyde. He had just received a message from a Police Constable in an outlying township requesting transportation for a young man with some sort of mental illness. He wanted him to be transferred to Preston Hospital for observation. It wasn't urgent so Joe and I took off just after lunch, after my radio consultations, and headed for the remote settlement at Bundarra, a hundred and fifty miles to the north-east.

It was three months since Joe had returned to duty after the near disaster at Salmon Creek. As we took off I joked with him that he was just about due for sick leave again. Later that day, neither of us appreciated the humour of the remark.

The flight out was pleasant and Joe and I spent much of the journey silent with our own thoughts. From the passenger seat I examined Joe's profile in some detail; his nose had not mended well and I felt that Fenwick's doctors had done a pretty poor job. The bulbous arrangement between his eyes was now, like much of the Third World, non-aligned. It did not add to the general appeal of his features, though I suppose it did lend them a certain character. Of course the only way to put it right would be to break it again, and re-set it. I didn't of course share these thoughts with Joe.

It was an uneventful trip and when we arrived at Bundarra the local Constable was waiting at the airstrip to meet us. After pleasantries had been exchanged he drove us into town to pick up our passenger. He had a strange tale to tell; and as the story unfolded it occurred to me that I might have met our intended charge once before.

The Constable told us that a team of geologists had been carrying out a survey in the nearby Doherty Ranges and one morning they had come across a small mine. At first they thought the mine had been abandoned; but as they were looking around they were suddenly attacked by a swarthy unshaven Latin, bellowing like a bull elephant and waving his right arm in imitation of a trunk. One of the party was knocked to the ground and the apparition then took off. The geologists, having armed themselves with rifles and axe handles from their four-wheel drive, eventually traced their assailant to one of the sheds, where they found him on all fours, with his head in a bag of oats.

Understandably a little unnerved, they lured the man back to their vehicle with the promise of sugar cubes. They then tied him up, put him in the back of the landrover and brought him to Bundarra, where he had languished for two days in the town's lock-up.

'He's the perfect gentleman most of the time,' the Constable said. 'In fact, there don't seem to be anything wrong with him in my opinion. But these geologist blokes ain't the sort that'd make up a story like that. Funny business, I can tell you. Don't know what to make of it.'

I asked the Constable the name of the mine where they had found the man and my suspicions were confirmed. Sure enough, when we reached the police station, I came face to face once more with my good friend Tony. He didn't seem to recognise me however, though he was very sincere in his greetings.

'How good of you to come,' he said, smiling his charming white smile. 'I hope I have not been the cause of any trouble.' It was the same rehearsed phrase he had used on me once before. I smiled.

'Not at all,' I said, and sat down next to him on the cell bunk. 'Now what have you been up to?'

'I no understand-a.' he told me, sadly shaking his head. 'Bloody thing. They-a say I break law. How-a can I break law? I there on my-a own. I just-a hope family no find out. They be so unhap-py.'

He seemed quite rational, though his memory was definitely fogged and on further questioning I found that he had only a slender recollection of the past two years of his life. Undoubtedly the solitude had disturbed the balance of his mind a little but he didn't appear to be violent.

'Well, look Tony,' I said at last. 'We'd like you to come with us into Preston. I think the rest would do you some good. You've probably just been work-ing too hard.'

'How very good of you,' Tony said in his 'Oxford don' voice. He smiled happily and slipped back into his accent. 'People here in-a Australia so friendly. Just-a like my country, yes?'

The Constable drove the three of us out to the airstrip and as he watched Tony disappear into the plane he looked as if a great weight had been shifted from his shoulders. He rarely had to deal with anything more sinister than Saturday night drunks

179

in Bundarra, so I think he felt a little out of his depth with an Italian who thought he was an elephant.

I told Tony he would be much more comfortable lying on the stretcher and I took the precaution of strapping his arms tightly to it, in case he became restive. I sat in the rear seat to keep an eye on him, but he seemed very calm. As we took off from Bundarra I anticipated an uneventful flight – which it was until we were about thirty miles from Preston.

The first signs of trouble were fairly subtle.

Tony had been quite passive during the journey. He just lay staring at the ceiling and smiling happily at God knows what. I was looking out of the window lost in my own thoughts when I was startled to hear a low growl.

I looked at Joe. 'Did you say something?'

'What?' Joe yelled back, over the noise of the engines.

'I said, did you say something?'

'What?' Joe yelled. Obviously, he hadn't. I looked at Tony who smiled sweetly up at me, a look of divine innocence on his face.

I shrugged my shoulders. I must have imagined it. I settled back in my seat, with a vague feeling of unease.

For some minutes there was silence in the cabin once more, with just the monotonous heavy drone of the engines outside. Then I heard it again – a low, rumbling sound, almost a snarl, like a tiger stalking its prey. I looked at Tony. He was still staring at the ceiling but now I could see his teeth moving apart as he brought the sound welling up from deep inside his chest.

He must have realised I had seen him, for he suddenly stopped and fixed me with his angelic, hundred-watt smile.

'You take-a me to the zoo?' he said.

'That's right,' I stammered. 'To the zoo.'

I noticed Joe stiffen in his seat and his hands tighten around the controls. I felt my own insides turn to ice.

'That's-a good,' Tony said. 'It must-a be close to feeding time.' And he suddenly let out a blood-curdling howl like a wolf baying at the moon. Joe, with his back just a few inches from Tony's head, shot vertically out of his seat, and only his lap strap prevented him from leaving us through the cabin roof. Tony started to wrestle with the straps that held him down and in a matter of seconds his face had contorted to a mask of savage, slathering fury.

Things happened very quickly after that.

I reached for the medical kit, deciding to sedate our patient immediately and head off the trouble. But I didn't have time. The leather straps on the stretcher were designed to prevent a sick man from rolling off the stretcher and onto the cabin floor, not for the prodigious strength of a madman who no longer wishes to be restrained. I was still fumbling through my black bag for a syringe when there was a horrible roar and a loud tearing noise.

The next thing I knew there was a hairy forearm around my neck, wrestling me to the floor.

For some moments we writhed and thrashed around the cockpit like a pair of old drunks brawling in a ditch while Joe shouted instructions from the front seat.

'That's it doc, stick to it! Watch his other arm,

doc! That's it, you've got him now!'

But I hadn't.

The young Latin managed to secure me in a fairly telling hold and by bracing his shoulders against one of the doors, he managed to kick open the other one.

'Christ, he's kicked the door open!' Joe yelled, rather unnecessarily, for it wasn't the sort of thing you could fail to notice.

All that was needed now was for the plane to bank a little to port and we would both pitch out into space. I reached frantically over my head for a hand hold and Tony seized this opportunity to bite me on the wrist.

Terror gave me a renewed surge of strength and I succeeded in dislodging one of the thick forearms round my throat. This only further enraged my Italian friend who kicked out now with his other foot, slamming Joe forward onto the control panel, smashing his nose and stunning him. He slumped forward and the plane went into a steep dive.

A few moments later we were hurtling towards the ground at the rate of a thousand feet a minute, all three of us lying in a heap on the control column.

Meanwhile two huge hands wrapped themselves round my neck and started to squeeze. Over the howling of the slipstream and the shriek of the engines, I could make out a ghastly choking sound.

It was me.

I struggled frantically for air and somehow Tony and I rolled sideways off Joe's back and lay pressed against the windshield on the passenger side.

Freed from our crushing weight, Joe began to pull desperately back on the controls. Slowly we levelled out of the screaming, pitching dive and Joe gained control of the plane once more.

I didn't even notice.

The pressure round my throat was increasing and purple spots flashed in front of my eyes. Soon I realised I would pass out and Tony would turn his attentions to Joe.

But Flying Doctor pilots are resourceful men. Joe had meanwhile reached beneath his seat and located a 7/8 spanner set aside for just such emergencies. He proceeded to pacify our troublesome cargo with two swift but effective blows to the cranium.

I pushed Tony's unconscious body off me, and fell on my knees on the cabin floor, gasping for breath. I once again became aware of the deafening noise of the engines.

'The door!' Joe yelled.

He banked the plane slightly to starboard and I scrambled into the rear of the cockpit and managed to fasten the door shut once more. I scrambled back into the front seat.

It was time to count the cost.

Blood was pouring from my wrist; and the front of Joe's shirt was also stained a lively red, as his freshly-mended nose yet again assumed a new and interesting shape. Joe's expression, with its strangely warped appendage was rather pathetic, and I could see he was about to indulge in a bout of self-pity.

He did, I suppose, have good reason.

I dragged Tony into the rear of the cabin. He was out cold, but I gave him a shot of phenobarbitone for good measure. I bandaged my wrist and quickly examined Joe's nose. It would have to be re-set.

Perhaps Fenwick's boys will do a better job this time, I thought.

'There's nothing much I can do about that nose right now,' I said to Joe, and then trying to cheer him up, I added: 'You might as well settle back and enjoy the rest of the trip.'

When we reached Preston the ambulance was waiting to meet us and Tony was offloaded on the stretcher, still groggy but conscious once more. As I helped to carry him to the vehicle, his eyes flickered open, and he smiled up at me as if I was a long-lost friend.

'Please. Thank-a your pilot for pleasant trip,' he said softly.

'I'll pass on your message,' I said.

His face once more took on that look of angelic sweetness. 'I hope I have not been the cause of any trouble,' he whispered slowly.

And then he passed out.

Some days later, Tony was flown to Perth for psychiatric tests. I found out later that he was discharged from the hospital some months later and had since returned to his native Italy. But I shall leave the postscript to his story to Matron Renford who called me at my Residence a few days later to discuss the case.

'Really,' she said, with the tone of voice one might use to a panic-stricken novice. 'I can't understand why you had so much trouble with the poor man. He's such a gentleman. All you had to do was be nice to him.'

I didn't even bother to answer her.

CHAPTER 16

In my second year of duty as Flying Doctor for the region. I began to form my own medical theories. The first was this: if a woman is going to have a difficult birth, she will always have it at night. I call it Hazzard's Law.

When the call for assistance came through from Quim Quim Downs it only provided me with further proof; it also left me in something of a predicament. After my previous experiences with night flying I was reluctant to fly out alone, but in the circumstances, it seemed I would have very little choice. I didn't feel that I could allow a woman in labour to suffer until morning.

I had weighed up all the alternatives. Joe, his eyes black and swollen, had his nose encased in plaster and was still having dizzy spells due to the latest outrages inflicted on his nasal attachments. He was certainly not fit to fly. Hoping to find myself a flying nurse I desperately tried to contact Sister Theresa at the mission but she was away in the country and none of the other nuns were able to leave. I did, in my innocence, try to appeal to the better instincts of Charles Fenwick, before discovering that he had none.

The situation was aggravated by the fact that it was, once again, cyclone season.

Preston had been battered by the remnants of a

severe tropical storm that had swept down across north-west Australia, having devastated parts of Indonesia. The worst of the cyclone had passed, but heavy rain was still drumming on the tin roof of the Residence, and the weather bureau had forecast severe air turbulence for at least another twelve hours.

If I had been flying with Joe, I think we would not have made the trip. Joe would have said the risks were too high, and he would probably have been right. After all, a dead doctor is no good to anyone, and the Service does not find its planes very easy to come by. I think perhaps that I allowed my confidence in the Beagle's ability to perform in heavy conditions to colour my perspective of what should have been an objective decision.

I decided to go.

Quim Quim Downs was one of the larger towns in the Kimberley, a hundred and twenty miles to the south-east, at the confluence of a major highway – if an unsealed dirt road on the edge of the desert can be called a highway – and three large rivers. The mission there was run by three nuns of the Order of St John of God. The patient was an Aboriginal woman, the wife of a jackaroo on a nearby station and it was to be her first baby. Unfortunately, from the information that the nuns had given me over the radio, I suspected a breech birth. The girl was in her twelfth hour of labour, and no progress was being made. The local doctor was out of town, and the nuns, in desperation had contacted me.

I passed on the usual request for flares at the aerodrome and half an hour later I took off from Preston.

In the buffeting head-winds and slashing rain, the trip to Quim Quim took almost two hours, a journey that I have made in fine weather in less than one. Sheet lightning flashed around the horizons and I flew through banks of dark, menacing rainclouds. However, the weather appeared to be breaking up by the time I arrived over Quim Quim.

I knew that the township would be a little easier to find than many of the small stations in the Kimberley that I had sought out before in similar conditions, but I was not prepared for what I saw when I made my approach.

As I brought the plane down through the clouds I peered anxiously into the gloom for the shallow ochre tinge of the ground flares. Instead, I found myself flying towards two parrellel rows of lights, sharp and very distinct, bright enough to do justice to a major international airport.

I was able to put the plane down on the airstrip with absolute confidence.

As I taxied towards the airport's single shed I saw for the first time that my landing lights had actually been car headlights; two rows of vehicles, of all makes and sizes, were parked in lines on either side of the runway.

One of the nuns from the mission, a Sister Barbara, was waiting by the hut to meet me as I climbed down out of the aircraft. I was ushered through the rain to the back seat of a waiting car. As she slid into the seat beside me the old nun looked at me with an expression of pride and amusement. She was a wizened old lady with thick-lensed glasses that were continually steamed-over in the humid, tropical conditions. They seemed to be of little value to her for they spent much of the time off her nose, being wiped on the folds of her cape.

I stared amazed at the two long rows of cars. 'Where did you get all those vehicles?'

Many of the headlights were being switched off now and the airport was returning once more to darkness.

'Oh, some folk had listened in on their radios and heard you were coming and drove out of their own accord. Then we got some of the boys from the mission to go round to the hotel and get all the men with cars to drive out here and help out, too.

'Incredible,' I muttered. She seemed to hug herself with delight and the Aboriginal boy in the driver's seat laughed and Sister Barbara wiped her glasses some more.

But there was little to enthuse over when we reached the mission. The poor girl lay on one of the beds heaving and crying with pain, while the nuns hovered round her, cooling her face with damp towels and giving what little comfort they could. She was a big girl – I guessed about thirteen or fourteen stone – and the two small nuns who attended her were having a lot of difficulty in keeping her still.

My examination confirmed my original suspicions; the baby somehow had its buttocks towards the opening of the uterus, which would explain its reluctance to be born. The girl was in terrible pain. I gave her an epidural anaesthetic and weighed up the possibilities.

There was little chance of realigning the child with surgical forceps. The girl was only eighteen and the opening of the uterus was just too small.

And to perform a Caesarian operation under the primitive conditions at the mission would be dangerous for both the baby and the mother.

'Put her on a stretcher, and find a van or station wagon we can use as an ambulance,' I told Sister Barbara. 'She'll have to come back to Preston with me straight away.'

Sister Barbara nodded, and the preparations were quickly made. In a few minutes we were speeding back towards the airstrip; I heard thunder rumbling ominously in the hills to the north of us. So much for the weather breaking up.

As we carried the poor girl into the plane's cabin I saw Sister Barbara kiss the girl gently on the forehead and press a small silver crucifix into her palm. She whispered a few words of encouragement to the girl, and as the car headlights switched to full beam all around us she said, 'God be with you,' and I said. 'I certainly hope so,' and with one last look at the darkening sky, I climbed into the plane.

My patient had never been on an aircraft before and the look of terror on her face intensified as I slammed the cabin door shut behind me. I gave her a few words of reassurance and climbed behind the controls; a few minutes later we took off, as a fresh spray of rain glittered on the windscreen.

We were twenty-five minutes out of Preston when it happened.

We had just passed through a break in some clouds, and in the thin light of the moon I could see a thick bank of cumulonimbus, a black anvil-shaped mass, looming dead ahead of us. I searched desperately for a way round it or through it, but there was none. We would have to fly straight into it.

189

I braced myself for the buffeting I knew was to come and prayed.

But although I was prepared for the storm, I certainly wasn't ready for what came next.

The science of medicine is a very exact art, as is the theory of aviation. Nature however is not as precise, and often confounds them both. How did it happen? I don't know . . . it shouldn't have. Perhaps the experience of being trapped inside that tiny plane on a black stormy night affected the girl's internal organs in some way. Whatever the reason, the baby somehow managed to turn itself round in the girl's womb and began to make its way naturally into the world.

The girl suddenly started groaning and threshing about on the stretcher, and I turned round to see what was wrong. I placed my hand on her distended belly and felt the movements as the child started to make its progress along the birth canal. Beads of cold sweat broke out on my forehead. Ordinarily, I could have put the plane onto automatic pilot and helped deliver the child. As it was, it was impossible for me to leave the controls.

I snatched up the intercom. 'Christ Clyde, she's started!'

Clyde's voice came in through the static, very faint. 'Message received, Six Charlie Tango. Good luck.'

We hit the cloud bank, bouncing through the turbulence like a cart on a rutted road. Suddenly the plane was caught in a fierce updraught and started to climb alarmingly. It was lifted like a sheet of paper and flung up into the air. There was nothing I could do. We were rising at the rate of two thousand feet a minute. Behind me, the girl screamed and I decided to join her. My mind went blank. For a few moments I had no control of the plane, the situation, or myself.

I put the flaps to full forward trim, but it had no effect. I dropped the undercarriage and finally, in desperation, stopped the engine. It did no good. I realised we could only sit tight and ride it out. I glanced at the altimeter. If we rose much higher we would need the oxygen.

Finally, tired of its little game, the strong upcurrent loosened its grip and we started to drop, a frail human cargo on the roller-coaster of the night.

I felt the girl's feet straining hard against the back of the seat. It was at this moment, after nine months in its peaceful incubated world, that the child decided to make its appearance. It could not have chosen a more unlikely or unpropitious situation.

The kid was obviously endowed with a sense of humour.

The girl groaned again and pressed her heels hard against the back of the seat and pushed me forward against the controls. Pitted against thirteen stone of straining, desperate woman it is pointless to resist.

Once again I was totally helpless.

The plane's nose tipped forwards and we began to dive down through the bumpy blackness, all the while pitching to the right and left. Unable to do anything to slow our descent, a crazy impulse made me put one hand behind the seat and I managed to catch hold of the greasy, slippery bundle that suddenly ejected itself onto the stretcher behind me.

With the birth of the child the woman gasped and the pressure of her feet against the back of my seat

191

relaxed, so I was able to force myself upright once more. With my one free hand I endeavoured to bring the plane out of its crazy dive. According to the altimeter, we were just one thousand feet from ultimate destruction when the plane eased out and launched itself into another updraught and once more we careened upwards into the blackness as the little bundle in my left hand wriggled to life.

After what seemed like an eternity, though it was probably little more than a couple of minutes, I regained control of the aircraft and the traffic tower at Preston started to guide me home.

Clyde's voice came through on the Flying Doctor network, asking me for information.

'She's had the bloody thing!' I gasped.

Clyde's natural curiosity got the better of him. 'Is it a boy or a girl? Over.'

'It's a little bastard!' I yelled back, as I struggled to keep the squirming bundle from rolling off the stretcher and onto the floor of the cabin. The mother was no help at all. Relieved to be finally rid of the lump in her stomach that had caused her so much distress for the last thirteen hours, she had lapsed into an untroubled sleep.

Landing the plane single-handedly – that is with one hand, and by the adroit use of my knees – was not a simple manoeuvre. Fortunately, we made our approach during a lull in the storm, and the fierce cross-wind had died to a gentle breeze as our wheels splashed onto the tarmac.

As if to emphasise that we were indeed under grace, the storm revived its fury just ten minutes after we had touched down, tearing sheets of corrugated iron from the roof of one of the storage sheds.

As the aircraft finally rolled to a halt in front of the hangars I saw the ambulance speeding towards us across the shiny concrete apron, and I was able at last to turn my attention to my passengers.

Examining the new-born infant I discovered what I had suspected all along.

It was a girl.

But there was little I could do for either of them. Suddenly released from the grip of half an hour of almost unremitting tension, my hands were shaking uncontrollably. One of the paramedics had to cut and tie the umbilical cord, and mother and child were carried out to the ambulance still sticky with dried mucus and blood.

My knees were trembling and one of the ground crew had to help me out of the cockpit.

As the stretcher was loaded into the back of the ambulance I noticed that the girl was still clutching the silver crucifix in her right hand. When it was finally taken from her at the Hospital, the doctors found she had gripped it so tightly during the flight from Quim Quim that the metal had actually bitten into the flesh, and it left a permanent, cross-shaped scar in her palm.

I'm not a deeply religious man, but somehow it struck me as a very appropriate souvenir.

When I got back to the Residence I found George waiting up for me. On the table in the kitchen was a steaming cup of tea laced with whisky.

As I came in the door George jumped up and started to help me off with my coat, fussing round me like a maiden aunt.

'Jeez boss,' he said grinning. 'I thought you bin

bugger up properly this time.'

'I nearly did, George,' I said, slumping into a chair and sipping gratefully at the tea. 'I nearly did.'

A few minutes later as I staggered into the bedroom, the phone rang. I stared at it in horror. Surely it wasn't a medical call? I couldn't go out again. Not in this. I just couldn't.

I picked up the phone tentatively, dreading that it might be Clyde. But it was worse than that. It was Fenwick.

'Do you call yourself a doctor, Hubbell?'

'Don't you ever go to bed?' I snapped.

'Not when there's work to be done.'

'Look, I'm tired. Fenwick. Call me in the morning!'

'Do you realise the mother could have got an infection? As I understand it, the ambulance driver had to tie the damned cord.'

'There were reasons for that, you know. We were flying through a storm.'

'A little drop of rain doesn't worry a true professional. This is the most clumsy, botched-up job I have . . .'

I didn't wait for him to finish. I slammed down the phone and took the receiver off the hook. I pummelled my fist into the pillow in impotent rage. The bastard.

Hell, I was too tired to care.

I sank down onto the bed and fell immediately into a dead sleep, dreaming of anvils and slippery fish and roller-coaster rides.

CHAPTER 17

After that incident, I don't think I would have been very sorry if I'd never sat behind the controls of an aircraft again – but Joe's incredible run of bad luck continued and in May he got the mumps.

It was about this time that two seemingly unrelated events brought about another confrontation between myself and Charles Fenwick.

The first incident involved the local Justice of the Peace, a silent, brooding man named P.F. Kirby. No one was quite sure what the initials P.F. stood for, though the local joke had it that it was 'Pissed as a Fart', owing to the man's prodigious alcoholic intake. He was taken sick unexpectedly and while recovering in hospital had a serious relapse which affected his mental condition.

Mr Kirby was no longer a young man, and it was considered prudent to transfer him to Perth, where he might receive better attention. Arrangements were made for me to fly him as far as Carnarvon, where he would be picked up by the Perth Flying Doctor. The date was set for the twenty-second of May.

The other seemingly unrelated event was the disappearance of Ethel.

I had noticed George mooning around the house for a couple of days but it had never occurred to me that there might be something wrong. It was hard

195

to realise when he was acting strangely because he never behaved in what you might term a normal fashion anyway. He was very much a mercurial character, with no regular habits and the uncanny ability to disappear for days on end but always show up if he was needed.

But suddenly he had become a nuisance.

I found myself tripping over his supine body on the porch and on the back steps. At other times I would come across him just sitting in the kitchen, staring into space, his face gloomy and morose beneath the flimsy brim of his drover's hat.

I put up with this for as long as I could stand it, but finally decided that something would have to be done.

That morning I found him once more littering the front steps, his long, bony body sprawled horizontally across the slats. 'Look, George,' I said as patiently as I could. 'Why don't you go and do something useful?'

'Yo-i boss,' George said and without reproach he got up and started to lumber off round the back of the house.

Stricken with guilt, I stopped him. 'George, for God's sake, come back here. Now – what's wrong?'

'She's right, boss.' George said, unable to look me in the eye. He scuffed at a stone with one bare brown toe.

'Well, something has to be wrong. You're wandering round the place like a cow that's lost its calf.' For some reason the analogy struck an intuitive cord in my brain and I looked at him sharply. 'Where's Ethel?'

'I bin lose her alonga poker.' George mumbled.

I shook my head in disgust. I might have known.

Aborigines love gambling as much as white men do, but what made the vice onerous to me was their peculiar system of betting. Often they will gamble item for item, regardless of the comparative value. I knew that they were not averse to putting up things of sentimental value as stakes, but I couldn't believe that my George would gamble with his pet emu.

'You gambled with Ethel?'

'Yo-i, boss,' George said, and scuffed the ground some more.

'What did the other fellow bet?'

'A sock, boss.'

'A sock?' I suddenly became sanctimonious. 'Well let that be a lesson to you, George. You shouldn't gamble.'

'No, boss. George doan gamble 'longa poker no more.'

'Good.' I couldn't help but feel sorry for him. I knew he and Ethel were good buddies. 'Would you like me to buy her back for you?'

'Oh no, boss,' George said, shaking his head firmly. 'I get Ethel back orright, doan worry.'

'How are you going to do that?'

'Tonight I win ber back 'longa two-up.'

The next day I took off very early to conduct a round of clinics in the south Kimberley. It was a tight schedule and the subject of George and his beloved emu didn't linger for long in my mind. After a hectic day I stayed overnight on a station called One Tree Downs and the next morning I flew out to the Doyles' place at Hawkestone River. I found them all in good health. Little Emma was growing taller each time I saw her, and was now completely recovered from the terrible illness that had nearly taken her young life.

Kate Doyle looked unusually flushed and excited; she told me she thought she was expecting another child and asked me to take some tests to confirm it for her.

Later on that morning I found myself alone with Tom, and I ventured to ask him just how big a family he intended to have.

'I'll keep going till I have a boy,' Tom told me. 'Girls are no good on a station.' But for all his talk of boys, I knew that Tom adored his daughters and they him, though in his gruff, proud way he did not like to show it when there were other men around.

As I was about to leave, Tom took me out to the stockmen's quarters and got me to look at two Aboriginal youths who had wandered onto the station the previous day. For some reason I couldn't quite understand, the men told us in broken pidgin that they had been made outcasts from their tribe. They were in a pitiful condition. Still in their early teens they had not been able to fend for themselves alone too well. They were both very thin and suffering from a complaint known as yaws, an eruption of sores over the skin caused by malnourishment.

As I bent down to examine them, they studied me and my stethoscope with a mixture of terror and awe, but fortunately they seemed willing to trust me and my 'whitefeller magic'. It was clear that they needed more medical care than I could offer them from the contents of my kit, and so I decided to take them back with me.

'We'll have to get them to a hospital,' I said to Tom, and we led the two youths out across the paddock to the airstrip. The poor boys were actually trembling with fright as I strapped them into their seats in the back of the cockpit.

'Pretty sorrowful specimens, ain't they?' Tom said.

'Yes. Still, a week or so in Preston Hospital ought to see them right.'

'What's wrong with 'em?'

'I think they've got yaws. See you in a couple of months, okay Tom?'

With that, I slammed the cabin door and climbed in behind the controls. The two native boys watched wide-eyed as the engines burst into life and we started to rumble across the ground to position ourselves for take-off. I waved to Tom as we took off, but he didn't wave back, just stood there staring, and I couldn't understand why.

When I got back to Preston I was surprised to find Ethel happily ensconced once more in a dust-hole in the back garden. As soon as she saw me she raced up to the back door and started pecking frantically on the fly wire. This was her signal to inform me that she wanted a beer. Somewhat resentfully, I opened a can out of the fridge and put it down on the back porch for her.

I wondered vaguely where George was.

Later that morning I got a call from a Constable Regan, who was the most recent addition to the town's three-strong police force.

'Doctor Hazzard? This is Constable Regan here. I heard you'd arrived back. I wonder if you wouldn't mind popping down to the station.'

'Why? What have I done?'

'It's not what you've done, it's a friend of yours I believe. George, he says his name is.'

I groaned. 'Oh no. All right, Constable, I'll be straight down.'

I drove to the police station.

George couldn't raise his eyes to look at me when the Constable led me to his cell. He just shook his head sorrowfully and stared at the cell floor, picking at a toenail.

'What the hell have you been up to?'

'Oh boss,' George intoned. 'I come a gutser this time for sure.'

'Well – how did it happen?'

'I dunno boss.'

'What did you *do* for heaven's sake?'

But George didn't answer, he just continued to stare at the floor and pick at the toenail. Constable Regan tapped me on the shoulder and with a conspiratorial nod of the head he led me outside.

We sat down at his desk, and he started to explain the course of events that had led George to this sorry state.

'It seems he was playing two-up behind the hotel. Evidently he got lucky and won an emu, would you believe! I should have thought that would have been enough for most fellas,' Regan said in his laconic way, 'but not your George. He used the emu as a mortgage for more bets and ended up winning a half bottle of whisky, a sock and a Holden Phoenix. Then he went on a bit of a celebration.'

I groaned and put my head in my hands. I could guess what was coming next.

'He drank the whisky, stuffed the emu in the back seat and took off. Fortunately, he was prevented from driving through the front wall of the lounge bar of the hotel by the presence of another car. The owner of the vehicle is understandably miffed by all this and is pressing charges.'

'Well, who is it?' I asked desperately. 'Perhaps I know him. I might be able to have a word with him.'

There were a number of people in the Kimberley I had treated over the previous sixteen months who had relatives and friends in Preston and I hoped my influence might stand me in good stead.

'Well, you probably do know him, Doctor Hazzard, yes.'

'Well, who is it?' I asked eagerly.

'It's that doctor over at the hospital. Fenwick. Charles Fenwick.

I paid George's bail and phoned Fenwick, offering to settle up for the repairs to his car plus a certain amount for the inconvenience he had been caused, if he would drop the charges. He told me to go to hell.

Poor George.

The next day I flew out to Clarimba, a small mission on the other side of Hall's Creek to pick up an Aborigine who was suffering from chronic arthritis. It had been arranged for him to receive treatment at the hospital in Preston. It seemed it would be a fairly routine trip.

The two nuns who ran the mission, Sister Agnes and Sister Chloe, accompanied me and the patient, who was known as Billy, out to the plane. I had settled him into the passenger seat, and was about to close the rear door of the cabin, when Sister Agnes put her hand on my arm and stopped me.

'What's wrong?' I said.

She leaned forward as if she had some guilty secret to tell and whispered something in my ear. Her voice was very soft, and she had an annoying habit of putting her hand over her mouth when she spoke, as if she was telling a dirty joke.

'You'll have to speak up,' I said.

'I said, "be careful",' she whispered.

I stared at her. 'Why?'

Sister Agnes looked round guiltily at her colleague Chloe, who nodded, silently encouraging her to continue.

'Yesterday he attacked me with a soup plate,' she mumbled into her hand.

Suddenly the day took on a whole new complexion. A routine flight was about to run into three lonely hours in a plane with a deranged psychopath. Memories of my encounter with Tony flashed through my mind.

'What do you mean, he attacked you?' I hissed.

'I don't suppose he meant any harm,' Sister Agnes said.

'Do you mean he's deranged?'

'Oh no, I shouldn't think so,' she said mildly into her cupped hand. 'But even if he is, we're all God's creatures after all.'

Little comforted by this information I slammed the rear cabin door shut with more force than was probably necessary, especially in the presence of two nuns. I went to the rear of the cabin, fished around in the toolbox and found an adequately sized spanner. Only slightly reassured, I returned to the controls and smiled amiably at Billy who fixed me with a stare of peculiar intensity. Preparing myself for trouble I slipped the spanner down the side of my seat and braced myself for whatever lay ahead.

We had been in the air for five minutes and neither of us had spoken a word. The tension was becoming unbearable. I decided to try and force some polite conversation.

'Have you been in a plane before?' I stammered. He didn't answer. He just turned his head, leaned forward a little in his seat, and stared. Sweat broke out on my forehead. I cleared my throat. 'I said, have you flown in an aeroplane before?'

He shook his head. Then, very loudly: 'No mister, first time.'

He was definitely a very queer specimen. The nuns had dressed him in an old pair of blue and white pyjamas and a dressing-gown, many sizes too big. His hair looked as if it hadn't been brushed for some months, giving it the appearance of a hedge that had been allowed to run wild. His eyes continued to watch me; on his face there was a look of intense and studied concentration as if he could see something incredibly interesting crawling out of my nose.

I decided that he had definitely lost his mind.

The effect of that long, silent stare was shattering. I felt my nerves going to pieces. I started to whistle but my lips were dry with tension and no sound came. I felt nervously for the reassuring hard metal of the spanner.

At last his interest was diverted to something he had concealed within the voluminous folds of his dressing-gown. A sudden icy panic overwhelmed me. Out of the corner of my eye I saw something glinting in his lap.

It was a knife.

Those bloody nuns had let this lunatic smuggle a knife out with him. I told myself to keep calm. He seemed to be having some trouble in getting it out of his pocket and while he fumbled around in his dressing-gown I casually let one hand slide from the controls and fall to my side, where my grip now fastened around the cool metal of the spanner.

My sinews were taut, ready to spring.

Suddenly he was waving the thing around in the air and in that same moment I raised my own weapon and threw myself sideways in the seat. We both froze in surprise, and sat there motionless.

I stared at the crucifix, and he stared at the spanner.

His face contorted into a frown, in an effort to comprehend. He blinked, looked at me, then back at the spanner.

With acute shame I realised that the 'knife' was simply a small silver-plated cross that the nuns had given the man as a farewell gift. It was all suddenly so absurd. I let the spanner fall to my lap.

Billy picked it up, held the spanner in one hand and the crucifix in the other and examined them for a moment.

'You wanna swap, mister?' he said.

I don't think he ever really made any sense of it.

I couldn't make any sense of it either until a few days later when I phoned the Hospital to check on the man's progress. I spoke to Matron Renford.

'He's progressing satisfactorily,' she told me, in

her hospital bulletin voice.

'Have you noticed anything unusual?' I asked.

'We are not in the habit of discussing our patients with outsiders.' You have all the subtlety of a freight train, Miss Renford, I thought sourly.

'But you must have noticed something. The way he stares all the time,' I said, persisting.

'Well, he's stone deaf of course,' she said as if it was common knowledge, and in a rush of comprehension I realised that Billy's peculiar habit of staring was only his studied efforts to lip-read, and that he had only attacked Sister Agnes with the plate out of pure frustration because of her habit of whispering and putting her hand in front of her mouth all the time.

I burst out laughing.

'Another man's afflications are not my idea of a joke,' Matron Renford said, and the line went dead.

It was the last time I was ever to get any patient information from that source.

CHAPTER 18

A hundred miles to the south of Preston lies the edge of the Great Sandy Desert, a vast arid region of scrub that extends over much of central and western Australia. The region is largely uninhabited except for tribes of nomadic Aborigines, but prospectors, geologists and other solitary expeditions sometimes encroach on the fringes of this wild place. To be lost out in that part of the country without water means a quick and dusty death, so when a man was reported missing out of Bucknall's Bluff, believed lost in the desert, all available aircraft in the area were called on to help assist in the search.

Sister Theresa volunteered to come along with me as my spotter. We set off early the next morning around dawn and headed due south over the Stirling Sound and the McDonald River. Soon we were leaving behind us the high timbered plateaux of the Kimberley, and flying out over a flat, monotonous saltbush plain.

The man we were looking for was a professional kangaroo shooter. These men make their living by hunting and killing kangaroos and are paid by the government for each carcass or fresh hide that they bring in. Kangaroos, indigenous to Australia, are widely regarded as pests; when they move out of the wilderness and encroach onto farmed land or pasture they damage crops, native forest and fences.

Our man knew the country well so it was unlikely that he had got lost. It was believed that his utility might have broken down or become bogged in soft sand. It was vital to reach him quickly, for the temperature in the desert often reaches fifty degrees in the shade.

And there isn't any shade.

The morning's search was fruitless. Our eyes ached from long hours squinting into the glare of mile upon mile of barren desert, a featureless wasteland of spinifex and gibber stone. We were running low on fuel and had already turned back to Preston when suddenly Sister Theresa grabbed my arm and pointed to a speck of light gleaming away on the horizon.

'What's that?'

'I don't know. Let's have a look,' and I turned the plane to port and headed towards it. I did not raise my hopes too high. It might just be a chunk of discarded metal or even a piece of mica quartz. After so many hours of fruitless searching we were prepared for disappointment. But as we got closer we both realised that it was something a great deal larger.

'We've found it,' Sister Theresa murmured. 'it's his truck. Thank God.'

'Amen,' I echoed. 'Let's hope he's still alive.'

The dusty and battered utility sat up to its axle in soft sand with half a dozen kangaroo carcasses lying in the back rotting in the hot sun.

But there was no sign of the man.

I radioed a message back to the search headquarters in Preston and told them that we'd found the truck. I gave them our position and began to circle the area, looking for a place to land.

I brought the plane down just a hundred yards away from the abandoned ute and we got out to investigate. I didn't venture any closer to the ute than I had to. The stench from the dead kangaroos in the back was appalling, and there was the inevitable thick cloud of flies around them which rose as I approached the vehicle.

There was no clue to what had happened to the 'roo shooter.

'You don't think he would have tried to walk in this heat, do you?' Sister Theresa suggested.

'No. He's an experienced bushman. He wouldn't leave his vehicle. Perhaps the sun got to him.'

Just then we heard the sound of raucous singing from a dry gully about two hundred yards away. We ran towards it.

Sure enough, we found our man sitting on the bed of the creek. He was stark naked, humming to himself, singing snatches of an obscene version of *Waltzing Matilda* and splashing the sand over his body as if he were in a cool bath. His clothes were littered over the gully bed.

Sister Theresa let out an astonished gasp, and looked the other way.

I started to clamber down the stony bank into the creek and the man noticed me for the first time. He stopped humming and looked up at me, open-mouthed.

He was a lot older than I expected. He was thin and wiry with a grey, grizzled beard and thinning white hair. As soon as he saw me, he started to get to his feet, swaying a little as if he was drunk. I noticed for the first time that his body was terribly burned, the skin hanging off his shoulder and neck in strips. There were blisters on his lips and face, and his scalp and body were covered in sand and red dust.

He was a horrifying sight.

'Come on mate,' I said gently, holding out my hand. 'Let's get you out of here.

'I don't want to go!' he yelled. 'I like it here in the water!'

And with that he turned and fled. In a few short strides I caught up with him and grabbed him by the arm. With surprising agility for a man of his age and condition he spun round and kneed me in the groin.

By now it was nearly midday. I was tired, sweating like a pig, and covered in flies. I was in no mood for that sort of treatment.

The old man was trying to clamber up the rocky slope on the far side of the gully.

Still wheezing with pain I tugged the old man round and dealt my coup de grâce with a right cross. It connected on his chin with a soft thwack like a cauliflower hitting a brick wall. He buckled at the knees and crumpled into the sand at my feet. I hefted the lobster-red body over my shoulder and started to make my way back across the gully. As she helped me up the far bank Sister Theresa glared at me reproachfully.

'Is that what they call a new breakthrough in medicine?' she asked.

'You have to be cruel to be kind,' I muttered, and we hurried across the burning plain back to the waiting Beagle.

George's predicament was weighing heavily on my

mind, and later that day I drove out to see Constable Regan and ask his advice. He had a sympathetic ear for George's cause but told me he was powerless to halt the course of justice.

'When's his case to be heard?' I asked, after we had gone through all the legal ramifications for the third time.

'Well,' Regan said, 'the new magistrate won't be flying up here till next week. I suppose I'll schedule it for some time soon after he arrives.'

Suddenly a curious thought flashed across my mind and a splendid image took hold. 'Look,' I said to Regan, leaning forward conspiratorially across the desk. 'Couldn't you schedule a hearing before then?'

'Not without a magistrate.'

'Supposing I find you one.'

'Who?' Regan said, frowning suspiciously.

'Kirby,' I replied, smiling a little.

'But the old bloke's gone daft.'

'And is easily led,' I added. 'A good defence council could twist him round his little finger.'

Regan looked out of the window, drumming his fingers on the desk nervously. 'Well, I don't know,' he said. 'Isn't Kirby supposed to be going down to Perth?'

'I'm picking him up tomorrow. If you make the hearing for around eleven o'clock I'll still have time to get him to Carnarvon before sunset.'

'I'll see what I can do,' Regan said.

At ten-thirty on Thursday morning I picked Kirby up from the Hospital and instead of driving straight to the airport we went to his offices just behind the Elders G-M warehouse by the jetty.

Kirby was still in his hospital dressing-gown, and had a day's growth of white, stubbly beard.

'Aren't we supposed to be going to the airport?' Kirby asked me.

'Constable Regan wants you to hear a case before you leave,' I replied.

'Nobody said anything to me about it.'

'It must have slipped his mind.'

'Well, what's it all about?' he said, frowning at me as though he was trying to peer through a thick fog.

'It's a very distressing case. An Aboriginal's being victimised by a white man. Blatant case. We wanted you to make sure justice is done before you leave.'

'Ah,' he said slowly. 'Discrimination, eh? I'll fix him. The Aborigine is put upon in Australia, you know.'

'Oh, I know,' I agreed. 'Something should be done.'

The hearing was attended by Fenwick, and a Mr Drysdale, the only solicitor in Preston at that time. George was hand-cuffed to Regan; and I had been appointed as counsel for the defence. As the medical officer for the region I also had the grand-sounding title of 'Protector of Aborigines in the Kimberley'.

Fenwick stared open-mouthed as I helped Kirby into the room and sat him down behind the large teak desk where his secretary had found stashed some four bottles of whisky and a hip flask of brandy after his departure to the Hospital the previous month.

'Now then,' Kirby said, looking round the room, the huge grey eyebrows knitted fiercely together. 'Let's get this straight. Which one's the Aboriginal?'

George raised his right hand, but it was handcuffed to Constable Regan's wrist, and his hand went up too. Kirby shook his head wearily.

'You realise,' he said to Regan, leaning forward with a sombre expression. 'You realise you're perjuring yourself, don't you?'

Fenwick groaned audibly on the far side of the room. I think he knew then which way the die was cast.

Kirby listened patiently as the circumstances of the case were read out to him, and finally he turned to George.

'What does the defendant plead?' he said.

George looked at me with a hangdog expression on his face.

'Not guilty,' I whispered.

'Guilty,' George mumbled.

'What was that?' Kirby said, cupping his ear in George's direction.

Fenwick raised his eyebrows heavenward. 'He said "guilty"!'

Kirby turned fiercely on Fenwick. 'I'm not talking to you.' He turned back to George. 'Guilty or not guilty?'

I gave George a sharp nudge in the ribs. 'not guilty!' I hissed.

But George was resigned to his fate. 'Guilty,' he said again.

Kirby seemed to digest this information for a while, then with an expression of great wisdom he straightened in his chair and looked directly at Fenwick.

'Case dismissed. Plaintiff to pay the costs.'

Fenwick's jaw practically hit the floor this time, and Drysdale jumped to his feet and started to bluster. Kirby waved his protests aside and ordered Regan to remove him from the building.

Justice had been done and George was once more a free man.

As I drove Kirby out to the aerodrome, he dozed peacefully for a few minutes, then asked me suddenly: 'What did you think of the case, young man?'

'I thought you handled it brilliantly.'

Kirby was not averse to a little flattery. He nodded in agreement. 'Points of law can be very tricky,' he said after a while. 'But I think I made the right decision. This is where experience comes in. Mind you, it was lucky for the Aboriginal chap that there was no incriminating evidence against him.

'Why was that?' I asked.

'Well – if I'd have thought he was implicated in the crime in any way,' Kirby said, stroking his beard, 'I was going to hang him.'

When he reached Perth Kirby was admitted for psychiatric care and it was the last I ever heard of him. But it wasn't the last I heard of Fenwick. Outraged, he wrote to the local Member of Parliament and to the Bar in Perth, but nobody showed much interest in the case. After all, it involved nothing more sinister than dented coachwork and a drunken native.

Troubled by conscience I made financial restitution to Fenwick who accepted what I thought was a generous offer with very little grace.

When Sister Theresa heard about it, she said she felt obliged to offer up a prayer for my soul.

When I got back from Carnarvon I took George down to the hotel to celebrate and afterwards we drove out to the Flying Doctor base to visit Clyde.

We found him, as usual, in the radio shed with a fistful of telegrams.

'Hello Clyde. What's been happening?'

'Ah, there you are,' Clyde said to me as I walked in 'I've been wondering where you were.'

'What's wrong?'

'That bloke from Hawkestone's been trying to get hold of you. He says it's important.'

'Tom Doyle?'

'That's the fella. Sounds real worried. I said the doctor from Berwick could get down there if it was an emergency, but he said he had to talk to you.'

'You'd better get hold of him.'

Clyde relayed the calling signal over the air and after a few minutes Hawkestone station responded. It was Kate. Clyde told her it was Doctor Hazzard for Mr Doyle and after a few moments Tom's voice echoed through the speakers and around the little hut.

'It's Doctor Hazzard, Tom. What appears to be the problem? Over.'

'I want to know when you're coming over to fix me up.'

'Fix you up? What are you talking about Tom? Over.'

'Those Aboriginals you took off the station the other day. They had some sort of disease.'

'That's right. It was yaws.'

'I thought so. Well if it's mine, I want you to come and cure me before I give it to the kids.'

CHAPTER 19

A flock of red and grey galahs were fossicking for seed on the red strip of the airfield, just the other side of the runway. The sky was a watery blue and the morning sun was warm, but without the early fierce intensity of summer. It was quiet. Somewhere among the white gums on the other side of the aerodrome a magpie was warbling its plaintive calls.

I drank in the moment. In a few minutes the serene quiet would explode with the sudden burst of the plane's engines.

As Joe went through some last-minute checks, my mind wandered to thinking about Megan Hoagan. She had been in my thoughts more and more often of late. For a long time she had been just someone I enjoyed meeting and talking to during my 'rounds' each month, a pretty face, a refreshing change from stubble and the smell of sweat.

But now I was aware of a far stronger emotion on my part; though I had no indication that she looked on me as any more than a cheerful visitor and a welcome contrast to the rough surly company of the station hands.

All in all, it was hopeless situation.

I saw her just once a month when we flew to the region for clinics, and I rarely had time alone with her. On the occasions that we did find time to talk, our conversation would often revolve around Sydney. She would want to know about Luna Park and what it was like to drive across the Harbour Bridge . . . what the people were like and how they lived and if I thought she'd like it there. She surprised me by knowing the names of all the leading nightclubs and taverns. She was interested in fashion; she had back numbers of *Vogue* flown out from Sydney – this from a girl I rarely saw in anything other than jeans and a shirt. She wanted to travel. I became aware very quickly of the sophisticated and adventurous spirit that longed to be free from the restraints of duty and the rigours and solitude of bush life.

Always at some point in our talks I would have to ask her the same question: 'Why don't you leave the station?'

'I can't.'

'Why not?'

'I'm needed here. What would Dad do without me?'

Once I snapped: 'That's not the point, is it? You're making yourself a martyr to this bloody station.'

Her eyes had blazed with indignation. 'You don't understand. He's getting old. He's sick. This is his whole life.'

'Perhaps. But it's not yours, is it?'

'He'll be selling up soon anyway.'

'When?'

'Soon enough,' she said. 'Anyway, what business is it of yours?'

That conversation had done me very little good. The next time I came to the station she had simply avoided me and I told myself that if I was to keep her friendship I would have to learn to be a little

216

more subtle.

I was scarcely aware of Preston aerodrome slipping away beneath our wheels and the embrace of the vast blue sky. Suddenly we were high above the almost surreal blue of Stirling Sound with the bright sun stretching its golden fingers into the cockpit. I looked at my watch. It was still not yet eight o'clock.

Thousands of feet below us the mottled blues and greens and indigos of the bays and tiny inlets, and the gold yellows of the creeks and sandbanks were like splotches of paint on some giant palette of subtly contrasting hues. And away on the far horizon I could make out the heat haze above the stark, forbidding plains of the Great Sandy Desert.

As Joe plotted our course west, my thoughts wandered back over the past eighteen months, and the way my life had changed during my stay in the north-west.

I had made a lot of friends, and these days I was never short of company. I spent many evenings drinking beer on the verandah with Joe, and I was always welcome at Clyde's, often availing myself of the opportunity to sample Mary Westcott's delicious cooking. Clyde of course always had a fund of stories to tell and they seemed to grow more fantastic as time went by.

I had come to know many of the people in Preston on a first-name basis. In the city I could have admitted to knowing just two or three people living in the same street as me; but out here I found people were far more conscious of their community and were not as aloof from one another. At night or evening, if you wanted company, all that was necessary was to squat on the front steps or on the verandah and sooner or later someone would walk by and nod hello and often come and join you on the steps. Now and then the process would snowball and on a couple of occasions what had started out as a quiet evening alone evolved into a raucous social occasion lasting long into the early hours.

Yet I was aware that there was something missing in my life, and as I became aware of it, so the loneliness increased and a melancholy settled over my inner world. Outwardly, I remained cheerful and efficient, but inwardly there was just a chill vacuum that craved the warmth and intimacy I had once known.

It was now almost two years since my wife and son had been killed. For some time I had blotted out the thought of there ever being another woman in my life but I knew that it was a decision made in pain. Now, as time eased away some of the despair of that loss, I began to think I should start rebuilding my life.

I looked out of the plane's window. There were just six months now until my term of service was due to expire. I wondered vaguely what life had in store for me until then.

Below us now lay the golden strip of the coast and the deep blue-green of the Indian Ocean. I could make out the shapes of a few turtles moving in and out of the sandy churn of the waves and a single shark cruising the reef, its long sleek body very dark in the light green of the water.

We were to make two scheduled stops that morning. Our main business was at Paccowarrie, a small township to the south of Broome. The Police

Constable there had requested my assistance to perform an autopsy on a dead Aboriginal. The other stopover on our day's itinerary was the lighthouse at Cape Leroche. The lighthouse-keeper's wife had been on my radio consultation list for some time, and as the lighthouse lay on the flight-path down the coast, it seemed like a good opportunity to make a house call.

The Cape Leroche lighthouse had been built on a bluff of dark granite, a lonely white-painted sentinel standing a hundred feet above the white water. It was here that Arthur and Mary Cusack, the two strangest people I have ever met, lived their solitary life, the only sounds the crashing of the waves on the rocks below and the haunting cries of the gulls.

Yet it certainly wasn't the most solitary of the outposts I had come across in the Kimberley, for just two miles away from Cape Leroche was the Mary Plains sheep station, a property employing over twenty men.

As we dropped towards the ground an eagle hawk suddenly appeared in front of us, pitching to the left and right, contesting manoeuvres with this giant noisy bird that had invaded its domains. Suddenly it veered away and out of sight and in a few moments we touched down on a narrow, sandy airstrip about half a mile from the cape.

As we landed, a small olive-green jeep came bouncing across the spinifex flats and pulled up alongside the Beagle. It was Arthur Cusack.

He was a tall, thin, saturnine man with hollow cheeks and crop of fair, wavy hair. To shake his hand was like picking up a dead fish – limp, cold and damp. Most of the people I met in the bush were enthusiastic about our visits, for in the normal run of events they can pass the year without seeing a new face. If Arthur was pleased to see us, he certainly did his best to hide it!

He sat in the jeep while Joe and I secured the plane with guy ropes and then we drove in silence towards the lighthouse.

'How's Mary?' I said, trying to force the conversation along.

'She's all right,' he mumbled.

'I bet it's a while since anyone's used the airstrip.'

'I suppose so,' Arthur said, with a shrug of his shoulders.

'It must get very lonely out here.'

'It's all right.'

I gave up my efforts at bonhomie and surrendered to the general atmosphere of gloom.

When we reached the lighthouse, however, Mary Cusack welcomed us as if we were royalty and seemed to have allowed herself the luxury of getting a lot sicker in order to make the most of this momentous occasion.

She was much as I had imagined her – a small, frail woman with the pallor one normally associates with those from much cooler climes. Although it was now mid-morning she still wore her dressing-gown, faded pink cotton from neck to ankle, and her hair had not been brushed. She was propped up in an armchair in the living room of their little bungalow, with her feet on a stool, looking wan but suitably brave.

I made the mistake of saying, 'Well, how are we today?' and for the next ten minutes she proceeded to tell me. It only reinforced for me the suspicion I had that there is definitely a link between hypochondria and loneliness; the need for attention surfaces in a number of phantom illnesses. Mary really was a case in point.

'Perhaps you should look at my back, too,' she said while I was trying to locate a particularly elusive pain that was moving around her knee and away from my probing fingers like an air bubble in an inner tube. 'I get terrible shooting pains. Like someone sticking a red hot poker in it.'

For a moment I thought of somewhere I would have like to have stuck the red hot poker, and I think it would have done a lot more good, but I am a professional man and so I said nothing.

I gave her a thorough examination and as I expected I found nothing much that was physically wrong. She had a touch of arthritis in one knee and she also complained of constipation, but I put that down to sitting around in the armchair all day. I suspected that a cure might be best effected by a change of scenery and perhaps, a change of husband – but that wasn't any of my business.

I had exhausted all my 'preventative medicine' on Aspirin so I wilted before Mary's insistence that she was a very sick woman. I gave her some placebos, three vials of what I called 'Joseph's Coats' (they were of many colours), along with detailed instructions for their use. She accepted them gracefully and I left fairly confident that my patient would survive the night.

As we drove back out to the plane I asked Arthur about the family which owned the Mary Plains station nearby. The man's name was Gerry Kavanagh and I had spoken to him several times over the radio when his wife Pta had come down with a mild kidney infection.

'They're all right,' Arthur said. And then, in a rare moment of abandon he added, 'I suppose.'

'Will you take me over to meet them?'

Arthur looked at me as though I had asked him to make me a packed lunch. Then he shrugged. 'If you like,' he said, with gloomy resignation.

It was only a short drive to the station. Arthur watched as we climbed out of the jeep and then I heard him slip the vehicle back into gear.

'Aren't you coming in?' I asked, in surprise.

'I've got some work to do,' Arthur said. 'Gerry will give you a lift back out to the plane.'

They were Arthur's parting words to us. He spun the jeep round and was gone in a small cloud of dust back in the direction of the lighthouse.

Gerry and Pta Kavanagh were delightful. They welcomed us effusively and Pta Kavanagh cut up some cold meat and boiled potatoes and Gerry produced some beers. It was like meeting old friends. Gerry chatted about the problems with stock and the on-going drought and Pta asked about friends she knew in Preston and talked about their son who was at university in Perth. The Cusacks were not mentioned.

Finally, my curiosity got the better of me. 'Your neighbours are a bit strange, aren't they?'

Gerry and Pta exchanged glances. 'The Cusacks? Yes, I suppose they are.'

'I expected him to stay and introduce us at least.'

The Kavanaghs fidgeted in their seats. Finally Gerry said, 'I think he's avoiding us.'

The thought of two families avoiding each other

out on the vast plain seemed rather absurd. 'Avoiding you?' I echoed.

'Well – it's hard to explain . . .' Gerry looked out of the window towards the lighthouse, where the only white family within a hundred miles had their home. 'It's just that we don't get on.'

'You mean . . .?'

Gerry nodded. 'We haven't spoken to each other for years.'

Paccowarrie is a small township lying between the sea and the main highway, a mining community with one main street, a general store, a church, and three hotels. The town's police force went by the name, of Constable Barry Murphy.

He was a huge, charming brute, with a ready wit and a girth that imposed a considerable strain on his uniform. Faced with the stark realities of policing an outback community he had long ago torn up the rule book and now ran the town and its environs in his own exemplary manner. He was a larger-than-life character who got on well with everyone and most people in the area were on first-name terms with him. Around town he was known simply as 'Big Bazza.'

I did not anticipate the visit there with much relish. Although it was not unusual to call in the Flying Doctor to perform an autopsy in an outback town, it was not a duty I particularly welcomed.

As we drove away from the town's tiny airstrip in his white Holden, he gave me the details of the case.

'They found this fella out on the road a few miles from here. Looks like he got himself a bit drunk and fell off the back of a lorry. Poetic justice, you might say.'

'Why's that?' I said, unacquainted with Murphy's sardonic brand of humour.

'Because he was the biggest thief in the north-west.'

We pulled off the track leading from the airstrip and onto the red dirt road that was part of the main north-west highway in Australia. It passed three miles to the east of the township.

'Where are we going?' I enquired, but Murphy pointedly ignored the question.

'All that's only supposition, of course. The bloke himself wasn't worth a crumpet, but I've got to put in a report, and I can't just go on the say-so of his mates. None of 'em exactly speak the Queen's anyway. And I've got to have a death certificate.'

'Do you suspect foul play?'

Murphy smiled. 'This is Paccowarrie, not New York. Though some of the darkies round here ain't too particular. There's plenty that had good reason to see him off.'

We were still heading north on the highway and Paccowarrie lay to the west. I decided once again to ask the pertinent question.

'So where's the body?'

'Well, that's where we're going now,' Murphy said. And with that he threw the Holden off the dirt road and onto the plain, and we bounced across the rocky ground for about half a mile, ploughing through spinifex bushes. Suddenly, Murphy pulled his car to a halt in front of a large boab and pointed to it.

'There he is.'

I looked out of the window. 'Where?' Then I saw a cloud of flies rise in a dark mass over something lumpy and black, halfway up the tree. 'You're joking.'

I stared at Murphy, thinking it was just another example of his bush humour. But he didn't smile.

'What's he doing up there?' I croaked.

'It's tribal custom. I daren't interfere. They took him away and laid him out up there with full ceremonial honours before I knew he was even dead.'

'But how long's he been up there?'

'About three days.'

'Three days?'

For what seemed like an eternity I sat in the car, just staring. It was quiet except for the drone of flies and the shallow breathing of the three of us in the car. Finally, Murphy decided it was time to make things happen.

'Do you want a shin up the tree, or what?'

'All right,' I muttered, and got slowly out of the car. I turned to Murphy. 'Why didn't you tell me about this?'

Murphy thought that was rather a stupid question. 'Because,' he said slowly, as if he was explaining it to a child, 'if I'd told you, you wouldn't have come – would you?'

'So what do you want from me?' I said.

'An autopsy. So I can have a death certificate. I have to know what he died of, don't I?'

'Have you checked the body yourself?'

'You must be joking,' he said laughing. And then he added, needing to justify it, I suppose, 'I'm squeamish.'

'Very well.' With Murphy's help I clambered up the tree to the corpse. The dead man was on a platform of bark and sticks, ceremonially laid out. The stench was appalling. Having lain in the hot sun for three days, at the mercy of all God's good creatures, there was not a great deal left to examine.

My post mortem was not particularly thorough. After several seconds I motioned to Murphy to let me down.

'You look a bit pale,' he said, as I staggered back to the car. 'I would have thought you were used to it, in your job.'

I fixed Murphy with a cool stare. 'Most of my patients are still alive. That's why I'm still a doctor.'

We got back into the car. Joe gave me a sympathetic pat on the shoulder. 'Just your luck,' he whispered.

'Well,' Murphy said impatiently. 'What do you reckon?'

'That's why you're here,' he said.

'All right. It is my considered opinion . . .'

'Wait a minute,' Murphy said, and he fumbled in his breast-pocket for his notebook.

'Are you ready?'

'Go on,' Murphy said, licking his pencil.

'He's dead.'

CHAPTER 20

It was not the last I was to hear of Constable Barry Murphy. Just a few weeks later, with the stench of the burial tree still in my nostrils, there was an emergency medical call from Paccowarrie. It was Murphy. I was at the Residence when the call came in, and Clyde tapped it through to me on the land-line.

The reception wasn't all that clear but I faintly heard the word 'Aborigine' and I almost groaned.

'Can you repeat that Barry? Over.'

Murphy must have started shouting at this point, because his voice suddenly came through very distinctly. 'I said, I've got a problem here with some Aborigines.'

My silence must have made him think I still hadn't got it, because he repeated it again.

'What sort of problem, Barry? Over.'

'Couldn't you just come out and take a look?' I could almost picture the practised look of pain and exasperation on his face that such a small request could be questioned. But I had rushed blindly to his aid for the first and last time. I wanted to know exactly what he was getting me into.

'You'll have to give me more details, Barry. Over.'

'Well, doc, I've got three of these blacks lying around in the lock-up here, and they're not dead and they're not alive, if you know what I mean. I don't know what to do with 'em to be honest. I was hoping you could fix it for me.'

'What do you want me to do? Over.' Fix it for him, I thought. Fix what for him?

'Well – I thought if they're dead you can give me a certificate and if they're not, you can fix 'em up. But I can't have 'em lying round here till Doomsday.'

'What are their symptoms? Over.'

'There ain't no symptoms. All they do is lie on the floor. They won't eat, they won't drink, they won't even get up. It's weird. It's giving me the proper creeps.'

'What have you got them in the lock-up for?' I asked him, now thoroughly confused.

'Because Harry . . . the publican . . . didn't want them lying round in his bar. He asked me to do him a favour and cart 'em off. I thought they were just drunk. Look doc, can you come down here straight away? The District Superintendent's coming round here on an inspection tour tomorrow.'

It all sounded very odd to me. But as the official Protector of Aborigines for the Kimberley District I considered it my duty to fly down there and see for myself what it was all about.

'Okay, Barry. We'll be down just after lunch.'

'Good on yer, doc. Over and out.'

It was while we were in the air, just ten minutes from Paccowarrie, that the second call came in.

It was one of the peculiarities of the job. Sometimes nothing happened for weeks, and then everything happened all at once. I listened to the call carefully, reflecting ironically that July had been very quiet up till now.

There was one occasion, on the way to an emergency call, when I ordered Joe to turn the plane round and go to another case that I considered even more urgent. This time however, it seemed that my immediate presence would not be required.

The call was from a Mrs Laird at Binyup station, three hundred miles away to the east. Her husband had been complaining of severe abdominal pains and was having trouble passing urine. It is in cases like this that the numbered medical kits that are kept on all of the stations, prove to be such a boon.

I pushed the button on the mike to transmit. 'All right Mrs Laird, now don't worry. I don't think it's too serious. It sounds like some sort of urinary tract infection, that's all. It might clear up in a day or so on its own. Now I want you to keep him in bed, and measure and strain the urine. Give him two tablets of number forty-four pethidine. Repeat that back to me, over.'

'Measure and strain the urine and give him two number forty-four.'

'That's it. Now I'm on my way to another call, so I'd like you to report back to me in another four hours, okay? Over.'

'Thank you, doctor. Over and out.'

Then I put the incident out of my mind and in a few minutes we came in to land at Paccowarrie.

This time, Constable Barry Murphy was not on hand to meet us.

Although it was winter, the temperature was well over thirty degrees, and we stood by the plane in the middle of the airstrip looking out over the flat

229

shimmering plains, in grim humours. Joe was all for taking off again and flying straight back to Preston. It was a two-mile walk to the township and I was not about to attempt something like that just to rid Constable Murphy of his three itinerants. I walked over to the tin shed at the edge of the field, hoping to find a phone. Locked.

I was about to take up Joe's suggestion and fly home again when I saw a car approaching along the dirt road. I flagged it down: it was an old battered Holden Phoenix, eaten with rust. The driver, a grizzle-haired Aboriginal, happily agreed to take us into the town. He guessed who we were, and wanted to know what we were doing in Paccowarrie.

He shook his head gravely when I told him about the men in Murphy's lock-up. 'Dem fellas bin die,' he said, showing us the whites of his eyes. 'Dey bin boned good.'

Boned. Suddenly, the situation became a lot clearer. I understood now why Murphy's three Aboriginals showed no desire to get on with life.

The Aborigines are, as a race, extremely superstitious and prone to suggestion. Like many primitive people, each tribe has a witch doctor; these men are attributed with supernatural powers and an Aborigine believes that if the witch doctor points a bone in his or her direction, accompanied by the correct incantations, he or she is assured of death within the next few days.

Our driver told us that it was rumoured around the town that these men had indeed been 'boned' and were therefore doomed.

Joe tapped me on the shoulder. 'What are you

going to do, doc?'

I shrugged. 'Boning' was a condition that had not been covered by my textbooks in medical school and I certainly hadn't come across it in any of my patients in Collaroy.

I turned to our driver. 'Where will we find Constable Murphy?'

'Big Bazza? He'll be down hotel, maybe.'

'At the hotel?' Joe said, outraged.

'Bazza's always down hotel 'bout now.'

'Will you take us there?' I said.

'Oh sure,' the man said grinning. 'Goin' there me'self.'

We found constable Murphy in the office out at the back of the Paccowarrie Hotel. Our unheralded arrival was greeted with much scraping of chairs and leaping to feet. Murphy snatched his cap from the table and grinned sheepishly in our direction.

'Christ,' he said cheerily, 'I forgot about you blokes.'

He turned to the publican and another man who were hurriedly trying to scramble cards and some one and two-dollar notes off the table and into the drawer of the sideboard.

'Now this is the last time I'm warning you, Mr Beasley. If I find you gambling again on these premises, I'll have to report you.' Murphy followed my gaze to the three cracked china cups on the table. They all contained a dark, amber liquid. 'And thanks for the coffee,' he stammered and ushered Joe and myself out of the door and led the way to the police car parked at the side entrance to the hotel.

'Sorry I missed you at the airport,' Murphy said

grandly. 'I was on a raid.'

'Looked more like a straight flush from where I was standing,' Joe muttered.

Murphy either didn't hear him or chose to ignore the remark. 'I hope you can do something about these Abbos,' he went on. 'Bloody blacks. All they do round here is die and cause trouble.'

'The fellow who gave us a lift told us they've been "boned",' I said, as we clambered into the hot car. Joe yelped as the hot vinyl on the back seat made contact with the bare skin on the back of his leg.

'You don't believe all that nonsense, do you?' Murphy said.

'It doesn't matter if I believe it. It only matters that your three friends believe it.'

'I just want them off police premises,' Murphy said, throwing the car into gear, and reaching for the bag of extra-strong peppermints that lay on top of the glove box. There was a faint smell of alcohol in the car.

'I think someone's been lacing your coffee,' Joe commented. Murphy turned round and glared, and we drove the rest of the way to the station in silence.

The Aborigines were indeed a sorry sight. They were full-blood tribesmen, naked except for the lap-laps around their groins. The three of them lay motionless on the hard concrete floor, staring vacantly at the ceiling.

It was as though they were hypnotized.

'Never seen anything like it,' Murphy said. He had left the cell door open, hoping they would leave, and go somewhere else to die. But I suppose they considered it as good a place as any.

I knelt down beside one of the men and examined

him. He made no protest as I poked and prodded with my fingers; his pulse was very faint. I tested his reflexes. He was, at least, conscious. But he continued to stare vacantly into space, almost as if I wasn't there. He looked to me as if he was past caring about anything.

For some reason I thought of the incident with the Aborigines at Brookton Downs and I had a sudden inspiration. I produced my thermometer from my medical kit and held it in front of the man's face. His eyes widened, and his body tensed very slightly.

It wasn't much, but it was a reaction of sorts.

There was only one thing to do, as far as I could see. If these men had been 'boned', then the only way to cure them was to 'de-bone' them.

White man's medicine, they call it.

'Come here, you two,' I beckoned, looking round at Joe and Murphy.

'What's up?' said Murphy, somewhat suspiciously.

'I need your help.'

'What do you want us to do?' Joe asked.

'A bone dance.'

Murphy looked at me as if I had gone mad. 'We're going to do a *what*?'

'We're going to de-bone these blokes. Make them think we've broken the spell over them. Only it's got to look convincing.'

Murphy must have thought I was having him on. He turned to Joe. 'What's he talking about?' Joe just shrugged. They both stared at me.

It looked as though it was up to me to get the party moving. I started off by rolling my trousers up to the knee – a pointless piece of showmanship I

233

suppose but I felt that bare shins were more in keeping with the spirit of the occasion. Then, hopping from one leg to the other, I began to hum *Tie me Kangaroo Down, Sport,* all the while waving my thermometer in the direction of the first Aborigine as if it was a sacred totem. After a while the other two natives started to take an interest and one of them even turned his head to get a better view.

I looked at my two compatriots. Their jaws had gone slack. They stood on one side of the cell with their backs to the door like two virgins at a high school dance.

'Well, come on them,' I shouted. 'Give me a hand.'

A little self-consciously perhaps, but with great verve, Joe snatched the stethoscope up off the floor and shook it at one of the Aborigines as though it was a coiled snake. The man flinched, possibly the first movement he had made in days. Encouraged, Joe began to torment him with it like a Roman galley-master with a whip.

Murphy, sensing which way the tide had turned, decided to join in. Groaning ominously, he started dancing round the cell like an overweight Apache, his enormous bulk wallowing around inside his shirt, held captive by just three small buttons.

It was indeed unfortunate that Murphy's District Superintendent should have arrived a day early. Much of the groaning and dancing stopped soon after his appearance in the doorway of the cell, spoiling what otherwise would have been a very creditable peformance of Aboriginal culture.

*

I never heard from Constable Barry Murphy again. He was transferred to Perth soon after, and a new man took over at Paccowarrie.

More interestingly, from a medical viewpoint, a few minutes after the arrival of the District Superintendent, the three Aborigines got up and walked out of the cell. This only helped to make poor Murphy's claims that the men had been sick look totally insupportable. As far as I could tell, the men were completely cured, although strictly speaking, they had never actually been ill.

I talked the whole incident over with George that evening as we sat in the kitchen sharing a bottle of beer. I felt that being one of that gentle but mystifying race, he might be able to enlighten me a little on the Aboriginal psyche. He listened attentively as I recounted the whole strange story, while Ethel nibbled irritably at the remains of the fly wire on the back door.

When I finished I asked him his opinion of the whole thing. After all, I said, medical science knows it is impossible for someone to point a bone at another person and kill him. There is nothing in an ordinary bone that can harm another living organism, unless you hit them with it. Yet these three natives would undoubtedly have been dead within another two or three days if I had not intervened. On the other hand, there is nothing in a thermometer or a stethoscope either, that can make a person well; yet these two simple diagnostic instruments had saved three lives as surely as a scalpel cutting away a cancerous growth. It didn't make sense.

George looked at me silently for a few minutes,

rubbing the short, black whiskers on his chin.

'I dunno boss,' he said at last. 'Sounds plenty queer to me. Mebbe there somethin' 'longa dis blackfeller mumbo jumbo after all.'

The next day I remembered that I had not yet heard back from Binyup station. I asked Clyde to raise them during the morning's medical session but there was no response. I grew a little concerned. Why hadn't the woman called back as I had asked her to? Supposing my diagnosis had been wrong and there had been an emergency while I was going through my weird calisthenics in Paccowarrie? Surely then Mrs Laird would have put out another call? And why were they not now responding to their call sign? It was very odd.

There was nothing to do but wait. Finally, near lunchtime, Clyde eventually got an answer from the station and patched his link through to me at the Residence.

'How's your husband?' I almost yelled into the phone, when I heard the woman's voice.

'Oh, he's fine. He's been mustering all morning.'

'I was worried when you didn't report back. What happened?'

'It quite slipped my mind, doctor. Sorry. We were all out this morning helping with the muster.'

'Well, I'm glad he's all right. Did you give him the pethidine?'

There was a strange silence on the other end of the line. The voice came back, sounding very sheepish: 'Well, we were all out of number forty-four. So instead of two of those, I gave him four number twenty-twos, and they worked a treat.'

CHAPTER 21

I was standing in the doorway at the radio base, watching Clyde relaying the day's telegrams. It was still early, not yet eight o'clock, but already it was very warm in the hut.

'Message here for Six Charlie Foxtrot, Fortune Creek. Are you reading me? Over.'

There was a crackle of static over the air waves, and then: 'Morning Clyde. Is that bastard Parker going to send me up the money?'

Clyde looked at me then flicked the switch on the receiver to 'transmit'. 'He's dead, Herbie.'

There was a pause. Finally *What was that?*

'He's dead, Herbie. Over.'

'He can't be.'

'I have a telegram here from a Muriel Parker, 23 Glynn Way, Mount Lawley in Perth. Message reads: JOE PARKER PASSED AWAY 30 JULY 1967 STOP WILL SEND FLOWERS ON YOUR BEHALF STOP PLEASE WRITE Message ends.'

'It's a trick.'

'Would you like to send a message of condolence? Over.'

'No I bloody wouldn't! I don't even want to send any bloody flowers.'

Clyde's face flushed angrily. 'Come on now Herbie, the old boy's dead. Isn't it time to bury the hatchet?'

'He did this deliberately so he wouldn't have to pay me back.'

Clyde sighed wearily. 'I have other messages to read, Six Charlie Foxtrot. If you would like to send a message of condolence, I'll be taking telegrams in about half an hour. Over.'

There was no response from Six Charlie Foxtrot, Fortune Creek.

Horses are still widely used in the Kimberley and so riding accidents are fairly common. Many injuries that I attended were due in one way or another to falls or kicks from horses. That afternoon we received an urgent request for assistance from McLaren station two hundred and ten miles to the north-east. A rider had been thrown from his horse and had sustained a serious head injury. We were in the air within the hour.

The man had been taken to the AIM mission at Weldon's Creek where the emergency call had been relayed to Preston. As we landed at the mission two of the nurses brought the patient out of the building on a stretcher and started to carry him towards the plane.

The injured man was still conscious and didn't seem to be in much pain; but he was very drowsy and had difficulty speaking. A cursory examination seemed to indicate a depressed fracture of the skull and possible spinal damage. The injuries were serious but there appeared to be no immediate danger.

Joe and I loaded the stretcher straight into the plane and then I turned to one of the nurses. 'Do you know the man, sister?'

'His name's John Simpson. He's a jackeroo on the McLaren station. He was up on Milligan's ridge and his horse put its foot down a rabbit hole and threw him. Three of his mates carried him two miles to the nearest track. They brought him in just after twelve o'clock.'

'How long ago did the accident actually happen?'

'Early this morning. Between seven and eight they reckon.'

Suddenly I felt a hand tapping me on the shoulder. I turned round. 'He never could ride 'orse. Serve him bleedin' right. He should have stuck to bein' cook and left the man's work to the others.'

'Who are you?'

'I'm his wife. Are you the doctor?'

Mrs Simpson was a thick-set, untidy looking woman. She had a mop of wavy black hair, going grey, and wore a man's dark check shirt and jeans. Her face was a blotchy red and she had the faint beginnings of a moustache. She reminded me of a gypsy fortune-teller I had once allowed to read my palm at a fair in Lithgow.

'He ain't gonna die, is he?' she said, nodding towards the stretcher.

'He doesn't appear to be in any danger. But we must get him to the Hospital straight away.'

'Can I come with you?' she said. 'I think I should be there with 'im.'

Now I never object to the relatives coming along with me where possible. Often it has a calming effect on the patient, and it also means that they do not have to go through the emotional torment of not knowing what is happening to their loved ones as they struggle for life hundreds of miles away. But on this occasion I just had the curious urge to lie and say there was no room on the plane. I wish I had.

Instead I said, 'You can come. As long as you don't excite him.'

'Oh, don't worry,' she said with a leer. 'I don't think I've done that for years.'

It started as soon as we were airborne.

The woman was sitting directly behind me, with her husband strapped to the stretcher behind Joe in the pilot's seat. Just as we were climbing away from the airstrip, the woman leaned forward and tapped Joe on the shoulder. Joe flinched, and turned round.

'Yes?' he said.

'It must be nice to be able to fly,' the woman said.

Joe stared at her for a moment, then turned back to the controls. 'Yes,' he said.

'Where did you learn?'

'At a flying school,' Joe said, trying to make it clear he was not interested in conversation.

'Do you have to take a test?'

'Yes.'

'Is it harder than a driving test?'

'A lot harder,' Joe said, looking at me out of the corner of his eye.

'Oh,' Mrs Simpson said, and then, after a pause, 'I don't think I'll get it then. I didn't get my driving test.' She reflected a moment on this bitter memory. 'I had a policeman do my test. Does a policeman do the flying test?'

'No,' Joe said.

'How did you do in the emergency stop?' Joe didn't answer, so the woman continued, 'I rolled the car. I think that's why he failed me.' Joe still

240

declined to comment so she leaned forward again and pointed to the instrument panel. 'What are all those little clocks?'

'Instruments,' Joe said.

'What are they for?'

'That's the oil pressure, and that's the altimeter.'

'What's that?' the woman said pointing to the seat adjustment.

'That's the handbrake,' Joe said with a sneer. 'And that,' he added, nodding towards the rev counter, 'tells me what time it is in Moscow.'

As we reached our cruising height I slipped out of my seatbelt and went into the back of the cabin to check on our patient. His condition seemed fairly stable and I anticipated an uneventful trip back.

I was able to get a good look at Mr Simpson for the first time. He was a thin, balding man with a sallow complexion and grey, tired eyes. He looked drab and worn, an old dishrag in the washing of life.

'Is he all right?' the woman asked.

'He's doing fine,' I said.

Reassured, she turned her attention to the majestic scenery now visible around us. 'It's nice up here, isn't it?' she said and leaned forward and nudged Joe in the back again. He sort of yelped and I saw his fists tighten around the controls.

'How high do you think we are?' the woman mused, looking down out of the port window. Joe, tight-lipped, checked the altimeter.

'Four thousand eight hundred feet.'

'Go on,' the woman laughed. 'You're just guessing.'

Simpson had lapsed into unconsciousness and after a while he became a little restless and began to groan. I decided to sedate him.

Mrs Simpson watched me put the syringe in her husband's arm, then suddenly leaned forward and poked Joe hard in the back with her thumb. Joe jumped in his seat, as if he had just got a thousand volts through his body.

'Can't we go any faster?' she complained.

'We're at our normal cruising speed,' Joe snapped back at her.

The woman looked out of the window. 'We're hardly moving.'

'We're travelling at a hundred and fifteen miles per hour,' Joe said, glancing at the speedometer.

'Then why aren't the trees flashing by?'

'I don't know.'

'When will we get to Preston?'

'Next Christmas.'

At this, Mrs Simpson leaned forward and jabbed him in the ribs again with her thumb. 'It's all right for you. It's not your husband, is it?'

Joe was close to boiling point. I put a calming hand on his shoulder and turned round to the woman. 'Your husband's in no immediate danger, Mrs Simpson. Now please, just relax. Everything's going to be all right. Our pilot knows what he's doing.'

This seemed to quieten her for a while but after a couple of minutes she leaned forward again and her index finger whipped into Joe's kidneys. Joe, who had been lulled into a false sense of security, gasped and shot sideways in his seat, hitting his head on the cabin roof. He turned round on the woman like a snarling beast. 'What do you want?'

'Where's the toilet, pilot?'

'We haven't got one.'

Joe considered this to be the end of their conversation and he turned round to the controls once more.

'Well – you'd better do something quick,' the woman insisted, 'or I'm going to disgrace myself.'

Joe looked at me. I shrugged. 'We'll be landing in Preston in about thirty-five minutes,' I said. 'Can't you wait?'

The woman wriggled in her seat. 'It's an emergency,' she whined. 'Can't you just stop somewhere? I'll go behind a tree.'

Joe looked desperately in my direction. 'We've got a bedpan you can use,' I said.

'I'm not using one of those things,' she retorted. 'Anyway, I want to do poo-poos.'

I suddenly had a vision of the cabin floor rolling with muck. We were still an hour from Preston. Our patient was in a stable condition. Perhaps . . .

Mrs Simpson was fidgeting in her seat. 'I don't think I can hold on much longer,' she said.

We were flying over Glenroy station. It had a good landing strip. I calculated we might lose only fifteen minutes at the most if we landed there. I turned to Joe. 'Put her down at Glenroy.'

'Just my luck,' Joe muttered. 'Just my luck.'

The woman leaned forward and nudged him in the ribs. 'And hurry up about it.'

A dark shadow passed across Joe's face. His lips curled into a snarl. 'Look, you silly b——'

I put a restraining hand on his arm. 'Forget it, Joe.'

He satisfied himself with a snort and turned back to the controls.

The airfield at Glenroy was well-maintained. It

was angled across a flat treeless plain three miles from the station. There was even an old tin shed at the far end with a windsock and emergency radio equipment.

As we made the approach the woman leaned forward once more and jabbed Joe in the side with her thumb. Joe yelped.

'This is no good,' she said. 'There's no trees.'

I turned round, furious. 'Just shut up!'

She blanched. 'I was only trying to help,' she said sulkily.

Three minutes later Joe taxied the plane to a stop in Glenroy.

'Okay, now make it quick,' I snapped, and jumped out the seat and threw open the cabin door.

'Got any toilet paper?'

'No.'

Mrs Simpson clambered out of the cockpit. I slumped back in my seat next to Joe who, with little sense of propriety I thought, continued to stare out of the window.

'What the hell's she doing?' he said.

I peered round. She was standing about fifty yards from the plane, looking at the scenery as though she was on a country hike. Finally she turned round and walked back to the plane.

We both stared as she climbed into the cabin and settled back in her seat.

'What are you doing?' I said.

The woman looked at me a moment, then screwed up her nose petulantly. 'I don't think I can go now.'

Joe had to be forcibly restrained. I could see it would make wonderful headlines in *The West*

244

Australian: 'PATIENT'S WIFE BEATEN TO DEATH BY FLYING DOCTOR PILOT' or 'INJURED MAN RECOVERS, HEALTHY WOMAN DIES.' Fortunately, Joe still had his safety harness on and I was able to wrestle him back down into the seat. We both glowered at her furiously.

'You mean we landed here for nothing?' I yelled.

'It's not my fault,' the woman said softly, staring out of the window. 'Oh, there's a kangaroo.'

I looked at Joe, and Joe looked at me. It occurred to me that the woman was a little simple, if not slightly deranged.

'It *was* the bloke who fell on his head, wasn't it?' he muttered.

The woman sulked for the rest of the trip. Occasionally we could hear her whispering words of encouragement to her husband – asking him if he was enjoying the trip, whether he'd thought to bring any money with him, things like that. The man was only semi-conscious and I doubt if he heard a word she said.

Air turbulence increased nearer to the coast and as we approached Preston aerodrome we flew into low cloud. As Joe began his descent he prepared for an instrument landing, with Preston traffic control advising that the cloud cover was as low as one hundred feet.

I was in the back of the cockpit checking on my patient when I saw the woman suddenly lean forward, her thumb shooting out like a snake and catching Joe just beneath the left shoulder blade.

'I can't see the ground'

'Neither can I,' Joe said, rubbing his back.

'Come out of the clouds.'

'Look, who's the pilot in this plane?'

I leaned across and put my hand on the woman's shoulder. 'It's all right,' I said. 'It's quite safe. Joe doesn't need to see the ground to land the plane. He can fly using the instruments.'

'He doesn't look that clever to me.'

'Why don't you shut up!' Joe snapped.

With great dignity Mrs Simpson drew herself up very straight in her seat. 'I wish I hadn't come now,' she said, pouting.

'That makes two of us,' Joe snapped back.

'Three,' I muttered, returning to my patient.

'Four,' someone whispered, and I looked down and Simpson had once more regained consciousness. The sad little eyes looked up at me, and in that moment they told a story that ten hardbound volumes could not relate.

Sadly, the man did not survive his ordeal.

At first I suspected incompetence on Fenwick's part but an inquest performed by an independent coroner from Carnarvon subsequently absolved the Hospital staff and the Flying Doctor from any blame. Indeed, although the death certificate records that the man died of heart failure, the actual cause of death remained open to conjecture. Fenwick and I both maintained that his injuries, though serious, should not have been fatal.

At one stage he seemed to be on the point of recovery. He was taken out of intensive care, and was sitting up taking solids. He was so well, in fact that they allowed his wife to spend half an hour with him.

The next day he died.

There were a number of theories about it at the time but I suspect that, quite simply, he lost the will to live.

CHAPTER 22

If you are a doctor, there is one particular hour during any twenty-four hour period when your phone is almost certain to ring. That time is midnight.

On this particular occasion, I fumbled for the receiver in the darkness and tried to find the lamp-switch with numb, groping fingers. I had attended two emergency medical calls that day; one in the morning to a man with a fractured arm on a cattle station, the other later in the day to pick up a geologist stranded in the Beverley Range with a suspected appendicitis. I was very tired.

I picked up the phone. It was Clyde.

'Hello? Doc?'

'Another one?' I mumbled.

'My word.'

'Who's calling?'

'Brookton Downs. I'll put them through.'

Straight away I thought: Jesse! His heart's given out at last. All my senses flooded back to me. There was a chill in the pit of my stomach as I waited for Clyde to feed the line through to the Residence.

'Hello? Doctor Hazzard here.'

Then came the voice I was least expecting. 'Doctor? Jesse Hoagan. I've got an emergency. Over.'

'Jesse? What's wrong?' Then another terrible

thought struck me. 'Megan all right?'

'It's Aspirin. He's taken sick. Over.'

'Aspirin?' I felt my spirits deflate. Was that all? 'What are the symptoms?' I asked mechanically.

'He's vomiting something bad. Rolling around on his bunk, moaning and all sorts. I think he might really have something wrong with him this time.'

'I see. Has he been complaining of pains during the day?'

'You know him. He's always complaining. Look, I know this is a bad time, but I really think you ought to come out. The way he's carryin' on, I'm frightened he's goin' to carc it. We can't quieten him down.'

Jesse sounded panicky. It wasn't like him at all. I seriously doubted that there was anything wrong with his sickly station-hand but I couldn't afford to take the chance.

'I'll be out there as soon as I can. Hold the line, Jess, Joe Kennedy might want to have a word with you. Over and out.'

I got out of bed and dressed quickly as I could. I silently vowed that if this was a wild goose chase, I'd give Aspirin something to really complain about.

We arrived at Brookton Downs at one-thirty in the morning. I was genuinely shocked by what I found.

Aspirin was in the bunkhouse; his bunk-mates were gathered round the bed in their underwear watching their stricken friend with grim, anxious faces. Megan sat on the edge of the bed dabbing his forehead with a damp cloth. Aspirin was groaning and tossing around on his bunk and I had to get one of the men to hold his shoulders to keep him still while I examined him carefully.

I was surprised to find that his temperature and his pulse were both close to normal. His dusky face was bathed in perspiration yet that could have been due to all the rolling around he was doing and the fact that, despite the heat, someone had thrown three blankets over him. The whites of his eyes were a little discoloured, but he seemed otherwise quite healthy.

I felt for swelling in the abdomen, but that too seemed fairly normal, although Aspirin assured me that every spot I touched was the source of unbelievable distress.

'Where's the pain?' I whispered, my fingers probing gently around the lower half of his belly. 'There?'

'Yes, there, there,' Aspirin gasped.

'What about there?' I said, gently pressing around the region of his appendix.

'Yes, yes. Oh my god, I think I'm going to faint,' Aspirin gasped. But he didn't.

'Is it a sharp pain or a steady ache?'

'Both,' Aspirin said, and with that he started to convulse and another two men were needed to stop him from throwing himself onto the floor.

I could feel all the eyes in the little lamp-lit hut watching me. What could I do? I couldn't really believe what I was witnessing here. Either the man was in his death throes or he had more acting talent than ten Marlon Brandos. I stalled for time.

I looked up at Jesse. 'What's he had to eat?'

'Stew. Same as everybody else.'

I looked down at the sweating, convulsing body

with the normal temperature and the normal pulse and tried to fathom it out. It just didn't make sense.

For a moment, Aspirin opened his eyes and looked up at one of the men standing by the side of the bed. 'Mick,' he whispered. 'I'd like you to have my stamp collection.'

The man called Mick nodded silently and lowered his eyes. This has to be an act, I thought. But what if he really is sick? What if he had some phantom virus that cannot be detected by ordinary means?

I made my decision. I had to be sure – I just couldn't take the chance. 'Okay Jess,' I said, straightening. 'Give me a hand to take him out to the truck. We'll get him to the hospital straight away.'

As we carried Aspirin out of the bunkhouse on a makeshift stretcher, he raised himself bravely on one arm and looked round at his bunk-mates. 'So long fellas,' he said in a hoarse voice. 'It was nice knowing you.'

The next afternoon I got a call from the Hospital. It was Charles Fenwick.

'Hubbord? Fenwick here.'

'It's Hazzard, not Hubbord.'

'Yes, yes . . .'

I took a deep breath. 'Do you have the results of the test?'

'I certainly do. You'll be delighted to know that your dusky friend has mild food poisoning.'

'Is that all?'

'You were quite right to bring him to the Hospital, of course,' Fenwick continued. 'I mean, it wouldn't do for all our coloured friends to have to go running round the Kimberleys with a stomach ache, would it?'

'But how did he get food poisoning? They all had the stew.'

'He's confessed to stealing food out of the kitchen while everyone else was out working. Typical black, if you ask me. Could have been any one of a number of items he thieved that made him ill.'

'I didn't know about that. I couldn't take the chance.'

'No, of course not. By the way, would you like me to requisition for a brain scanner? It could be very useful. Every time one of these fellows gets a headache you can rush him straight in here to test for a tumour.'

'Have you finished?'

'You won't go wasting my time like this every week, will you, Hubbord? We are seriously under-staffed, you know. There are some white people around here who do get genuinely sick. Not that you'd know about that.'

'Thank you for calling,' I said, and hung up. I cursed Aspirin to the mercy of all the devils in hell. He'd really done it to me this time.

One night just three weeks after Aspirin returned to Brookton – the 'Resurrection' as Jesse called it – the phone rang again. I turned on the light and peered at the clock. Just as I thought – five minutes after midnight.

It was like déjâ vu. I heard a familiar voice on the other end of the line saying, 'Doctor? It's Jesse Hoagan.'

'Jesse? What's the problem?'

'It's Aspirin. He's sick again.'

My head fell back on the pillow. 'Oh no.'

'He reckons he's got this headache. Been complainin' about it for days. Now he's doing his dying swan in the bunkhouse again.'

'Has he had any knocks on the head recently?'

'Couldn't have done. He's been sitting on his bunk for the last week.'

'What about fainting fits?'

'No. Not that I know of.'

'Dizzy spells? Loss of balance?'

'You know him. He's always having dizzy spells.'

'I don't think it's anything to worry about. Give him a couple of aspirin and call me back in the morning, Jess.'

Jesse did not protest. 'I've had it with this bloke. I can't put up with all his carry-on any more. I've told him he's through here.'

'I can't say I blame you.'

'Know what he said? He said, "You can't fire me, I'm dying." What a load of bullshit. He just wants to delay putting in the new electrical engine for the water pump. I've told him, tomorrow morning I'm kicking him off the station.'

But the next morning Aspirin had the last laugh on Jesse Hoagan, by passing away silently in the night.

I flew to Brookton to perform the post mortem. For the first time in his life Aspirin really had been sick. He had died of a massive brain haemorrhage. I discovered a congenital weakness in the cranial region that meant the slightest knock on the head could have proved fatal. The only miracle was that he had survived as long as he had.

I stayed on for the funeral.

The day was a little cooler than usual, and overcast – dressed in grey for the occasion. It had been arranged that Aspirin would be buried on the station, on the small knoll overlooking the bunkhouse and the water pump that he had never got round to fixing. The parson from Fitzroy Crossing come up to perform the burial service. Jesse, dressed in his best brown cords, Megan, Joe Kennedy and myself, stood at the head of the grave, the rest of the men gathered round in a circle, hats in hand.

As I watched Aspirin's friend Mick, and three of his bunk-mates carry the coffin out of the bunkhouse and up the hill, I had to remind myself that even if I had flown out to Brookton when I got the call that night, there was nothing I could have done that would have saved him. Even so, it was hard not to feel a pang of guilt over the way the whole affair had ended.

All was silent save for the lazy drone of flies and the lonely call of a magpie away in the acacia trees behind us. As the parson read out the burial service Mick and the other three pall-bearers began to lower the coffin into the grave.

Mick was the first of the men to notice the bungarra asleep in the bottom of the hole.

Now a bungarra is a very strange creature. Apart from its enormous length, this prehistoric-looking lizard has another daunting peculiarity; when frightened or disturbed its instinctive reaction is to dart up the nearest tree – but if a tree is not available it will run up anything in the vicinity that resembles one, and dig in.

Mick realised that in this instance, the nearest available tree was going to be the parson. The situation called for drastic action.

The parson made the sign of the cross over the coffin and on Mick's signal the men then released the guy ropes.

Thunk!

There was a stunned silence. The parson stopped in mid–sentence and stared.

Mick however, was not satisfied. The men took up the slack on the ropes and he peered down into the hole. The lizard was stunned but it was still moving. The four men pulled hard on the ropes and the coffin appeared at the lip of the grave for the second time.

The parson looked imploringly at Jesse. Jesse shrugged.

Thunk!

'I knew he was good for somethin',' I heard Jesse mutter, close to my shoulder.

Mick peered down the hole. Satisfied, he made the sign of the cross twice – once for Aspirin, and once for the bungarra.

It was a short service, but a fitting one. One by one, the men filtered by the grave to pay their last respects. Having no wreaths to present, there was a rousing chorus of *For he's a Jolly Good Fellow,* followed by three cheers.

Then one and all retired to the house.

Jesse, although now three generations removed from his Irish ancestry, still kept up the old traditions, and a wake had been prepared. However, because of the heat it was considered prudent to have the funeral first. Beers were passed around, and we all assembled out on the porch to mourn.

'He was a good bloke,' somebody said, nodding in the direction of the hill, and the fresh mound of earth.

'Yeah, he was a top fella,' someone else agreed.

'One of the best,' Mick observed. 'Mind you, he did bung it on a bit.'

'It was a good send-off, weren't it? I think he would have been happy with that. Especially having the doctor here. That was a nice touch.'

'Yes, it was a good send-off,' Mick agreed, pouring himself another beer.

'Strange the way he went like that.'

'Just when he was about to get the shove. Almost like he couldn't bear to leave the place.'

'Yeah, seems that way, don't it?'

Suddenly a louder voice imposed itself over the low murmur of conversation. 'All right, everybody, 'ush down!' It was Jesse, standing legs astride at the end of the verandah. He had decided, like a good Irishman, that he couldn't allow the occasion to pass without giving some sort of speech. 'I'd just like to thank the parson here for comin' all this way to do the service, we all appreciate it very much, don't we, boys?'

There followed another rousing chorus of *For He's a Jolly Good Fellow*.

Jesse continued, 'Now as you all know, Alexander,' – for that indeed was Aspirin's real name – 'Alexander and myself had our differences of opinion, but I was very sad when he kicked orf, as I'm sure all of you were. It's a pity that in his short life he didn't have time to leave behind some sort of memorial – like a new generator for the water pump – but I suppose that's the way it goes. It would have been nice if every time we looked at the water pump we could have said "why, our dear departed friend Alexander fixed that" but unfortunately we won't be able to, because he didn't do it. I'm sure, if the Good Lord had given him a little more time, he would have gotten round to it. But never mind, let's not think ill of the departed. I'll just have to get someone to come all the way from Fitzroy Crossing to fix the bloody thing, that's all. So, having said that, let's all charge our glasses and drink a toast . . . to Alexander, wherever he may be.'

And, while we all raised our glasses, the familiar drone of the generator in the background faded and died, as the pump that Aspirin never fixed joined him in the land of the late departed.

Jesse's expression changed from one of surprise and puzzlement, to red-faced fury. One by one the gathered multitude discovered that the day was getting on and they had to get back to work. Jesse's fists clenched and unclenched in impotent rage and he strode across the compound, his face towards the heavens, the muscles in his neck contorting into reef knots.

'I hope you're satisfied, you lazy bastard!' he shouted. 'When I die, I'm goin' to get you for this!'

Aspirin had very few belongings. His stamp collection, such as it was, went to Mick. I was presented with the bulk of his personal effects which consisted of four books: *Common Diseases and their Symptoms*, *Modern Pharmacology*, *The Power of Positive Thinking* and of course, *Livingstone's Pocket Medical Dictionary*.

Three vials of assorted tablets and pills came with them. When analysed later, they were found to contain everything from dialgesics to Smarties. Last of all was a stethoscope with no identifying marks.

Aspirin now reposes on that hill overlooking Brookton, and a small stone cross bought by his workmates marks his final resting place.

The inscription reads: *Alexander Brophy, late 1940's–1967. There, I told you I was sick.*

CHAPTER 23

We found him slumped across the table next to the transmitter, the breath of life barely in him. The grizzled old head, with its thinning mop of white hair, lay face down on the pages of an old notebook.

I had flown down with Sister Theresa, for just the day before, Joe had broken out in a rash, which later turned out to be measles. He was sent to the Hospital and put into quarantine, and I took over as pilot once more.

The next afternoon, Clyde received a somewhat garbled message from Six Charlie Foxtrot – Herbie at Fortune Creek. Clyde said that the message made no sense but it sounded as though he was ill or in trouble. I decided to go out and investigate the call and we arrived there just an hour before sunset.

We found Fortune Gully by following the bed of the Hardy Creek south from Fitzroy Crossing for seventy miles, right to the edge of the desert. It was here that Herbie lived his solitary life.

I landed the Beagle on the flat plain next to the Creek. As I stepped out of the plane I got something of a shock. I had had no idea that Six Charlie Foxtrot Fortune Creek was so remote and so desolate.

'My God,' I whispered. 'What on earth would make someone come here?'

Herbie lived in a rusty iron humpy, built on the

banks of the Creek. This was Fortune Gully; a number of tunnels had been cut into the steep brown banks under the twisted roots of a gnarled red gum, and these were the mines where Herbie had spent most of the last ten years in search of that elusive band of gold.

There was no sign of life; the desert air was deathly still. As we approached the humpy a dog ran out at us, snapping at our heels, its little yellow teeth bared into a snarl. I kicked out at it, and it retreated a few paces, growling.

Soon after, we found the old man.

'Is he alive?' Sister Theresa whispered to me as I felt for signs of a pulse.

'Barely.' The small purple veins on his cheeks and the stained wax paper of his skin were evidence of his age. There was a heavy white stubble on his chin, and a pervading smell of gin and cheap tobacco.

I lifted him upright. 'Give me a hand, Sister.' Together we carried him over to the old iron bed on the other side of the room. The dog watched us from the doorway, whining.

Herbie's eyes fluttered open.

'Get me some water,' I whispered to Sister Theresa. I looked down at the old man. 'How are you, Herbie?'

'Buggered,' he murmured.

'We'll soon have you in hospital. Now take it easy.'

'Christ, I'm too old to get better,' Herbie whispered. 'What's the point?'

Theresa came back in with a pitcher of water from a well she had found behind the hut. She poured some into a cup, and holding the old man's head with one hand, she gave him some sips of water.

I looked around the room. The only table was an upturned orange box next to the bed. One corner of the humpy was dominated by an ancient green kerosene refrigerator; some tattered scraps of linoleum covered part of the earth floor.

Something moved in one of the darkened corners. A pink and grey galah was perched awkwardly on top of an old iron cabinet, watching us warily, moving from one foot to the other like a schoolboy about to wet his pants. As I got up and walked towards it, it fluttered away to the other side of the hut.

I had noticed a yellowing photograph in a black wooden frame on top of the cabinet. Two men were smiling at the camera, shaking hands. One of the men I recognised as Herbie, in a younger day. His hair was still dark and fewer wrinkles were etched into his face. It must have been taken ten or fifteen years before. I didn't know the other man.

There was a handwritten inscription in the corner of the picture. 'With best wishes, Joe Parker.' So, that was him.

I heard the sound of coughing behind me, and the tin cup rattled to the floor.

'That's enough. I can't stand wimmen fussin' over me,' Herbie protested weakly.

Sister Theresa stood up and looked anxiously in my direction.

'It's all right, Sister.' I sat down on the edge of the bed. I knew there was little I could do for the old man. It was a three and a half hour flight back to

Preston, and I doubted that he would even be able to live out the trip. 'Anything I can do for you, Herbie?'

A grimace of pain passed across his face and he looked up at me. 'Look after me dog.'

'What's its name?'

'Joe,' he murmured. 'I called it Joe after that other bloody mongrel in Perth.'

The evening shadows were falling across the doorway. In the desert there is a deathly quiet, strange and almost frightening to a man who has lived most of his life in the city and its suburbs, as I had done. Silence, total silence. Even your own heartbeat sounds a little too loud.

I checked the old man's pulse. It was very faint now. He looked up at me through one rheumy eye and beckoned me to come closer. I pressed my ear close to his lips.

'Thanks for coming,' he whispered.

'Would you like Sister Theresa to pray with you?'

'Ain't prayed for a good many years, son,' he croaked. 'Bit late to start bungin' it on, now.'

'Any regrets?'

'A couple. In nineteen thirty-seven I found a vein of gold in Coolgardie thick as me arm. Went back to town to get supplies, and then I couldn't find the bastard again. I'm sorry about that.'

'What else?'

'Only one other regret,' he whispered, and a flicker of cunning passed across his face. 'I didn't get me hundred quid off that bastard Joe Parker.'

A few moments later the flicker was gone, and Herbie lay quite still. I left the Sister alone with him for a while to pray for the repose of his soul, and then we carried him out to the plane.

I came back to look for the dog, but it was gone.

That night we flew to Fitzroy Crossing and handed the body over to the authorities there. The feud was over.

The next morning, we flew back to Preston. It was a clear blue day, and I put the plane on automatic pilot and relaxed, enjoying the side panorama of the Kimberleys. After a while I reached into the top pocket of my shirt and took out the letter that had come for me from Melbourne just the previous morning.

Royal Flying Doctor Service
Headquarters
Melbourne
Victoria

Dr Michael Hazzard
PO Box 12
Preston
West Australia   *15/9/67*

Dear Doctor Hazzard,
It has come to my attention that there has been certain friction between yourself and the administrator at the local Hospital, a Dr Charles Fenwick. He has communicated with me on several occasions to make formal complaints about your attitude and claims that you have so far shown little willingness to cooperate with him or with his staff. He cites a case a little after your inception as medical officer for the region, when you refused to render your assistance at the hospital, while they were short-staffed and trying to cope with an epidemic.

While I am conversant with Dr Fenwick's attitude towards the Service, and am more than satisfied with your performance with us over the last eighteen months, I must point out that it is in all our interests not to antagonise him further, especially with regard to the fifty-mile limit. I would therefore ask you to be more circumspect in observing this rule, to avoid further conflict with the principal and staff of Preston Hospital.

With very good wishes,
JOHN K. LYNOTT
(Director, RFDS, Melbourne)

What a rat. 'Little willingness to cooperate with him . . .' Indignation and outrage welled up in my throat. My fist tightened on the letter. One day, Charles Fenwick, one day . . .

I scowled and put the missive back in my pocket. Still, I'd heard that Fenwick was going on leave for a couple of weeks, so at least he would be out of my hair for a while.

I looked at Sister Theresa. Her small white Bible lay open on her lap, but she was staring out of the window, and seemed somehow preoccupied.

'A penny for your thoughts, Sister.'

The nun looked round at me, pursing her lips thoughtfully. 'Doctor Hazzard,' she said slowly. 'What do you think of dancing girls?'

The question caught me unawares. 'In what sense do you mean, Sister?'

'In every sense, Doctor Hazzard.'

'May I know why you're asking me that question?'

'Are you aware of what's been taking place this week at the Preston Hotel?'

'Ah, you mean Cindy Sunshine.'

'If that is the woman's name, yes.'

Cindy Sunshine was the stripper who had recently completed a three-week season at the Union Hotel in Preston. Although fast approaching an age when other ladies are turning their thoughts to diets and children's exam passes, Cindy had nevertheless proved very popular with the local male population, particularly the lunchtime trade. There was talk of further attractions being provided in the coming months.

'The other Sisters and myself,' Theresa continued, 'are very much concerned about the effect this lady has had on the spiritual and moral values of the community.'

'It's just a little harmless fun,' I said, laughing.

'Have you seen this woman, er, perform?'

'I was in the Hotel one day having a social drink and she happened to come on, yes.'

'A doctor should set an example to the community,' Theresa muttered reprovingly. 'I believe she removes all her clothing.'

'She does have . . . tassles . . .'

'If God had meant us to go around naked, Doctor Hazzard, He wouldn't have given us a moral fibre.'

We were interrupted at this point by Clyde, urgently repeating our call sign over the Flying Doctor frequency. I snatched up the intercom.

'Six Charlie Tango, receiving you Clyde. Over.'

'Yairs, there's been a car smash on the highway near the Gilliuga Roadhouse. Will you take it? Over.'

I groaned. I had crossed swords with Fenwick over a traffic accident near the Gilliuga Roadhouse once before. This was exactly the sort of situation Lynott was warning me to avoid.

'That's inside the Hospital boundary, isn't it, Clyde?'

'It will take the ambulance over half an hour to get there doc,' Clyde said. He sounded frankly disgusted that I should be worrying about rules and regulations when there was work to be done. 'You'll be over the area in about five minutes. Over.'

I sighed. It didn't seem to me that I had much choice. Fenwick would probably raise hell for me again, I thought, but better that than leave some poor sod to bleed to death while I fly right overhead.

'All right, Clyde. I'll take it. Over and out.'

We banked twenty degrees to port and a few minutes later were over the Roadhouse. I took the plane down to a hundred feet and we spotted a cluster of three or four vehicles about two miles to the north. I brought the Beagle in to land on the flat plain just fifty feet from the roadway.

There was only one vehicle involved. A vaguely familiar mustard-yellow Mercedes diesel, it lay on its back on the other side of the road. Judging from the wheel marks in the gravel on the highway shoulder, the car had skidded off the blue metal at speed – the driver may have fallen asleep, or swerved to avoid an animal.

Three other cars had pulled off the road and the occupants were clustered around the two victims who lay twenty yards apart on the red dirt.

As I jumped down out of the cockpit one of the men ran towards me.

'What happened?' I asked.

'I saw the whole thing,' the man said breathlessly. 'I was driving about half a mile behind them. They just semed to veer off the road for no reason. They were both thrown out of the car when it rolled. It looks pretty bad.'

I raced over to the nearest of the two bodies. It was a man. As I bent down to examine him, I gasped in shock.

It was Fenwick.

He opened one blood-smeared eye and glared. 'What are you doing here, Hubbord?' he croaked. 'You're inside the fifty-mile limit.'

I checked him over quickly. One of his legs was crumpled awkwardly beneath him, and there was a long ugly gash along his forehead. He had at least three broken ribs, and I guessed internal injuries to go with them. He was in a bad way. I pulled a syringe of morphine out of my bag and started to prepare the injection.

'The ambulance should be here in about half an hour. Would you like to wait?'

Fenwick groaned and said nothing.

I gave him the morphine and ran over to the other body. I got an even bigger surprise this time.

It was Cindy Sunshine.

She was conscious, but bleeding profusely from her scalp and her thigh. She had a number of abrasions on her face and neck and was covered in blood. She was a shocking sight, but her injuries looked worse than they really were.

I am embarrassed to confess that because of the blood, it wasn't her face that I recognised first.

'Ow Christ,' she moaned. 'Men'll be the death of me.'

'It's all right, Cindy,' I said. 'We'll get you to a hospital as quick as we can.'

She opened one purple and swollen eye and looked up at me. 'Christ, you're the first bloke what's recognised me with me clothes on. Am I hurt bad?'

'Not too bad,' I said. 'Are you in much pain?'

'I'm all right.' She put her hands up to her chest. 'As long as me tits are okay. Worth their weight in gold, they are.'

'Must be worth a fortune then,' I heard one of the men behind me murmur.

'This wouldn't have happened if he'd kept his eyes on the road,' she said.

'How *did* it happen?'

'He made a grab for me whatsits. Couldn't wait till we got to Carnarvon, dirty bugger. Ow, I told him this would happen.'

I put dressings on her thigh and her head and one of the men helped me carry her to the plane. We took the stretcher out of the back of the cockpit and rushed back to Fenwick.

'I'm afraid you'll have to cancel your holiday,' I said. 'This leg's broken.'

'I know that,' Fenwick said. 'I'm a doctor too, you know.'

'It looks as though you're going to be on your back for a while.' And then I added, somewhat cruelly, 'But probably not quite the way you planned.'

The morphine was starting to make him drowsy. 'Miss Sunshine and I are just . . . good . . . friends,' he slurred.

Sister Theresa frowned at me. 'Evil he who evil

sees,' she murmured.

With the help of some of the men, we li[ft]
Fenwick very gently onto the stretcher. His ri[ght]
leg was a mess and I guessed he would be in plast[er]
for at least six months. With any luck, I thought, we
might get a new administrator at Preston Hospital.

As we carried him to the plane he reached out and
grabbed my arm.

'Hazzard,' he whispered. 'What am I going to
do?'

'Take it easy,' I said. 'We'll have you in hospital in
no time.'

Then he said a very strange thing. 'What will I do
when Margaret finds out about Cindy?'

'Is that your wife?'

'No, not her . . .'

'Matron Renford?'

'Women are such passionate creatures,' he murmured and then he slipped into unconsciousness and
I never spoke to him again.

Charles Fenwick had fractured his right leg in three
places and was not able to walk again for nine
months. Happily, there were no internal injuries,
and he eventually made a complete recovery. He
flew down to Perth to convalesce with his family
and a new administrator was sent up to replace
him.

I never heard of him again, and I hope I never
shall.

Cindy recovered and went on to brighter and
better things in Sydney. She was left with a few
small scars on her face, but as she said to me, 'Who's
going to notice?'

As for Matron Renford – a few weeks after Fenwick left she applied for a transfer to Perth. She must have forgiven him I suppose.

But then, he was such a lovable man.

CHAPTER 24

It happened the day after Joe fell down some steps and twisted his ankle.

The monthly round of clinics was due in the west Kimberley, and by now I didn't think twice about filling in for him. I now considered myself an experienced bush pilot and Joe a dispensable luxury.

'Keep an eye on her,' Joe warned me before I left. 'She's been playing up a bit lately.' He was sitting propped up in bed, solemnly surveying his swollen, heavily-bandaged ankle.

'Have you had her checked over?'

'The mechanics have given her a good going-over but they can't find anything wrong. I don't think it's serious. Just keep an eye on her, that's all. If she starts to run rough, bring her home.'

'What's been the trouble?'

'Port engine's been dragging a bit. Might be nothing,' he said and then he added the words that should have forewarned me of impending doom. 'Shouldn't worry. She'll be right.'

But, when I had the plane airborne she performed well enough, and I could feel none of the 'drag' that Joe complained of. Lulled into a false sense of security I started on my round and the next day I arrived without incident at Brookton Downs.

I was shocked when I saw Jesse Hoagan. He looked pale and tired and I was sure he had lost weight. He was sitting on the verandah in one of the cane chairs when I arrived. That in itself was a surprise because Jesse was the sort of man who hated sitting – he ate, drank and talked standing up.

'What's the matter, Jess? Not feeling well?'

I thought I detected a hint of fear in the steely grey eyes, but he remained typically evasive. 'Just a few too many beers last night, that's all.'

'Like me to have a look at you?'

Jesse scowled and stood up. 'Christ, you're worse than a feed salesman,' he said and went inside, slamming the door behind him.

It looked as if it would be no more than a routine afternoon's work. A small group had assembled on the verandah and I was laying out my equipment on the mahogany table when Megan suddenly rushed into the room.

'Doctor! There's a call for you. It's the radio base at Preston.'

I followed her down the verandah to the small room at the back of the house where the station's transmitter was kept.

'Doctor Hazzard here. Is that you Clyde? Over.'

'Doc? I've had a call from the air traffic control at Preston. A light plane's gone missing over the desert. The Air Force are sending out two Hercules and they've asked us if we'll help them in the search.'

'Who are they?'

'It's a geological team from the Giles Experimental station. Last reported position two hundred miles south-west of Fitzroy Crossing. That was at eight o'clock this morning.'

'All right, Clyde. Tell Preston I'll be in the air

within a quarter of an hour. Over.'

'Okay, doc. They'll give you the search coordinates. Over and out.'

I turned to Megan. 'Looks like I'm off again.'

'Where's Joe?'

'He's not with me. He's hurt his ankle.'

'Would you like someone to go with you?'

'Well, I suppose . . . who do you have in mind?'

'Me. You'll need help. Four eyes are better than two.'

'Well, okay. Jesse won't mind?'

'Why should he?'

'Okay. We'd better be going.'

An hour later we were flying over the edge of the Kimberley plateau and out across the wilderness vastness of the desert. The sparse, scrubby plain spread out endlessly ahead of us, a huge silent continent of emptiness.

The search was to be centred in an area within a fifty-mile radius of a volcanic outcrop with the ominous name of Desperation Rock. But as we neared the search area, strong easterly winds began buffeting the plane as we flew into a fierce dust storm that was blowing in off the central desert. It grew steadily worse and it soon became evident that we were wasting our time. The horizon was hung with an impenetrable curtain of red dust, a fog that obscured everything around us. We radioed to Preston that we were turning back but the storm was disrupting the radio transmissions and their response was garbled and very faint.

Fierce winds were starting to throw us around through the air and the controls were responding sluggishly. They felt strangely heavy. We were losing height. A glance at the instruments indicated that the revolutions on the port magneto were dangerously low.

I remembered what Joe had told me before I had left Preston and a chill wave of panic swept over me. 'Dammit. Not now.'

Megan looked at me. 'What's the matter?'

'Something wrong with the port engine.'

'Is it that bad?'

'It's not that good.'

We were still losing height. I did a quick mental calculation, and I reckoned we had a fifty-fifty chance of making it to Fitzroy – provided I managed to keep the plane dead on course. With these cross-winds and an under-powered engine, and practically zero visibility I realised I had all the odds stacked against me. The one thing I wanted to avoid was a crash-landing in the desert, so I decided to head for Girrilie mission, which I knew was somewhere in the vicinity. I brought the plane down to three hundred feet, hoping to dodge under the thick curtain of dust and get a visual sighting on the mission.

But the ochre haze remained impenetrable.

I broke out in a cold sweat. What if the winds had blown us too far to the west? There was no way we would make it to Fitzroy Crossing now. We had to find the mission.

I tried to raise Preston on the radio, but the dust storm had created a barrier of static. Occasionally we got voices, but they were very faint and distorted. I began relaying our position and trying to explain our predicament, when suddenly the ridge loomed up ahead of us.

I pulled back hard on the controls but the belly of the craft hit the ridge with a sickening jolt and the port wing smashed against something hard and swung the plane around. Turning through a hundred and eighty degrees the Beagle skidded on its belly down the leeside of the ridge and crunched over the stones and rocks for another two hundred feet before coming to a halt with the tail hanging over the edge of a dry gully.

It was over in seconds.

There was a little time to react. We rode out the sudden and horrific landing, braced for a final impact that never came. Then there was silence, save for the rushing of the wind, and the storm-blown sand beating against the frame of the aircraft.

Megan was the first to speak. 'Did we land or were we shot down?'

I reached for the radio and tried to raise Preston. Nothing. It was dead. I turned to her. 'Are you all right?'

'I think so. You're the doctor.'

I swore under my breath. I couldn't believe it had happened. One moment we were in the air, and the next . . .

So much for the experienced bush pilot.

'I'm going to check the damage,' I said, knowing very well what I was going to find. I clambered out of the cockpit. Immediately I had to suck in my breath as the wind whipped the sand into my face and body. I shielded my eyes against the sandblasting with my hands and felt my way along the side of the fuselage. The swirling clouds of dust were so thick I could barely see more than a couple of yards but it didn't take me too long to confirm that our little Beagle had taken its last flight.

The port engine had torn away from its mount-
ings and was nowhere in sight, leaving just three or
four feet of the port wing still intact, like the stump
of an amputated limb. Our radio aerial had gone,
and the tailplane had almost snapped away from the
main fuselage and hung down the rocky bank of the
gully. Another few feet and we would have slid
down into the creek and the cockpit might have
been crushed.

We were lucky to be alive, but there was no cause
for celebration. I had brought us down into an alien
wilderness in the middle of a sandstorm with no
food and just a little water on board. I was angry
and frightened; but most of all I couldn't work out
how the hell it had happened. The altimeter had
been steady on three hundred feet when we hit the
ridge; the maps had indicated that there was no high
land around Girrilie. The only ridge of that height in
the whole area was well over forty miles to the
west. Could the wind, and the failing port engine
have taken us that far off-course?

I looked at my watch. Three-thirty. Well, there
was nothing anyone could do until the dust storm
cleared. The traffic control would not be able to
organise a search for us until morning at the earliest.
Where would they start looking? On my last
transmission I had given our position as five miles
south of Girrilie mission, but I was sure that they
had not received the message.

We had twelve litres of water on board; a
precaution that Trenton had impressed on me
before he left, and I silently blessed him for it. It was
going to be pretty stale; I hadn't changed it for over

four months, but taste wasn't a primary concern right now. At least we would have enough water for the two of us for three or four days, in desert conditions.

But we were going to be very hungry. The only food we had with us was a hundred and thirty malted milk tablets that I kept in the medical kit. They were a favourite with the little Aboriginal children and I used them as a bribe when they shied away from having treatment.

You're due for a taste of your own medicine, I thought grimly.

I clambered back inside the cockpit. 'Well,' I said, turning to my hapless passenger with a smile. 'Guess what's on the menu tonight?'

It was going to be a long night. The veil of dust hid the moon and the stars and it was as if we were on another planet. Outside, the wind was whipping itself into a frenzy.

Megan was lying on the stretcher behind the pilot's seat, her cigarette glowing in the darkness. I had made a sparse bed for myself on the floor of the cabin with a few spare blankets and a couple of towels as a pillow.

'Will they find us?' Megan said.

'I radioed our position to Preston just before we hit the ridge,' I said. That of course was true, but it was also a lie. Even if they had received my message, which I doubted, it was probably incorrect by up to forty-five miles. I felt it was better she didn't know that. I tried to exude confidence.

'When do you think they'll start looking for us?'

'First light is around four-thirty. I imagine they'll

start the search then. The storm should let up by that time, another lie. Some of these dust storms lasted two or three days. 'I know this sounds pretty feeble,' I added, 'but I'm sorry.'

'What for?'

'Well – I don't think it was particularly bright, flying straight into the side of the only hill for four hundred miles. Anyway, I shouldn't have let you come with me. I had no business bringing you along.'

'I volunteered.'

'I feel badly about it, that's all.'

'Don't. I'm glad I'm here. You'd be stranded on your own, otherwise. Just think of it as my good deed for the day.'

I fell silent. I was acutely aware of being alone with her, and it seemed to me somehow absurd that my thoughts should be so persistently carnal when we were in such a desperate situation.

Perhaps she could read my mind for she said suddenly, 'What are you thinking?'

I smiled in the darkness. 'About what we can do when the storm dies down,' I lied. If we had had food and an artesian well I would have been content to let it blow for weeks. 'We'll have to set up some sort of smoke signal if we can. It will be pretty hard to spot us out here.'

'I wonder what happened to that other plane.'

I'd forgotten all about the geologists. Another strike against us, I thought bitterly. 'The Air Force will be busy tomorrow. Now they've got two planes to look for instead of one.'

But I was wrong. With supreme irony the geologists' Cessna landed at Fitzroy Crossing approximately five minutes after we hit the ridge. Their radio had failed and they had continued with their scheduled survey unaware of the panic they had caused.

A few hours later, when we failed to return to Brookton or Preston, the alarm was raised once more. As I assumed, our radio messages had not been received and Preston traffic control organised a search to be carried out on the basis of our planned flight path to and from our search coordinates.

The Air Force was advised that in their opinion we had come down fifty miles to the south of Girrilie mission.

By early next morning the storm had died down. We had got lucky at last.

A gusty hot wind still blew across the plain but visibility had cleared and we found ourselves staring up at the brow of the ridge, surrounded on all sides by a barren spinifex plain and a few scattered stunted mulga trees.

I climbed out of the cockpit and clambered up the rocks to scan the area with field glasses. Nothing. There was no sign of water, so we would have to rely totally on the little we had with us.

The morning brought with it a new problem. Flies. Even after two years in the Kimberley bush I had never experienced anything quite like it. They arrived in dense clouds, scenting out our perspiration and the smell of warm blood. They seemed to come from nowhere, persistent and bold to the point of contempt. Some of the larger ones had a penchant for drawing blood. They were maddening. They drove me closer to insanity than the heat of the sun could ever have done.

We breakfasted on five malted milk tablets each, washed down with a mouthful of water. I have enjoyed more satisfying meals, but at least, as Megan remarked with her typical practical charm, there wasn't any washing-up to do.

'What now, skipper?' Megan said.

'We'll see about getting some sort of fire going. There's an axe in the cabin. I'll get some branches and some brushwood. I'm making you chief fire-warden.'

'Promotion already?'

The heat of the sun soon took its toll. After half an hour's work I was exhausted. Sweat was pouring out of every pore in my body, and in my mouth was the taste of the dry, orange sand. I was covered in dust and grime. The flies, encouraged by the sweet warm perspiration on my body, took to me with renewed fury. Each blow with the axe to bring down a thorny branch or a small spiked bush was followed by a fevered attempt to keep the filthy buzzing creatures out of my face and eyes.

After a quarter of an hour of pawing at them with my bare hands I took to them with the axe.

Megan had erected a small lean-to against the side of the plane using a couple of sticks and one of the blankets from the cabin. It gave us a little shade at least.

Eventually I slumped beneath it exhausted and watched Megan light a fire with the branches and the spinifex that I had collected. The dry wood flared briefly and burned quickly through. My half hour of labour was enough to fuel the flames for just ten minutes and the strong, gusty wind soon dispersed the smoke before it had risen more than a few feet into the air.

'Well,' I said, 'that's about as much good as a negligée in a nunnery, isn't it?'

Megan looked at me encouragingly. 'Someone might have seen it.'

'Look – I'm sitting here, and *I* couldn't even see it.' I got up and threw a tremendous right hook, catching one of my tormentors right across the snout. 'Oh, these bloody flies!'

I retreated into the cockpit but it was suffocatingly hot under the perspex. In a very short while I was back under the lean-to, rejoining battle with the flies. An uppercut sent one buzzing off in a bewildered retreat but his two million companions remained undaunted.

'What now, skipper?' Megan said again.

'Well, in the happy event that someone gets us away from these bloody flying maggots in the near future we're going to want them to be able to land without breaking a mainspar. We'd better clear a landing strip.'

Megan looked at me sympathetically as I contrived to catch one of my little friends in my balled fist, and crush it. I unclenched my fingers to gloat on its mangled remains and it flew away.

'It's best to try and ignore them,' she said.

'I can't. Not when they're like this.'

We chose a spot two hundred yards away, on the other side of the gully. It was brutally hard work. It wasn't yet ten o'clock, but I guessed that it was already over forty degrees. We set about clearing the strip, knowing we would not be able to work much longer that day.

Megan used the surgical scissors to cut some pieces of surgical lint into strips for markers and I paced them out in two parallel lines, twenty yards apart, keeping the lint in place with large stones. Then we rolled any large rocks clear of the strip and burned off the few stunted trees and spinifex by lighting fires at their base. Finally, Megan cut out two pieces off a red blanket in the shape of a flag and I tied them to the stretcher poles and dug them in at the top of the ridge.

At last we sought shelter in the lean-to, exhausted. Heat and dehydration sap energy much quicker than any amount of labour, and for a while I did not even have the strength to wave away the host of tiny tormentors from my face.

We lay there motionless, our ears tuned to the silence, hoping and praying to hear the drone of an aeroplane, but the only sounds on that day were the buzzing of the flies and the gusty howl of the easterly.

As the afternoon wore on I sought refuge from the flies in a pillow slip, which I pulled on over my head when the torment grew too great. I would thrust my head into the folds of cotton, laughing triumphantly as the tiny black maggots flew disjointedly round my head, frustrated from entry. But I couldn't keep it up for long. The pressure-cooker heat and the need to breathe brought me out from my refuge and available once more to their crawling embrace.

Megan must have wondered if the sun had got to me. But if she did, she didn't comment on it. She seemed not to mind them; occasionally she would brush a languid hand across her face but most of the time she bore their trespasses with equanimity.

Our other problem was water.

We had used up far more than I had anticipated. Originally, we had only three four-litre plastic containers and we had drunk one and were halfway through the other on our first day. I decided that on the following day we would have to rest in the shade and conserve our body fluids as best we could.

With dusk, the last of our hopes for a quick rescue faded. As darkness fell the flies at last retreated to their satanic hideaways and left us in peace. We returned to the cockpit, exhausted by the heat and the silence and now – the hunger.

We ate our meagre ration of six malted milk tablets and went through the ridiculous charade of nibbling them slowly to make them last longer. Hunger and thirst dominated my thinking, and longing thoughts were now starting to become actual hallucinations. During the day I had found myself beginning to fantasise about a water melon; juice for my dry throat and pap for my empty stomach. A large rock a few feet away from the lean-to seemed to turn green and ripe and at one point I almost picked up the surgical scissors to see if the skin would splice apart to reveal the soft flesh.

It had worried me. My mind had begun to deteriorate after just one day. Another couple of days and I was frightened the good Dr Hyde might turn into a raving Mr Jekyll, punching flies and trying to chew on rocks.

I just hoped they found us soon.

CHAPTER 25

I lay on the floor of the cockpit, looking up out of the window at the desert stars, which were very bright, very close. Somewhere, from far off, came the lonely haunting howl of a dingo. Megan lit a cigarette, and for a long while we lay on our back in silence.

'Mike,' she said softly. 'Can I ask you a question?'

'Sure.'

'Were you ever married?'

'For a while, Nine years, ten months and five days.'

'What happened?'

'Someone got drunk at a party and tried to overtake on a double bend. My wife was coming the other way, with our son in the back of the car. The other driver gets out of prison next week.'

'How long ago did it happen?'

'Two years last September.'

'How do you handle something like that?'

'For a while you get eaten up with hate and bitterness. Then you just get sorry for yourself and resent anyone who looks as if they're happy. But in the end you find that life has to go on. You still love and care about people, even when the ones you cared about and loved the most aren't around. If you decide not to love or care any more, you might as well be dead yourself. That's the way it happened with me, anyway.'

There was silence. I heard her draw on her cigarette and exhale slowly. 'Will you get married again?' she said after a while.

'Providing one of those bloody planes shows up tomorrow.'

Megan rolled over on her side so she was looking directly down at me. I could see only her silhouette moving in the darkness, but occasionally her face was lit by the glow of her cigarette. 'Anyone in mind?' she said at last.

'Who'd have me? I'm never home.' As soon as I'd said it, I wished I'd treated her question seriously. *Yes, I've had you in mind.*

'Now can I ask you a personal question?'

She sounded a little wary. 'Okay.'

'Is there a man in your life?'

'She laughed. 'Yes. My father.'

'It can't stay that way forever.'

'So you keep telling me.'

'Do you want to leave the station?'

'I've never wanted anything more,' she said, with sudden surprising venom. 'But Dad won't quit the place. He told me the only way they're going to get him off Brookton is when they carry him off. I can't leave him, Mike. I know I should – but I can't. I have to stay with him.'

'Is that what he wants?'

'I don't know,' she said softly. 'But if I left and anything happened to him, I couldn't live with myself.'

I sat up so that my head was level with hers. 'Have you spoken to him about it?'

'No. I can't,' she said. I thought of Jesse and his

complaints about his daughter's 'moods'. I could picture their life together – Megan , silent, resentful and bored, hating every moment she spent on the lonely cattle station, increasingly irritable and restless, and Jesse, nonplussed by his daughter's behaviour, realising it was probably high time she had a life of her own anyway but dreading the day she would no longer be around. He was in effect trying to stall the natural course of life.

I said, 'My guess is that old Jess loves you very much and he can't bring himself to force you out of the nest. But I think the last thing he wants is for you to be unhappy.'

'When Mum died . . . he was so hurt. I was only little, but I remember it like it was yesterday. I thought I'd die, seeing him like that. I just wanted to take care of him . . .' her voice trailed off.

'You can't be his wife. You're his daughter.'

'I know that,' Megan whispered in the sort of tone people use when you have told them an obvious truth that they won't – and don't – hear. She believed, and I think she was right, that for all his domineering bluff, Jesse would fall to pieces if he didn't have her to lean on.

'It's not fair to you,' I murmured. 'You're such a beautiful young woman.'

It happened very quickly. One moment I was sitting up talking to her, wanting to help, then suddenly the words came spilling out of me and something else hit me, a wave of something very strong, then she had her arms around my neck and I was kissing her and the good doctor finally broke all his own rules and fraternised with a patient, to the fullest possible extent of the word.

*

We sat under the wing of the aircraft, holding hands; with my other hand I waved away the flies. A strange way to romance, covered in dust and dried sweat, our lips swollen and cracked from the hot wind, our faces and arms burned and blistered.

The day wore relentlessly on and still there was no sign of rescue. Towards afternoon I felt the first twinges of panic; I had refused to believe they might not find us, but now I began to wonder if on this occasion I had tempted Providence a little too far.

We were both weak with hunger, but although it was a discomfort, I knew it wasn't an immediate danger. The body can withstand up to forty days of starvation without permanent harmful effect – indeed, there were recorded cases of up to seventy days.

But in the scorching fifty-degree heat of the desert, dehydration can sap life-giving moisture from the body in seventy hours. Another day in this furnace and rescue might be too late.

'Will they come soon?' Megan asked, echoing my thoughts.

'They will,' I replied, trying to disguise my own doubts. I couldn't understand it. They knew our original search coordinates. Any organised rescue operation should have brought a plane near us by now.

'Have you got a hand mirror?'

'A small one. It's in the cabin. Is this a good time to worry how you look?' she said, with a half-hearted smile.

'Keep it handy. I remember when I was looking for this old kangaroo shooter in the desert a while ago. It was the sun reflecting off the windscreen of his car that helped me find him. We may need to use the mirror in the same way.'

I reflected on my own experience of flying over desert terrain. You could lose a battleship in the middle of the Great Sandy unless it was painted a bright blue. A search plane could fly right over us and not see us. It would be up to us to attract their attention.

'Okay skipper, I'll get it,' she said. 'And whatever happens, it's been nice being stranded with you.'

'It's been nice being stranded with *you*, Miss Hoagan.'

I turned to face her. What would I have done without her? While I swung axes at flies and put my head inside pillow slips and railed against the heat, Megan had been calm and serene and full of humour. I moved my head forward to kiss her but a small fly, obviously a squadron leader or something, began to crawl up my nostril. I gave a sort of sneeze and the moment was shattered.

'Bloody flies,' I said, and tried to mangle it but only succeeded in slapping myself in the face.

So much for love in the desert.

It was late afternoon again.

The sun had lost some of its ferocity and had begun its descent towards the barren plain. I was resigning myself to another night out in the desert, with the solemn thought that the way things were going, there wouldn't be many more to endure.

Then I heard it.

It was very faint at first. It lasted just a few seconds and I thought I had imagined it.

Then it came again, much louder – the unmistakable hum of aircraft engines. We looked at each other and scrambled shakily to our feet, beginning to scan the horizon for the small, dark speck we had waited on for two long days.

Megan spotted it first. It was about two miles to the west of us, travelling north.

We waved and shouted, instinctively I suppose, although we both knew it was pointless. Almost as soon as we saw it we realised, with sudden horror, that they weren't going to see us. The plane was too far away to see the landing strip or the flags.

Megan reached into her breast-pocket, pulled out the small hand mirror and held it up to the sun.

'Keep moving it!' I said. 'They're more likely to see it flashing.'

We stood and waited and prayed.

But the small speck continued to move north; almost level with us, very soon they would be gone.

Then suddenly the miracle happened.

We watched the plane bank to starboard and come towards us.

'He's seen us!'

It was long minutes before the plane, a three-engine Drover, made its first pass overhead, very low. Someone leaned out of the cockpit and shouted at us.

It was over.

We jumped up and down like a pair of schoolkids and hugged each other. We had been in the desert for just forty-nine hours. It seemed like years.

The Drover banked a half a mile further on, and made its approach to our handmade airport. It made a perfect landing and a few minutes later we were scrambling across the gully and out onto the plain towards the aircraft, that was now taxiing towards us.

The first man out of the plane was Joe Kennedy, still on his crutches, limping across the gibber-stones. Impulsively, he hugged us both.

'You old bastard,' he grinned. 'I thought you were buggered for sure.'

'So did I. How did you find us?'

'Preston reckoned you came down south of Girrilie in the search area. They thought you would have allowed for the easterly. I said you were a rotten pilot and it would have blown you off-course. I was right!'

I felt the smile freeze on my face. 'Look, the port engine was running rough . . .' I started to say.

'Oh, for Christ's sake, not here,' Joe said. 'Let's get you on the plane.'

'Whose plane is it?'

'Friend of mine from Broome,' Joe said. 'I told him it was an emergency. Christ, Mike, Headquarters is crying bloody blue murder about all this. When you get to Preston, I reckon you're going to wish we had left you here.'

Soon, the desert and the remains of the Beagle were far behind us. Joe slapped me painfully on the back over and over, grinning like a madman.

'I thought you'd had it for sure, doc,' he kept repeating. 'I didn't think you had sense enough to keep yourself alive out there.'

I took the uncertain compliment in good part. Then Joe turned to Megan. 'Your father's sure been worried about you.'

'Poor Dad.'

'He's really been fretting. I don't think it was being lost in the desert that worried him, but your being alone for two days and nights with Mike.'

He grinned, first at Megan, then at me. But as he took in the glance that passed between us, the grin fell away. He coughed, and the red bulbous nose blushed a deep maroon.

'Just your luck,' he muttered.

CHAPTER 26

The day after my return to Preston I was summoned to the aerodrome to the office of the airport manager.

Bill Hardaker was an easy-going, middle-aged man with thinning, sandy hair and a sunny disposition. But, like the north-west, he occasionally had his storms, and I knew this was going to be one of them. I guessed that he had had his ear chewed by his superiors in Perth, and I was to be the next one down the line.

As I walked into his office, he turned a grim countenance in my direction and silently indicated the chair in front of his desk. I sat down.

'How are you feeling?' he said solemnly.

'Fine,' I answered, smiling. 'No ill effects.'

'Well, I've had a few.' He leaned back in his chair and tried to look stern. Bill had given me plenty of rein during my two years as the Flying Doctor and now I'd gone and hanged myself with it. We had been good friends but now, unwittingly, I had put him up to his neck in trouble.

'I've been getting my ears burned all yesterday and today. As we both know, you're not supposed to pilot a Flying Doctor plane, pilot's licence or no.'

I shrugged. 'You know how it is, Bill.'

'It doesn't matter if I know how it is,' he said, leaning towards me across the desk. 'The point is, *they* don't know how it is. And they don't want to know, either. They must think I'm running a bloody flying circus up here.' He softened a little. 'Have you heard from Melbourne?'

'They're not pleased.'

'What about Joe?'

'I told them he knew nothing about it. I didn't see why he should have his head in the noose. Besides, he needs his reputation more than I do.'

'They were on to me as soon as you went missing. Wanted to know why I gave you clear-ance.'

Poor Bill. He'd taken a lot of the flak that should have hit me first. I didn't know what to say. 'Sorry,' I tried at last.

'Do they know about all the other times?' he said.

I winced. 'I don't think so.'

Bill shook his head. 'It's all going to come out in the wash, you know.' He picked up an old brown pipe from the desk and tapped it on the edge. He started to fill it with trembling fingers. 'Look Mike, this isn't anything personal. You know I'm on your side. But I've also got a job to do, and my superiors want to see some action. I'm afraid I'm going to have to revoke your licence pending an enquiry. I'll have to ask you to hand it in.'

'My licence?' I said. He nodded. 'I'm afraid I haven't got one.'

Bill shot forward in his chair as if he had been hit in the back with a blow dart. '*You what?*'

'What I mean is, I have a licence but it's expired. I was going to renew it but I needed a medical and the only doctors in Preston were part of Fenwick's crew and they always said they were too busy. There was old Smithy, but he's sick all the time and I never quite managed to fit it in.' I realised I was gibbering. 'Sorry,' I finished lamely.

'Oh, Christ, what am I going to tell the Department?'

'I suppose it does make things a bit awkward,' I muttered.

'Get out,' Bill said softly, and as I closed the door behind me I thought I heard George saying to me from somewhere: 'I think you bin bugger up properly this time.'

Clyde had arranged a 'welcome back' party for me that afternoon at the Flying Doctor base. Mary Westcott had made a few dozen scones especially for the occasion and baked a whole barramundi which Clyde claimed he had caught off the jetty the previous night. None of us believed him. George, Joe, Bob Harper – Joe's friend and my rescuer, Sister Theresa, even some of the ground crew came along.

We all gathered out on the balcony sipping beers and waving away the flies that were trying to land on the buttered scones. As I looked round at the chattering, animated faces I realised with a pang how much I had come to love the hot, dirty, stinking little town. Suddenly, so far from the place I called home, I was surrounded by friends.

And what an odd crew they were. A loud-mouthed war veteran, an Aboriginal itinerant, a nun, a brooding, accident-prone pilot . . . the sort of people I suppose I would once have avoided. Yet they had helped to give me a new lease on life when I was at my lowest ebb.

After everyone had arrived, Clyde climbed up on a stool to give me a formal welcome back to the land of the living.

'Yairs . . .' he began, precariously perched on a rickety wooden stool. 'Well, the doc here nearly came a gutser the other day and on behalf of all youse here I'd like to say good on yer doc, and welcome back. Yairs. In my many years of service in the Flying Doctor . . . ow, Christ!' He started to topple backwards off the stool and George stepped forward and made a timely grab at Clyde's braces. Recovering, Clyde shot an apologetic glance in the direction of Sister Theresa and crossed himself. 'Beg your pardon, Mother,' he muttered. 'As I was sayin' – in my many years with the Service, I've seen a lot of these blokes come and go, but I reckon Mike's got my money as the bloke with most guts.' The stool teetered perilously beneath him. 'Now I know that some people reckon he does some pretty daft things sometimes, and he gets all over the place like a madwoman's custard, well that's as maybe. But the things he does, he does for the right reasons and in my book that's all that matters.' There was a small trickle of applause. 'So good on yer doc. I don't know why we all wasted our time worryin' – the bastard'll probably die in his bed at ninety-two of syphilis anyway, eh?' He gave a raucous laugh and then remembered again that Sister Theresa was present. He looked sheepishly over in her direction and crossed himself. 'Sorry, Mother.'

Sister Theresa smiled and nodded graciously to excuse him. George helped Clyde down off the stool, and everyone resumed the drinking of beer. Sister Theresa accepted a lemonade from Mary

Westcott and turned to me, smiling.

'Well,' she said. 'All I can say is it was a terrible waste.'

I thought she meant the plane. 'Yes, but they're fully insured, you know.'

'No, I don't mean the aeroplane. You may not know this, but the other Sisters and I held two masses for the repose of your soul, all for nothing.'

I laughed. 'Well, I'm sure they'll come in handy one day.'

'And how's the young girl?'

'She's fine. She stood up to the ordeal better than I did.'

'There has been a lot of gossip in the town you know,' she confided. 'Of course she is a very attractive girl so it's natural. But as I've told everyone, Doctor Hazzard is a gentleman beyond reproach.'

'Thank you, Sister. Idle tongues love to talk,' I said, looking pointedly in Joe's direction.

I knew there had been a certain amount of speculation about Megan Hoagan and myself – most of it justified, I suppose. That, in itself, did not concern me. The real problem wasn't the past but the future. We were lovers, but nothing else had changed all that much. Megan was still reluctant to leave Brookton, and Jesse's attitude was certainly unlikely to alter. Since our ordeal in the desert his opinion of me was little different – he just disliked me more.

Our problems were solved rather dramatically.

I was speculating with Bill McCormack on what could have caused the trouble with the port engine just before the crash when I heard the tinny crackle of voices from the radio hut. In the same moment, Clyde had put down his beer and was running down the verandah steps.

I knew what it meant. Another call. Everyone had fallen silent. I followed Clyde to the hut, with Joe limping along behind me on his crutches.

When we got there, Clyde was already crouched over the transmitter, pencil in hand, speaking urgently into the mike. He looked up at me as I walked in. 'It's Jess Hoagan,' he said. 'He's collapsed.'

So it's happened at last, I thought. His heart's given out on him. There was little satisfaction in being proved right. I just hoped that the attack had not been a serious one.

Clyde stood up and I took over. 'This is doctor Hazzard. Who's calling? Over.'

'Hello, skipper.' It was Megan. She was trying to be composed but she sounded very close to tears.

'Megan. Is he conscious? Over.'

'Sort of . . . he's just lying there . . . mumbling. I should have made him quit this bloody place!'

'Where is he now? Over.'

'He's lying on the bed. Two of the men helped me carry him in. Over.'

'Okay, now don't panic. I want you to loosen all his clothing and keep him calm. And try to get him into a sitting position – prop him up with pillows. Have you got that? Over.'

'Yes. I'll do it. over.'

I spoke to Megan for a few minutes to calm her down. I told her to give Jesse a couple of the digitalis I had prescribed for him. 'We'll be there as soon as we can.'

I turned to Joe. 'Better tell your friend the Flying Doctor would like to requisition his Drover for another emergency.'

The flight took just under an hour. One of Jesse's boys was waiting to meet us in the ute. Bob Harper stayed with the plane while I took the stretcher and jumped into the ute to go to the station.

By the time I arrived poor Megan was close to hysteria. Jesse was in a bad way. His cheeks were tinged with blue and he was breathing only with the greatest difficulty. I got two of the station hands to bring in the stretcher from the ute.

I looked at Megan. 'How did it happen?'

'I don't know. He was out on the verandah. I heard a crash and when I came out – he was just lying there.'

'Okay. Let's get him to the plane.'

As we started to lift him onto the stretcher Jesse opened one puffy eye and fixed me with its glazed stare. 'Go away,' he mumbled, 'I'm all right.'

'Take it easy, Jess,' I said. 'You're coming with me.'

Jesse shut his eye again, too weak to resist. 'Bloody doctors,' he muttered and slipped into unconsciousnes, not coming round again until he woke up the next day in Preston Hospital.

I took Megan back on the plane with us, and she went with Jesse to the Hosptial. Fortunately, he had suffered only a mild heart attack and the doctors at Preston were confident he would recover fully – providing he had the proper rest. That night Megan stayed with the Westcotts and I picked her up the next morning to drive to Fraser Point. For hours we sat on the beach and talked. Finally, we got in the car and drove to the Hospital.

Jesse was sitting up in bed, sedated but still defiant. He was staring sullenly out of the window when we came in, his arms folded petulantly across his chest.

'Well, how are we Mr Hoagan?'

He fixed me with a cold stare and said nothing. He turned back to the window. Megan kissed him quickly on the cheek and sat down on the edge of the bed.

'I brought some flowers. To brighten up the room,' she said smiling.

'I don't want any flowers.'

Megan looked in my direction, unsure of what to say next. I decided to take a different tack. 'The doctors say you're going to be fine.'

'Of course I am. So when are they letting me out of this dump? There's work to be done. It's not right for a man to be sitting round in bed of an afternoon.'

'You'll be out of hospital at the end of the week.' Megan said.

'End of the week? And who's going to keep me here? I'll walk out now if I want to.'

'Dad . . .'

I decided it was time for me to chip in again. 'Look, Jess, I've talked about your condition with the doctors here and they agree with me that you've been overdoing things. You need to rest or your heart's going to give out on you again. Only next time you might not be so lucky.'

'I'll take my chances.'

Megan got to her feet. Her lower lip quivered but

she stuck out her jaw defiantly like a true Hoagan. 'Well then, you'll have to take you chances on your own.'

A shadow passed across Jesse's face. He looked round at Megan. His shoulders seemed to sag. 'What . . . what are you talkin' about, girl?'

'I mean I don't want to go back to the property, Dad,' she said softly.

'But it's our life,' Jesse stammered. Suddenly he looked terribly vulnerable, and very old.

'It's *your* life, Dad. Not mine.'

For a moment he looked as lost and forlorn as a homeless orphan; then he recovered and his mouth tightened in grim determination.

'All right then. I'll carry on alone. You've been in the way on the property, anyway. I'll be glad to get you out of my hair.'

'Jesse,' I said. 'It is the opinion of myself and the other doctors here that if you go back to the property, you're going to have another heart attack, a serious one, within months. That sort of life is far too strenuous for a man in your condition . . .'

'What do you mean, "in my condition"?'

'Listen to him, Dad.'

'And you should very seriously consider retiring.'

Jesse's world was crumbling round his ears, but he refused to admit defeat. 'No,' he said. 'It's my life. I can't give it up.' He was pleading now, but not with me, and not with Megan. With Life. He knew he had been stalling for more time for years, and now he wanted to bargain some more.

Megan put her hand over his. 'Please, Dad. For me.'

The deep lines on his face were etched with his

fear and his hurt. 'I can't,' he mumbled.

'You can buy a little place down in Perth. Somewhere with plenty of space for kennels. You've always said you wouldn't mind breeding dogs. I'll help you.'

'Come back to Brookton with me,' he whispered. 'I promised I'll take it easy.'

Megan shook her head. 'No, Dad.'

Jesse looked at her, then down at the covers. I could see he was preparing to resign himself to the inevitable. Finally he looked up at me, and on his face there was no little resentment.

'Well? Is there any other good news you've got for me?' he growled.

'Yes, sir. I'd like to marry your daughter.'

There was an uncanny silence in the room. Jesse just stared at me, his face as stony as a cliff. Finally he took a deep breath and looked out of the window, over the reticulated lawns of the Hospital and out to the brown hills beyond.

'Why didn't you let me die?' he whispered. 'That would have been the kind thing.

CHAPTER 27

It was just a week later that Tom Doyle's fourth daughter was born in the back of the new Cessna on the way back from Hawkestone.

Dawn's first grey fingers were inching through the scudding clouds as I drove back from the Hospital.

I was exhausted. I hadn't slept for twenty-four hours. I was wet through and my clothes were caked with ochre mud. I was promising myself a hot bath, a clean bed and a cup of George's strong tea.

Behind me Tom was draped over the back seat, a shocking wraith-like figure. His hair was dirty and matted, and there was a heavy ginger stubble on his chin. He was snoring.

When I reached the Residence I got out and left him asleep in the car. George, as always, was waiting in the kitchen with the kettle boiling on the stove and the cups ready on the table.

'Yo-i boss. You look longa dead man I think.'

'Yes,' I said. 'I need some sleep.'

There was a letter for me lying on the table. It was an RFDS envelope with a Melbourne postmark. Mechanically I picked it up and ripped it open. I read it through quickly and stuffed it in my shirt pocket.

It was from Lynott informing me that my two

years of service as regional medical officer would shortly be completed, and I would not be required to continue. My services had been most valuable etc.

I was getting the sack in the nicest possible way. I couldn't say I blamed them. I'd been expecting it.

I'd wrecked an expensive plane, flouted the service's rules on a number of occasions by flying alone and a local doctor had submitted complaints about my professional behaviour.

Not an auspicious record.

I looked out of the window. It was the quiet time of early morning, those precious moments before the first brilliant sliver of sun edges over the horizon. There was an odd scratching at the back door, as Ethel gnawed at the fly wire, eager for her first beer of the day.

I got up and went into the bedroom.

I was starting to take off my shirt when I noticed a small red and white package lying on the bed, with an envelope underneath it.

There was a Christmas card inside. 'To the Bloody Red Baron. A rotten pilot but the best doctor in the north-west. We all got together to decide what you needed most. The vote was unanimous. Happy Christmas, doc. Clyde, Mary, George, Joe, Sister Theresa and Ethel.'

I picked up the package, which was wrapped in Christmas paper, with pictures of Santa Claus trudging through the snow.

Inside was a tiny brown box. I opened it.

It was a St Christopher's medal on a gold chain.

I felt a lump in my throat. They were right. The perfect gift for a rotten pilot.

There was a shuffling sound from the doorway. I turned round. It was George.

'Yo-i, boss,' he mumbled.

'What's up, George?'

'You goin' longa Sinney, now boss?'

For a moment I wondered how he knew. Then I remembered the RFDS letter must have been there all day and that George didn't only boil the kettle to make tea.

'No, George. I'm *not* going back to Sydney.'

'You sure, boss? Letter fella says . . .' George stopped, realising he had given himself away.

'Don't worry, George. They're not getting rid of me that easily. Anyway,' I said, picking up the St Christopher from the bed, 'if I don't stay – when will I get the chance to use this?'